The Twin Sister

THE TWIN SISTER

YVETTE DAVIES

JOFFE BOOKS

Joffe Books, London
www.joffebooks.com

First published in Great Britain in 2025

Cover art by Nick Castle

ISBN: 978-1-80573-288-4

TRIGGER WARNING

*Please note this manuscript contains scenes of sexual assault,
which some readers may find upsetting.*

For Paul, Amy and Matt. You are my world.

PROLOGUE

He takes in the upturned vehicle lying across two lanes of the motorway. The roof crumpled and squeezed like a discarded tin can. Fragments of glass, glinting like ice cubes, and other debris strewn across the road. An item of black clothing lies abandoned. Who is the owner? Experience tells him the atmosphere among his colleagues is the best barometer as to the fate of the occupants. Faces are pinched, hardened to what they must deal with. He smells it in the air, carried on the wind. Death.

It never fails to amaze him how the start of the most ordinary of days could become anything but for some people. Life pivoting and changing based on split-second decisions. Someone's mother, father, son, daughter, brother or sister is still trapped in the wreckage.

Barrier tape has already been put across the motorway; crowd-control is essential for the safety of all. He's been informed that Fire are on their way; specialist hydraulic equipment is needed for this incident. He lets the first responders do their job and awaits confirmation on casualty numbers. He sucks in a deep breath and braces himself for what is evidently going to be a long afternoon.

An abrupt movement in his peripheral vision catches his attention. A woman with striking auburn hair ducks underneath the tape and runs towards the RTA vehicle. Terror and panic etched into her face. He lunges and manages to grab her by the arm.

'No, Miss. Stop.'

BEFORE

CHAPTER 1

Beth

I've been stewing all day like a casserole on a slow simmer about to reach boiling point. Here's my dilemma: I was sorting through the laundry basket and checked David's jeans pockets. Something I do routinely as he's always leaving stray tissues, which make a right mess in the washing machine. No tissues, but I did pull out a receipt for an expensive meal for two with a bottle of wine at a fancy restaurant. It wasn't me who dined with him. What am I supposed to think:

a) Great. My husband works so hard that he deserves to splash out.

b) Lucky me. He's obviously giving it a test-run for a surprise thirteenth-wedding-anniversary romantic dinner he must be planning.

c) He's having an affair.

Answer c). What a scumbag.

David's key turns in the front door and, boy, am I about to erupt. He'll be taking off his suit jacket and draping it over the banisters, loosening his tie. Six strides down our small terrace hallway and he appears in the kitchen doorway. I sniff hard and swallow.

I dangle the crumpled receipt in front of his nose. He deliberately ignores me as he makes a beeline for the fridge.

'What the hell is this?'

He turns to look at me, smile fading. Clutching what I'm sure isn't his first after-work beer, he directs a cursory glance at me.

'And good evening to you too, my little praying mantis. That, darling wife, looks like a receipt of some sort.'

Do I catch flames of guilt licking that face? My mouth forms the words I don't want to say.

'Be honest with me. Are you having an affair?'

'How the hell did you draw that conclusion?' David screws up his face like a five-year-old who's been forced to eat a Brussels sprout.

'You're not denying it, then?'

'Of course I'm denying it. You're kidding me, right?' Frowning, he pulls his bottom lip in below his teeth and chews on it for a second. Is he buying time to concoct a story? I grit my teeth.

'Explain. Now.'

'Explain what, exactly?'

'This receipt. I certainly didn't dine on Dover sole and a bottle of Chablis,' I say, holding it out for him to see.

David shrugs, barely giving it a glance. 'Oh, that.' He prises the top off the beer bottle and takes a swig. 'It's from when I had lunch with the new company sales director. I told you about it, I'm sure.' Did he? I don't recall. 'And I'll be able to claim it back on expenses if that's what you're worried about.'

David wears his well-rehearsed butter-wouldn't-melt look. He is a supreme master of casual denial and defusing situations. He closes the fridge door and gives me a peck on the cheek as he reaches to open the messy top drawer.

'Takeout tonight? What do you fancy?' He holds up Indian and Chinese takeaway menus with a flourish.

Confused innocence or a deflection technique? He does look genuinely baffled. Am I overthinking this? Every bit of me wants to believe him. David has never given me cause to doubt him before, but things haven't been good between us lately. Years of trying for a baby take their toll. I know that, but I've always taken David's faithfulness for granted. Things may have crumbled around our once cosy cocoon, but I still thought we were a given. Now I'm not so sure. How do I get to the truth?

'Think I'll go for the crispy chilli beef. We can share an egg fried rice. What are you having?' David puts a hand on my shoulder and gives a reassuring squeeze. He pulls out a chair and sits at the kitchen table with his back to me, scrolling through his phone to call the Chinese. 'Oh, by the way . . . I'll be away Friday and Saturday night. I've said I'll go to Gavin's golf stag weekend after all.'

Suspicious thoughts circulate again at alarming speed. I can't quell them. Will he be out on the green or in the arms of someone else?

'I thought you weren't going? We agreed to save the money.'

'Gav persuaded me. Besides, it'll give us a well-earned break, *BeBe*, do us both good. And you could go away with Cate. It's this weekend — that cottage thing, isn't it?'

'If a break is well-earned, why do we have to take it *separately*?'

David lets out an exasperated sigh. 'Because I've already promised the lads I'll go. And because you're so strung up and stressed out that if we spent it together, we'd end up talking about the baby thing. Again. At least you would. Constantly.'

'I so wouldn't.' Has he chosen to focus on our infertility issues to mask the other capital I in the air? Infidelity.

'The subject is parked, Beth. If we're not together then we can't talk about it, can we? It's a metaphorical pause button, that's all. I'll be back Sunday night.'

'So, can we agree to discuss another round of IVF on Sunday? And maybe revisit the topic of adoption?'

David pushes back his chair, stands up and runs his hands through his hair. He's not avoiding my gaze now.

'For Christ's sake, Beth. Stop. We can't afford more IVF at the moment. And I'm telling you right now — I will not be raising someone else's child. This has become a total obsession with you.'

'Well, I'm not surprised we can't afford it if you keep going on piss-up weekends. And don't you dare call me obsessed. I thought we were in this together. How could you?'

'You're not here, Beth. Not anymore. Can't you see what you're doing to us?'

The pressure-cooker effect steaming inside my head all day intensifies. I want to slap him but make do with jabbing my finger.

'What do you mean, I'm not here? You're the one who comes home late. I don't know where the hell you are most of the time.'

'I mean . . . You're. Not. Present in this . . . relationship,' David says, spelling it out slowly for maximum effect. He takes a step towards me. I mirror it by taking a step backwards. I shrink into myself, not wanting to hear any more. 'Some couples are always destined to lose at the baby-odds table. That's us, Beth. We both have to accept it.'

What is he saying? I stand mute as the tears start to fall. I can't. I can't accept it.

'And perhaps once we do, our sex life can become less mechanical too. Spice it up with a bit of that thing called spontaneity,' David says with more than a hint of sarcasm. And then the killing blow. The passive-aggressive Exocet, delivered in a tone more pertinent to informing me that he'd rather not holiday in Majorca again this year.

'Nearly ten years of trying is enough. I can't do this anymore.'

He puts both hands up towards me, palms facing, and slices them horizontally through the air to indicate the conversation and my dreams of us having a child are over.

CHAPTER 2

Beth

It's Sunday morning and with David away, I've joined my perfect sister, Cate, and her perfect family at a perfect rented cottage in the New Forest. Do I believe David's on a golfing weekend? Like hell. Especially after having shared my suspicions with Cate.

'Read the signs, Beth. I'd perform a Bobbitt and stick his dick in a blender. That'll teach him.' She really has no idea what it's like for me; everything seems to fall in to place for Have-It-All Cate.

Dishwater-grey light filters through the chink in the curtains. I'm in no rush to get up, exhausted from thinking about David. He's not even bloody phoned. I want to kill him.

Cate and Giles are awake as well. An iron bedhead rhythmically bangs against the paper-thin bedroom wall next door. Grunting noises too — like a warthog. How romantic.

I can't believe David's called time on us ever trying for a baby again. My mind keeps spinning. Infertility . . . Infidelity . . . cause and effect.

'Come on, Cate, come on.' Giles gasps through the wall.

There's no sound from Cate. Not even a whimper. I imagine my sister lying there, bored, allowing Giles to perform. Dear, cumbersome Giles. Sunday-morning perfunctory sex. I suppose this

8

is the price Cate pays for the security of a dull but loyal husband and a seriously overloaded bank balance.

'Mum-eee. Where are you?'

Oops. I leap out of bed and poke my head around the door into the hallway. 'Boo!'

'Auntie Beth!' Georgie clutches her threadbare teddy. She bounds over and wraps herself around my pyjama-bottomed legs.

'Hey, gorgeous. Whassup?'

'I don't know the doors. I can't find Mummy and Daddy.'

'Think I heard Daddy snoring so let them sleep, huh? Want to come in my room?'

Georgie comes and sits with me on my bed, and I pull the bedspread over her bare legs.

She eyes my phone on the bedside table. 'Can we go through the photos again, Auntie Beth?'

'Sure thing, chicken wing.'

Georgie snuggles up beside me. We scroll through the photos I took yesterday on our walk. We were near the mill pond in Beaulieu and came across a drove of donkeys. Dozens of them. Grey ones, brown ones, baby ones. Georgie and her older brother, Charlie, were ecstatic.

'Can I have some of the pictures to take to school? I can show them to Esme and Willow. They'll be sooo jealous.'

'Pleasure, treasure. I'll send them to your mum.'

'I love you,' Georgie says as she flings her arms around my neck to give me a hug.

Wham. It hits me again like an express train emerging full pelt out of the tunnel.

'Love you more,' I manage to reply.

She squeals with delight as I tickle her. The most wonderful, infectious giggle. It's rising up from the pit of my stomach, though, passing through my soul, through my very being until it leaves an acrid taste in my mouth that threatens to choke me. I pretend for a second I've got a stray lash in my eye. It's always the same feeling on repeat. I couldn't love Georgie more, but it's not enough. I want to be loving my own child.

My attention turns back to the activity in the room next door as the hideous grunting stops. No post-coital tender snuggling — within seconds their bedroom door creaks open, the bathroom door opposite bangs shut, a bin lid clunks and the toilet flushes. Giles appears to be done as he thuds downstairs.

I glance at the door. 'I need to nip to the loo, honey. You can borrow my phone and show Charlie the pics if you like?'

Georgie doesn't need any more encouragement. She leaps off the bed. 'Charlie. Charlie! Look!'

* * *

Perched on the loo, the bathroom bin is right opposite me. It's one of those metal pedal-bin types. I extend my right foot over the lever, wiggle my toes and the lid shoots open. I don't have to rummage far to find the holy grail of what I've been looking for. It's neatly wrapped in tissues like a little gift.

Minutes later and I'm back in my room taking a few more moments before I face the day. I lie topsy-turvy on the bed, splayed out on the ditsy-print patchwork quilt, my pelvis elevated on a pillow. With a little wiggle, I manipulate everything into place and we're ready for the send-off. I lean my legs up against the wall at right angles to the rest of my body. A yoga pose, of sorts. I need to relax. If I can clear my mind of my cheating husband, then, you never know, this could work.

Dishwasher-emptying duty has clearly been bestowed on Giles. The clatter of utensils as they're flung onto the granite worktop reverberates around the cottage. The echo of stainless-steel sauce-pans being thump-stacked together crashes through my brain.

Then it's the turn of the china plates as they're bump-slid into the rack above the sink. The inevitable breakage — or that could almost certainly be plural — arrives with the shattering of glassware on the stone-tiled kitchen floor. Not just a tinkle, but a cascade of vessels meeting their end. They're probably only Ikea, but even so. *Oh, gosh, Giles — what a bumbling buffoon you can be!* At least he can easily afford the security deposit.

The cacophony shakes our weekend rental to life. The latch on the bathroom door snaps open and Cate yells down the corridor. 'What the hell, Giles?' followed by a mutter, 'Can't fucking do anything right . . .' before she slams the bathroom door shut again. Georgie and Charlie charge out of their bedroom and thump down the stairs like a herd of baby elephants eager to get a look-see into their father's mess.

Baby Edward starts to whimper from next door. Within seconds he's going full throttle. I'm done here now so I swing my legs over the side of the bed, grab my dressing gown and go to placate Ted. Cate hasn't shown any signs of leaving the bathroom yet, which should be my next destination, but I don't need an excuse to grab a cuddle of the gorgeous baby. Lifting him out of his travel cot, I cocoon him in my arms, bringing his head to rest upon my shoulder. I breathe him in deeply. He smells sweet and new. Of powder and milk. God, I want this.

'There, there, little one,' I whisper in his ear as I bounce him up and down to soothe him.

I plant little kisses on the top of his soft head when my doppelganger walks in. My twin sister, Cate. My identical twin, to be precise. Same height, same auburn hair colour, same dress size. You name it, same everything. Although I do have longer and stragglier hair as I can't afford the regular trips to the salon like coiffured Cate. I am forgetting the one major difference, though — our wombs, apparently. She's the fertile one who's had the temerity to produce three children in the last eight years. And at thirty-nine years of age, I fear I will now never have the opportunity to catch up.

'Thanks, babes. You're a doll. I won't be a minute, my little Bear.' Smiling at me, she pulls a lemon sundress over her head. Cate wanted to call Ted Bear, but Giles, a stickler for tradition, was having none of it.

'Auntie Beth's reward for taking such good care of my little Teddy Bear is going to be a scrummy full English. Let's get to it, shall we? And maybe that clumsy man downstairs can change your nappy and give you a bottle?' Sighing, she takes Ted from my arms and adeptly places him over her right shoulder with a muslin in place.

'I'll do it.' My empty arms crash back down by my sides, making me feel bereft already.

'Oh, God, I wouldn't. First guzzled bottle of the day and that'll end up all down your back.' Cate contorts her face in revulsion. 'No, we'll save that pleasure for Thunderclap Daddio, won't we, baby Bear? You go and grab a shower, and start packing. We've got to be out by twelve anyway. Do you mind helping with the kids' things, though? There's bound to be socks and crap under the bed. And don't forget the stuff they've probably left in the garden. I'll start on brunch. How do you want your eggs?'

'Fertilised, please.'

Cate doesn't hear my response. She's already whisked Ted away. Leaving me alone, totally deprived save for relishing the prospect of having to clear up the weekend's debris. *Deftly done, Cate. Deftly done.*

CHAPTER 3

Beth

Cate's brunch, while delicious, made a hell of a mess in the kitchen. She cooked so wasn't expecting to clear up, declaring she needed to finish packing her toiletries. Giles remembered an important business phone call and made a beeline for the seclusion of the garden. I set to and handwashed the caked-on-scrambled-egg and baked-bean pans, fearing the dishwasher wouldn't cope, and gave Charlie and Georgie tea towels to help with the drying-up.

Charlie rubs the largest saucepan to see if he can make a genie appear. Georgie polishes away at a stainless-steel baking tray, admiring her distorted reflection. They burst into fits of giggles at their antics as Cate reappears. She looks at her phone with a grizzling Ted in her arms.

'He's so tetchy, this one. I've tried to get him to nap, but he's having none of it. I don't suppose you've seen the Calpol syringe, have you? That sometimes does the trick.'

'Sorry, no. It must have been packed somewhere.' I turn away from Cate so she doesn't see the guilty-as-charged look on my face.

Giles saunters in from the garden with a huge grin showing off his blinding veneers. He rubs his hands together.

'Are we set, then?'

'Nearly ready, sweetie,' Cate replies in a panting voice as though she's the one who's been dashing around for the last hour. 'The stuff in the hall can go in the car,' she adds, referring to the bags I had packed earlier, the toys I'd put in a bin liner, and the coats and shoes I'd collected together.

Another ten minutes and we're all outside with Giles's Range Rover loaded. Charlie and Georgie are in the back debating what movie they're going to watch.

'Have a good week back at school, guys.' I blow them a kiss. 'I've emailed the donkey photos. Love you both.'

'Bye, Auntie Beth,' they reply in unison as Georgie waves the arm of a cuddly toy monkey at me. Cate and I are returning in her Mini Clubman; she'll drop me home in Twickenham on her way back to Richmond. Ted, who's travelling with us and is already secured in his car seat, starts to ramp up the whining again. I make shushing noises at him, but he isn't placated.

Yesterday's heat has been replaced by a brisk, flirty breeze with blankets of cloud skirting overhead. Such a contrast to Saturday's glorious weather. The kind of overnight temperature displacement that only the UK can deliver. I shroud my shoulders with my black leather jacket as I wait for Cate to lock up the cottage. She places the key in the security box while fiddling on her phone. I wish she'd hurry up.

'All done. We'd better get started.' Cate drops her phone in her handbag and throws it on the back seat next to Ted.

'You okay? I ask. 'You look pretty tired.'

'Thanks,' Cate replies with a grimace. She glances at the bag she's put in the back.

'I'm a bit bothered by — oh, I don't know.' She shrugs her shoulders. 'It's not important. But . . .' Cate trails off, staring at the ground.

'But what? Come on. You know you can tell me.'

'It's complicated.' Cate hesitates again. 'I'll tell you in the car.' She looks up at me with pursed lips. I know that expression — she's hiding something. Something she's avoided telling me, but she is now on the verge of dropping one of her bombshells. Her face softens; she's letting the moment pass. 'To be honest, Beth, I feel shattered today. Didn't sleep too well last night — I've got a splitting headache and it's freezing. Should've brought a cardi.' She rubs at her bare arms as the wind whips her auburn bob across her face. I feel the chill on the back of my neck, having clasped my longer hair in a claw clip earlier when clearing up.

'Take my jacket. I'm fine.' I remove it and put it around Cate's shoulders.

'Thanks. Giles will have buried my coat somewhere in the back.'

Ted starts to scream. I see him through the window, clenching his fists, his little legs kicking wildly. Cate looks skywards with a heaving sigh. 'Give me a break. Not again.'

'Look, let me drive?' I say.

'Really?'

'In fact, why don't you go with Giles? Don't worry about Ted. I'll cope. Try to grab a snooze. Charlie and Georgie are occupied with a movie.'

'What about dropping you off?'

'I'll get a cab back from yours. Or David can pick me up — assuming he's home in time.' I try not to let David's whereabouts torture me. Can Cate tell how delighted I am about the prospect of a couple of hours alone with my nephew — even a grizzling one?

'Ted might need a feed,' Cate says.

'I'll stop off at the Winchester or Fleet services if he's not settling and give him a bottle. It doesn't matter if I'm a bit behind you.' I can tell that Cate is tempted by my proposal, but she's still hesitating.

'But you'll be driving my car. What about—'

'I'm a driving instructor.' I interject. 'I have specialised insurance that will cover me. And, to be honest, if you're not feeling well and are that tired, I think it's safer, don't you?'

Cate's eyes flash wide.

'Don't you fucking dare go there,' she mouths silently. Giles beeps his car horn.

'Come on, girls.' He pokes his head out of the driver's window. 'Are we leaving together or what?'

'Coming,' Cate says, giving me a defeated look. 'Change of plan. I'm travelling with you.'

'I'm sorry,' I mouth back at Cate, regretting my reference to her driving skills. She brushes past me with resignation on her face, handing me the car keys, and lightly touches my arm. I get the message. Twin secrets should stay that way.

* * *

The traffic on the M27 is busy for a Sunday lunchtime, but I recall it's the end of half term as I spot another loaded-up family heading back to London. Mum and Dad in the front; 2.4 kids in the back. At thirty-nine, I thought this was what David and I would have been doing by now. Instead, we're hardly speaking to one another and I'm piggybacking on my sister's life.

I glance across at Ted's adorable, sleeping expression. I moved him to the front seat to keep him close. Cate needn't have worried; he nodded off not long after we left the cottage. I'm enjoying my snatched time alone with him even more than driving Cate's brand-new car. This must be what it would feel like if I had a baby of my own — private contentment.

I reflect on my conversation with Cate. I didn't mean to upset her by having a dig at her driving. It's about the only area of our lives where I have the upper hand. I'm a good driver, always have been, and I sometimes wonder whether I took up driving for a living to act as a constant reminder. In this, at least, I am the superior twin and I never want her to forget it.

I'm on the inside lane on the motorway and intermittently move out into the middle to overtake. Giles has stubbornly remained in the middle lane, occasionally moving out then back to the middle. I keep increasing my speed to keep them in sight. I'm averaging seventy-five mph so Giles must be topping eighty plus. He's always dangerously close to the car in front. Tailgating is a habit I abhor and he's had to brake countless times as he's not anticipating the road ahead.

As we approach the entry slip road of junction six on the M3 from Basingstoke, a white transit van joins the carriageway at considerable speed. Brake lights illuminate up ahead as it barges its way into the stream of traffic, making it to the outside lane. I accelerate to move into the middle lane as I don't want to drop too far behind Giles.

By the time I get there, I notice that the white van has slowed down considerably — I'm catching up with him. *What was the hurry, dude?* He's allowed quite a gap to open up in front of him, so cars are bunching behind. I apply my brakes as I'm not going to undertake. He must have done the same, because now we are driving side by side. What's happening here? Discomfort settles in my stomach. I glance across at the van. The beanie-hatted driver stares at me intently and then breaks into a smile. I think he's waving? Or is that a salute? Weirdo. The motorway is not the place for flirting. Although I'm a teeny bit secretly flattered. I ignore him and focus on the road ahead. The white van accelerates and is now weaving in and out of the middle and outer lanes. He cuts up a Toyota RAV4. Jesus, that was close.

The Range Rover still sits resolutely in the middle lane. The van moves up at speed behind Giles and the two vehicles look like they're almost interlocked. Yes, he's an absolute idiot of a driver, but *move*, Giles. There are children in the car. Has he even looked in his rearview mirror?

Cars are accelerating in the outside lane. The van's brake lights repeatedly flash on and off as the guy grows impatient. A small gap appears and he veers sharply into the inside lane without indicating. Equally as sharply, he cuts in front of Giles to undertake him.

Slow down; drop back.

Brakes screech and the Range Rover swerves to the outside lane. A horn blares. Did the van clip them or has Giles lost control doing an emergency stop at over eighty miles an hour? Every vehicle is braking hard. Red lights, red lights. With my heart pounding in my chest, I slow the Mini down safely.

Giles doesn't have control. They make impact with the central reservation barriers, then ricochet back into the middle lane. Holy shit. The Range Rover rocks side to side as it continues careening. I don't know if he's clipped another vehicle, but they're now veering back towards the central barrier, side on to the traffic. The Range Rover goes over rain-gully dips on the far side of the outside lane at speed, causing it to tilt. They hit the barrier again. This time the impact causes them to flip into the air. As if in slow motion they gain height and for a nanosecond appear suspended. Then they roll and disappear into the path of traffic on the southbound carriageway.

CHAPTER 4

Beth

The traffic in front comes to a standstill. I struggle to grip the steering wheel as my hands are shaking so much.

What have I witnessed? This can't be happening. I've got to get to them. Nothing's moving. I consider getting out of my car to go and help. I could easily climb across the central reservation barrier as it's one of those lower metal-balustrade-style ones. No, that would be crazy and dangerous. I can't do that with Ted in the car, either. *Think straight, Beth.*

I must call the emergency services. I reach for my leather jacket for my phone. It isn't on the back seat — only Cate's Mulberry handbag. Shit, Cate has my jacket. I can't call, I can't do anything. The pounding in my chest turns to a tightness as the air is squeezed out of me.

* * *

I'm frozen and don't know how much time has passed, but the traffic ahead is starting to creep forward. So many cars must have witnessed the accident, but there's no blockage on this side of the motorway. Distant sirens are audible. Thank God, help is coming. I've got to get across to the southbound carriageway. I turn on the

Mini's satnav. Junction five for Hook is only about three miles away so I can exit there and double back. Less than six in total and I'll find them.

The traffic flow gradually picks up and we're now at fifty mph and accelerating. The sign for the next junction looms so I indicate to get into the left-hand lane. There's a queue on the exit slip road on the approach to the roundabout. The traffic continues to build and the slow progress is excruciating. By the time I'm on the roundabout, I've come to a standstill again. I can guess what's happening — the southbound carriageway is blocked so the traffic is starting to back up. Jesus Christ, this must be bad. I tremble and my eyes fill.

The emergency sirens get louder and louder. A National Highways Agency vehicle with flashing blue lights negotiates the roundabout. Cars find inches to move to let it through. This is my chance. I activate the hazard lights and follow, weaving in and out of the scrum. Cate and her family need me.

I accelerate down the entry slip road for the return carriageway, which is clear as vehicles have avoided joining the motorway. As soon as I reach the merging lane, it's jammed. What am I going to do? There is only one option: the hard shoulder. Emergency access only, but this is an emergency. I follow the Highways vehicle, which is now some way ahead. Flashing lights beckon in the distance.

* * *

I've never seen anything like this. Vehicles are strewn across the road at odd angles; some have collided. An articulated lorry has jackknifed. My heartbeat quickens further. My mouth is very dry and it hurts to swallow. A motorbike is on its side in the road, but mercifully the rider is standing. People have left their vehicles; some are leaning against their cars with arms folded and heads bowed as if afraid to look up. Others are standing on their bonnets peering ahead to get a better view. This is scary. A crowd has gathered on the verge; some are sitting. I scan the faces looking for Cate, the children.

The sense of shock in the air is palpable, even from inside my car. I reduce speed, gingerly continuing along the hard shoulder. Onlookers obediently move out of my way but give me cold stares.

The Range Rover comes into view. It looks like a shiny, upturned cockroach straddling the outside and middle lanes. It's surrounded by traffic cops in high-vis jackets. One is lying on the ground, reaching into the vehicle. I don't think I can breathe. Have they got them out already? Are they all still inside? This can't be happening.

I am forced to come to a stop by a police security tape across the road. I don't want to block the route for emergency vehicles, so manage to squeeze into a small space between one of the halted cars and a police car. Checking that Ted is still asleep, I open my door and duck under the tape. Then I run. I run towards my sister and her family. I run towards the people I love.

An officer throws himself towards me and grabs me by the arm.

'No, Miss. Stop. This is a serious incident and we have to preserve the scene. You can't contaminate anything. You shouldn't be here.'

The tears fall.

'The children . . .' I point towards the upturned vehicle. He looks at me intently and follows my stare towards the wreckage, then back to scrutinise my face. He's still holding on to me tightly. I must make him understand.

'My sister. Giles. Please, please. My family! Oh, my God, the children . . .' But the words won't come as every last drop of air is exhaled. My knees give way and I crumple to the ground, sobbing uncontrollably.

The officer calls a colleague for assistance and the pair of them lift me back up on my feet as though righting a toppled chair.

'Miss. We're going to ask you to rest over here a while,' the officer says as I'm guided away from the accident site. I vaguely catch an exchange between them, but everything has become muffled and distorted as though I'm listening through water. Except one word uttered, which sticks and reverberates around my brain. They seat me on the grassy bank at the side of the motorway.

'Assistance will be here in a moment, Madam,' the officer who stopped me says. 'Can you give me your name?'

I lift my head to stare at him. Have I heard right? Did they say the word *deceased*? Who? *Please, God, no.* I'm rendered speechless, paralysed. I'm conscious of sirens and flashing, pulsing lights as more and more vehicles arrive. The air takes on an orange-and-blue hue, colours intermingling. I'm suspended, like in a dream. I scrabble in my subconscious to find reality. I need to wake up. I'm present, but not really here. I want to stand up, but my limbs are heavy, weighted down with shock. I am incapable of moving. I feel the comfort of a blanket placed around my shoulders and a hand gives it a solace squeeze.

'Ensure a family liaison officer is appointed asap,' a voice says. One officer moves away, but another loiters nearby, occasionally glancing in my direction. I'm left to observe the scene. Is this for real? It is. This is no dream.

* * *

The motorway has been closed on both sides of the carriageway now and is strewn with emergency vehicles — fire engines, ambulances, police cars, Highways agency patrols and a van with *Collision Investigation Unit* emblazoned on the side. The Range Rover has been screened off and I can see a team of firemen working around it. *Please get them out.* There's activity everywhere.

The scene swims before my eyes. I can make out ambulance crew attending to a few injured. *Please help my family too.* Cate. The children.

'Excuse me, Mrs Mildenhall?' a female voice says. 'Mrs Mildenhall,' the voice repeats. I look up, realising that a police officer is addressing me.

I try to focus on what she is saying. Her face looks kind. I'm willing myself to speak.

'We need you to return to your vehicle, please,' she says, pointing at the Mini. 'Your baby has woken up and started to cry. Here, let me help you up.' She reaches out an arm.

'Ted.' I manage to croak out his name as she pulls me to my feet. My gaze focuses on her badge. *Hampshire Constabulary, Emma Jenkins, Police Constable.* She's real.

'I think —Ted, is it — needs you, Mrs Mildenhall,' PC Jenkins says kindly, escorting me back to the Mini. Christ. I need to wake up. How could I have left Ted alone in the car? He could have choked. Been snatched. Anything.

'Please. Can you tell me what's happened to my family?' I implore PC Jenkins as I find my voice. Tears stream down my face as I unclip Ted from his car seat and rest him on my shoulder. His sobs start to subside as mine dial up.

'I was travelling separately behind. Are they all going to be okay?'

The police officer's face clouds.

'The emergency crews are doing everything they can for them,' she says in an overly considered tone. PC Emma Jenkins has chosen her words carefully. I'm no fool.

I've been told to stay close to my vehicle so I sit with Ted in my arms in the back of the car, soothing him with a bottle of milk.

Doing so brings me some composure. I need to think. A tall figure casting a blinding, yellow reflection approaches. It's the male officer who stopped me getting to the car. He's close enough now that I can make out his name badge — *Police Sergeant Anthony Radcliffe*. PS Radcliffe is carrying an amber-coloured grain-leather Mulberry tote. I didn't even notice it had gone.

'This one's a Millie,' Cate boasted earlier this weekend, giving it a loving stroke. Cate can afford handbags that come with names.

'For safekeeping, Mrs Mildenhall,' the sergeant says, holding it aloft so that I can see it before he opens the front passenger door and places it in the footwell. So that's why they're calling me Mrs Mildenhall. The police think Cate is me.

* * *

It's getting stiflingly hot sat in the back of the car without the aircon on. It's still breezy outside, but the fresh air isn't making it into my lungs. Ted has finished his bottle and it'll be easier for me to wind him standing up. I grab a muslin from his baby bag and we step outside. I lock the car this time. The sheer volume of parked-up vehicles on both sides of the motorway makes me imagine that I could be in the long-term at Heathrow. Except this is no pre-holiday park-up.

Holding Ted against my chest helps me regulate my palpitating heart. I decide to risk leaving the car momentarily, I certainly wouldn't be the only one. As I walk away, PC Emma Jenkins appears by my side. She must have been keeping an eye on me.

'Can I help you, Mrs Mildenhall? It's best you stay with your vehicle.'

'Please, just a few minutes. I need to get some air.'

'Just a moment, then. Can I get you some water?' I nod appreciatively. 'I'll be straight back.' She heads for a police car nearby.

With her back turned I briskly move from the crash site in between the cars. After about fifty metres I cut across to the hard shoulder and double back, weaving among the crowds. No one takes any notice of me; I'm just a delayed traveller with a baby. The air is restless with impatience. Car crashes are nothing more than inconveniences to most. I can hear mutterings of 'It's been nearly two bloody hours' and 'We've got a dinner reservation at seven'. I want to scream at them.

A group of police officers are deep in conversation a few yards ahead. I sidle as close as I dare without drawing attention to myself, straining to hear what is being said. They're discussing opening up the opposite carriageway. One of the collision investigators is explaining they've finished collating evidence where the Range Rover made contact with the central reservation barrier and have taken all they need from that side. The southbound carriageway won't be reopening yet, though.

'We need to finish photographing,' one says.

And then I think I'm going to be sick.

'. . . and then the bodies can be removed.'

A block of concrete has been dropped on my chest from on high. I knew it, but now I *know*.

I cling on to Ted tightly. Is he an orphan? Focus. A nappy change must be due. I'm about to head back to Cate's car when I spot PS Radcliffe emerging from behind the cordon. My trusty leather jacket is slung over his arm, and he's holding my mobile phone and mini black wallet that I always carry in the pocket. I think of David. He bought me that wallet for our third wedding anniversary nearly a decade ago. I've always loved it. Leather is the traditional gift for three years — to signify flexibility and dura-bility. A material that is used to protect, keep you warm, safe and secure. I look down at my wedding band and engagement ring. *So, where are you, David? Who's going to protect me now?*

I watch as PS Radcliffe looks at the cards inside: bank and credit, my Tesco loyalty card. He scrutinises my precious driving licence. An officer approaches him with clear plastic bags, and my jacket and wallet are all placed individually inside and sealed. Good. I want those back later. As my phone is about to receive the same fate, as if on cue it starts to ring. The 'Mouldy Old Dough' ringtone stops me in my tracks. PS Radcliffe and the other officer look down at it simultaneously and exchange a glance. I know what it says on the screen — ICE HUSBAND. David has finally decided to call. It's only taken him all bloody weekend.

I should run over and explain but I can't. My legs are like lead and I'm rooted to the spot. A tremor surges through my body and renders me speechless. I'm paralysed, my stare fixed on the two police officers. If the police think I'm Cate Mildenhall then . . .

PS Radcliffe answers it. He turns his back and starts to walk away, so I can't hear what's being said or even try to lipread. Is he telling David that his wife has been involved in a fatal car crash or do they save that for later?

* * *

I stand on the edge of a precipice here. How is David feeling about what he's hearing? I don't want him to suffer, but would he even miss me? Will he be heartbroken? But should I care? He doesn't want IVF, he won't adopt a child — so maybe he deserves to suffer. So be it — let him! The tug at my heart knowing that David is on the other end of the phone is both tangible and terrifying, but that's what the wreckage of our marriage and my life has come to.

'I'm not going to leave you, little one,' I whisper to Ted.

I remember the nappy change, so will my body to move. As my limbs start to mobilise, movement from the screened-off area catches my attention. An ambulance has been manoeuvred into place adjacent to the cordon. I hold my breath. I glimpse a stretcher covered with a sheet. It's being carried by two ambulance workers. There's a sickness in my stomach. From its size I doubt it's Charlie or Georgie, but — I have to definitively know: is it

Cate? Clutching Ted, I urge my legs to gather pace until I reach PC Emma Jenkins who is standing by the security tape, scanning the crowds with a look of concern. She's been looking for me. PS Radcliffe is further ahead up the motorway, still on the phone. All the uniformed police are occupied. It's now or never.

I stand directly in front of PC Jenkins. Her face relaxes.

'There you are. I got you that water. We must take care of you.' She raises her right arm as if to guide me away. I shake my head. 'Mrs Mildenhall, you really must—'

I take my chance, confident she will respond, and thrust Ted towards her. Emma's reflexes comply as she grabs him with both arms. I summon all my strength, duck under the tape and run towards the ambulance crew. I reach them as they're loading the body into the back of the vehicle.

'Please! This is my family.' I reach under the cover and grab Cate's arm. Intuitively I know it's going to be her. She's my identical twin after all — even in death now as well as life. I'm right. She feels soft to the touch, but cool. Has she really gone? I caress her hand and raise it up to my face, kissing her as I do so. Her engagement ring scratches my cheek. Emotion bubbles up. I'm almost blinded by the tears streaming down my face. *This is it, Cate. The end. Just me now.* To my surprise, the crew allow me a moment. I'm not sure they know what to do with me.

'You will be able to visit soon, Miss,' one of the guys says in a soft tone. I feel a pair of strong arms land on my shoulders and I'm steered away from the ambulance. It's PS Radcliffe.

'I'm so sorry. This is terribly traumatic for you,' he says. 'Best let all the emergency services do their job and we'll get you home. We have a car for you and your baby — it's parked just over here. We'll arrange to get your car back to you.'

'My family. Please can I see the children? Where is Giles?' I ask pleadingly. PS Radcliffe takes a deep breath, purses his lips. PC

Emma Jenkins approaches with Ted in her arms. He looks at her as if for moral support before placing his hand on my shoulder.

'I have confirmation that all occupants of the Range Rover are deceased. I'm so, so . . .'

I don't hear the rest. What I do hear is a strangulated cry. It's come from within me. I didn't need them to confirm it. I knew. But I didn't want to hear it. I look at Emma as the tears cascade.

'We're going to get you home, Mrs Mildenhall. A family liaison officer will meet you there and explain everything.' Her face is sympathetic. She offers Ted up to me. I take him gratefully. Even though he is starting to get restless, Ted has the ability to soothe me. We'll get through this nightmare together.

Within minutes I find myself in the back of a police car with Ted strapped into a baby seat beside me. The fabric seats have a synthetic smell. They feel soft and yielding. Perhaps the foam within them will envelope and consume me, prevent me from ever getting out of this car and stop me from what I'm about to do. PC Jenkins is sitting in the passenger seat; an officer unknown to me is driving. He may have introduced himself, but I don't recall. Everything is blurred. I'm grateful that we're getting out of here, away from this hell.

'Can you just confirm the address for me, Miss?' the driver says.

I give it to him. We're heading for Cate's house in Richmond. I'm not sure what I think I'm going to do when we get there, but Ted needs to be home. Apprehension tightens its grip at the prospect of what lies ahead. I still can't believe what has happened. The constrictive, invisible band around my chest is squeezing all rational thought from me.

I can't take my eyes off Ted. We're both caught up in the same storm, but I think it's safer if we travel together in the same boat from now on. I can't take the risk that we won't be allowed to. As the thought takes hold, I realise that I'm playing anxiously with my rings. I glance down at my left hand. Cate's Tiffany baguette-cut diamond sparkles as it catches the early-evening sunrays, which are starting to appear from behind the clouds. It's heavy on my finger. I think of my diamond micro-chips encircling a miniscule sapphire engagement ring, along with my thinning gold wedding band. Both of which now reside on the left hand of a cooling corpse. *I'm so sorry, my precious Cate.*

I offer Ted my index finger. He grips it tightly. *We're going home, Teddy. You and me.*

AFTER

CHAPTER 5

David

No. No. No. I throw my weekend things into my holdall. Where are my sodding car keys? I pull the duvet off the bed in a panic. A waft of scent fills my nostrils. A painful reminder of what I haven't been able to resist.

I regret leaving it so late to call, but now I know why she's not been picking up. Is this for real? Jesus Christ. Hang on . . . Slow down a minute here and calm down. Think this through. What if this is all some sick joke? Loopy Loo punishing me. I wouldn't put it past Beth. Some perverted retribution she's concocted in Cate's company. Could it be? Surely? Yes. Sussed it.

'We've clearly got nothing to say to each other so no point in calling,' Beth said before I departed for my golf weekend. Deep down I know she didn't mean it. Beth often says the opposite of what she means, but a bit of space from each other is what we both need.

But she's gone and done it now. Beth's crazy. Total batshit crazy. Egged on by that poisonous twin of hers. I imagine the pair of them having a good laugh at my expense. They've been waiting for me to call and probably coerced some guy in the pub to pick up Beth's phone and impersonate the police. Bought him a couple of pints. Thinking about it now, he said something about a female in a yellow dress. He slipped up there. That's not Beth. She rarely wears dresses and, while I may not be completely *au fait* with my wife's wardrobe, I'm pretty sure there's no yellow. I remember being with Beth once when she tried on a sunflower-yellow dress. She laughed hysterically saying she looked like a mustard pot. I thought she looked gorgeous and told her the colour suited her. She pulled a face and joked she might surprise me one day by buying a yellow dress, but she'd make sure it was a much more expensive one. The police-imposter caller must have been looking at Cate when he was speaking. I can't believe I fell for it.

Beth has got it into her head I am having an affair. Unbelievable. She has no evidence whatsoever save for the fact that I bought a few new clothes. But who knows what goes on in that overripe imagination of hers? So now we're going to play some weird charade.

You might not believe it, but once upon a time sex and laughter were the heart and lungs of our relationship. Sex has now become by prediction-stick-appointment only and the sense of humour we both shared has all but evaporated. Where did it start to go wrong? If only we could turn the clock back. Take the other week when she told me off for grabbing a Friday-night beer.

'It'll destroy your sperm count,' she said, snatching it away.

'Come on, Beth. It's been a long week. A man's gotta unwind.' I leaned over her, grinding my hips into her backside, nuzzling her ear while trying to reach the bottle in her outstretched hand. An action that once would have, at the very least, earned me a gentle crotch stroke and a display of the infectious Beth giggles. Not anymore.

'For Christ's sake, David. No. You know how important this is. I'm beginning to think you really don't care?'

'Babe,' I said. 'That's not fair. Be reasonable. One? Pretty please?' I put on my what-used-to-be-irresistible puppy-dog face while realising that she'd probably already smelled the after-work beers on my breath.

'Don't "Babe" me. It doesn't cut it right now,' Beth replied through gritted teeth. She slammed the beer bottle down with force on the counter before flouncing out of the kitchen in the most dramatic way possible.

'Come on, sweetheart — don't be like that.' I pleaded with her, but Beth wasn't listening as she stomped up the stairs and banged the bedroom door shut.

I imagined she'd be calling Cate to discuss my failings and scrutinise my inadequacies. A heart-to-heart with Cate is always a fresh source of ammunition to fire at me. If that was the case then I thought I might as well console myself, so I picked up the beer bottle off the counter. Bad move.

The base gave way and the amber liquid gushed out everywhere, creating a giant, fizzing puddle that immediately started cascading down the cupboards to the floor. I was that miserable in my pathetic desperation for more beer to help blot out the debacle of my marriage, I sank to my knees and started lapping it up. An even worse move.

Beth must have come back in. I hadn't noticed, I was too busy wondering whether the five-second rule could be applied to spilled alcohol. Okay — I'll admit I was already a bit tipsy. She started yelling obscenities at me. I'm sure I can remember a time when she didn't even swear.

'You just don't fucking get it, do you?' Her voice rose to a shriek. 'Or maybe it's that you don't actually give a shit. Our family isn't that important to you. You miserable imbecile, pisshead apology for a husband!'

The tirade continued and the language got worse. I knelt there beside the beer puddle, dumbfounded at her reaction. I reached out a consolatory arm to catch her hand, but she backed away and yanked open the freezer. The next thing I knew she was ripping open a bag of peas and shaking the contents over my head. Then followed a bag of frozen prawns. The peas ricocheted all over the kitchen floor like little green bullets; the prawns landed with an apologetic splash in the beer slick. Between Beth's sobs I caught her say, 'My period started today and you didn't even bloody ask.'

Shit. I should have remembered that vigil. My major bad. Beth was inconsolable and wouldn't let me touch her, so I did the only thing I could to help. I cleaned up the mess.

* * *

Result. I've located my car keys in the bedside drawer. The hotel notepad looks up at me where, at some point this weekend, I doodled a cartoon baby with two front teeth and sticky-out ears. The subject isn't going away and I do owe Beth an honest explanation. Avoidance is a weak strategy. *Must do better, David.*

I'm worried, though. Beth seems so unstable these days that even if we could afford another round of IVF, I don't think we should. She's in no fit state for the physical and emotional rigours of all those injections again. This cooked-up scheming with Cate and the phone call confirms where her head is at. It's all designed to put pressure on me. But we genuinely can't afford it — we don't have another five grand to spare. Or, more accurately, we don't anymore. I've screwed up big time on that score and at some point, I've got to come clean. But maybe we're even now after this little round of gameplay. She's pushed it too far even though I know Beth is heavily influenced by Cate. But this is cruel. Sicko. What she's planning for the big reveal? Should I call back and see who picks up? No, I'm a step ahead of you on this one, *BeBe* babes.

I'm going home. I'll take a shower. Open a bottle of wine. Wait for her to appear expecting me to be in bits. Act all cool like. That'll floor her and maybe then we can have an honest and long-overdue conversation.

* * *

As I turn the corner into our road, my lungs constrict. There's a police car parked up in the street. No. No. Can't be. Tell me this isn't happening.

I park and get out the car. My mind clutches at straws. You can hire guys in police uniforms, can't you? But there's a very official-looking car.

The words of the police officer come slow and weighty, like a wrecking ball.

'I am sincerely sorry to confirm, Mr Brown, but your wife has been involved in a fatal car accident.'

My body shakes and heaves. I can't believe it. No prank — it's true. What was Beth doing with bloody Giles? How am I ever supposed to live without her?

The officer helps me get my keys in the door and follows me inside. I turn to him, my brain having gone into confused overdrive.

'Are you sure you've got this right? There's two of them, you know. Twins. Beth and Cate. And there was mention of a yellow dress. That's not likely to be Beth.' I shake my head before resting my forehead in my hands, trying to assimilate everything I've been told. 'At least, I don't think so. And I don't get why she was with Giles, Cate's husband.'

'I'm so very sorry, sir. We have confirmation that it was your wife travelling in the Range Rover with Mr Mildenhall. Mrs Cate Mildenhall was driving her own vehicle with her baby a short distance behind. She witnessed the accident. The police at the scene will have spoken to her and verified everything.'

'God, it was to be with the kids — wasn't it? Oh, Beth!'

'I'm sure that's a plausible explanation, sir.'

Fuck. My beloved Beth has gone.

The police explain and give me more detail of what happened, They're all gone — Giles and the children too, except for Cate and the baby.

It's bizarre what sticks in your brain. Moments ago, I learned my wife has died and the image I have of Beth in my head is from well over a decade ago. She's wearing her denim dungarees, her gorgeous auburn hair tied up with a red-and-white spotted scarf, scalpel in hand stripping the woodchip from the walls of our terraced house. A smattering of freckles covers the bridge of her nose and her brown eyes are flecked with sparkling gold. Whenever a tune she likes comes on the radio she dances around the room, finishing right in front of me to plant a kiss on my lips.

Once the police have left, I stumble into the living room and collapse on the sofa. I convinced myself it was Beth's fault for what was happening between us. Why did I do that? Words used as weapons to inflict maximum damage where my fertility was concerned didn't help. I decided Beth was thirsty for conflict and was building up a long list of grievances, so I justified my indiscretion as fresh fodder for her mental notepad.

The clamp in my chest is guilt, though. Black, sodden guilt. The truth is my wife was drowning and no one was there to throw a lifeline. It was all too much for her and she was sinking beneath the waves. I didn't notice, I was that busy polishing my excuses. It's all too late. She's gone. Some lifeguard I've turned out to be.

I reach for my phone in my pocket. I appreciate I walk a moral tightrope here, but we all deal with grief in different ways, don't we? I can't help myself. I am a master at making situations worse, after all. I take first prize for weakness, but I can't face this alone. Maybe it should be Cate that I call? Christ. She must be in a dreadful state too. My fingers hover over the keypad. I put my phone on the coffee table. I can't face her. I'll contact Cate tomorrow. I pick it up again, gasp in some air and press the call button before the morality police turn up too. After three rings, Adrianna answers.

'*Olá!*'

'Hi.'

'What's up? It's not Tuesday.'

'Something's happened. I need to see you. Right now.' The words stick in my throat. 'P-please. It's important.'

There's a pause on the line. 'Where do you want to meet?' she finally asks, with a fleck of flirtation.

'Here. I want you to come to my house. I'll give you the address.'

'I know where you live, David. I'll be there within the hour. *Tchau.*' And she hangs up.

CHAPTER 6

Adrianna

Que inferno. What the hell was that all about? David was distraught and could hardly speak. Something's up that's for sure. I'm in Knightsbridge after a Harvey Nichols shopping trip. This is not what I planned for the rest of my day. I call an Uber. Three minutes.

I was liking this guy. He has serious potential. And it's been easy this far. Like putty in my hands, as the English say.

I first spied David in a coffee shop in Richmond. He was clutching his Starbucks container while talking on his mobile. I could tell he was agitated, if not a tad stressed and exasperated by the way he tensed his shoulders. I wanted to massage those tight sinews in his neck and shoulders right there and then. Adrianna could ease those troubles away — I just needed to orchestrate the opportunity. He'd raise his cup to take a sip, then put it down again in frustration. I moved to the table behind him so that I could eavesdrop.

His suit jacket was slung over the back of the chair next to him. I clocked a name badge — *David Brown, Regional Sales Manager.* Evidently, he worked for a mobile-phone company that had a Richmond branch. Convenient. He leaned back in his chair, oblivious to my presence. He was so close I could smell his after-shave. Ylang-ylang, plum and patchouli with a touch of black truffle. My money is on Tom Ford. Years of working on the perfume counters at John Lewis and Bentalls in between acting jobs had fine-tuned my nose. A sophisticated choice, Senhor Brown.

He ran his fingers (displaying a wedding band that no longer shone) through his hair, which was thick, dark brown on top, tapering into a low fade. Very business professional, Senhor Brown. I'm guessing he was talking on the phone to his wife.

'I am listening — I am . . . Can we talk about this later, Beth? Okay, yes, got it . . . I should finish about six and, yes, I'll come straight home. Promise. I said I would, didn't I?'

He let out a big sigh as he finished the call, and put his phone down gently and with precision as if to try to calm his nerves. Even without a proper introduction, I already knew his name, his wife's name and his place of work. Check, check, check. Good-looking and fragrant too. He was perfect. Until this afternoon's phone call.

Still, this could be interesting, particularly as I've been invited to his house. Where's the wife? Has she left him? I say this could be interesting, but what I mean is *I am interested*. I shouldn't be, but I am, and I haven't felt like this for a long time.

David is the latest in my little romance-scam sideline. Just a *pequeño* — a little something to supplement the income here and there. Don't judge me. I've taken enough crap from men — one in particular — and this is my way of evening up the score. Sol is to blame. This is my self-therapy, taking back for the hurt done to me. A crazy external solution to an internal problem. It's perverse, but you'd do the same if you'd been through what I have.

Sol gained more pleasure from forcibly taking something rather than getting it for free. Lying there, pinned down by someone you thought loved you with their hands around your throat as they pound and thrust into you can make you do some screwed-up things.

40

I'll admit my form of retribution has been starting to get out of hand — like a payday loan, these things do have a tendency to spiral out of control. The last guy, who I didn't sleep with, was planning to leave his wife of nearly twenty years so that we could move in together and take our relationship to the *next level*. I had to get out fast. I've been wondering if David could be the one to put a stop to my scheming? I like him. He's got a vulnerability about him that I want to cherish. Maybe I'm about to get the opportunity.

'Here, I want you to have this,' David said last month, pushing a thick envelope into my hand. It contained five hundred pounds in cash. I was incredulous considering we were only six or seven dates into our *relationship*. It isn't normally that easy. He knew about my financial problems. Being an actor, not knowing when I'd get my next paycheque. My landlord on my back — all my usual routine. But still, I normally had to work harder. I feigned protestation but David insisted.

'I think your need is greater than mine. In fact, maybe you'd be doing me a favour,' he said with a mock laugh, without explaining what he meant. He appeared with another five hundred a week later.

'A little something for safekeeping.'

I usually have to make promises about paying the money back, but he wanted to give it away. For the first time since I've been scamming, I carried guilt on my shoulders.

I got the idea for all this from the invisible-performance module at drama school. After roleplay in the studio, we'd be sent out on a mission, in pairs, to a local coffee shop, park or bus stop. There we'd act out a given scenario engaging members of the public, convincing them we were someone other than our true selves. Persuading them that we were members of a famous pop band was a favourite of mine. Unknowingly, they became both audience and participants. I've been perfecting my street-improvisation drama combined with a catfishing sentiment for years now. David is Sting Twelve.

The rush of it, not just the money, is what makes it worthwhile. Pulling it off, but feeling I'm living dangerously close to the edge, is the reward. After I've got what I want from each relationship, I end things and move on. And after each *romance* ends, I raise two fingers to Sol.

The way it works is that David gets sucked into my plight because he doesn't think I could be lying to him. So far so good. I've gained his trust. I always make sure there's an element of romance so it feels genuine, but how far that part goes depends on their fuckability score. David is a definite nine. That's rare. I don't make a habit of it, but things in that department moved on at a pace with David.

I can see the Uber crawling along the kerb towards me. The driver is scanning the pavement. I raise my hand and the car pulls over. I open the cab door and get inside. I feel like a hooker. I give the driver David's address. It occurs to me that I told David I already had it. That was a rookie error. The state he was in caught me off-guard. I'm going to have to come up with an excuse for that one if he asks. Hopefully I've dodged a bullet. We're soon speeding along the Cromwell Road towards west London. The cabbie is chatting away about good job it wasn't yesterday as it was a nightmare around Twickenham Stadium, but I'm not listening. I can only think of David as I clutch my Harvey Nichols booty, courtesy of his generosity. The situation is unprecedented. Is it about the money? The wife has found out and he's in deep shit. But he sounded inconsolable. I know her name is Beth, but it's safer if I refer to her as *the wife*. Never reveal what you already know. I got caught out on that one once. Never saw the guy again. Weeks of work wasted.

Or maybe the wife has found out about us? I did meet David at his hotel on Friday before his golfing weekend, but he said she was away until today. No — it's something else. A feeling of trepidation is curling its way up my body like a plume of smoke. What am I walking into?

I step out of the cab and check I'm at the right address. It's a late Sunday afternoon in June, but the curtains are partially closed. I hope David's not brought me here under false pretences. Just fancies a quickie while the wife is out. I'll be seriously pissed off if that's the case. I walk up the small front path. As I extend my arm to ring the bell, the door swings open. David stands there looking dishevelled; he appears to have been crying.

'You came. Thank you. I knew you would.' He pulls me inside.

'David. What is this about?'

'She's gone. She's gone.'

'Who's gone?' I mustn't say Beth. She's left him. Interesting.

'Beth — my wife. She's dead.' David collapses into my arms, his body heaving with sobs.

What? Of all the scenarios that've been going around in my head, this certainly isn't one of them. His wife has gone and fucking died? I'm not prepared for this. Don't know how I'm supposed to react. I'm not sure I signed up for this. David must know that I shouldn't be the one here. He clings on to me tightly.

'Please don't leave me.'

I let him hold me, but focus past his shoulder on the dust motes dancing in the sunlight that streams through the gap in the curtains. I think I'm about to embark on my most challenging role yet.

CHAPTER 7

Beth

We pull up in the road outside Cate's house. A police car is parked in the driveway and two plainclothes police officers step out to greet us. I'm not sure I'm ready for this. What am I supposed to do next?

Waves of emotion engulf me like a fast-moving tide. The grief I feel for the loss of my sister and her children — even Giles — is so monumentally physical, I can't believe I'm still living when my heart has been shattered to smithereens. My brain isn't connecting either; I can't think straight.

Is it ever too late to do the right thing? What even is the right thing? Maybe that train has already left the station; instead, I'm standing on the final-decision platform. It's the last call. Glancing over at Ted, I know I've already climbed on board and chosen destination Cate. We are two halves of one whole, after all.

A woman, mid-forties, with shoulder-length mousy hair, approaches the car. She straightens the jacket of her grey trouser suit and fleetingly looks over at her colleague as if for moral support before opening the rear passenger door.

'Mrs Mildenhall, please let me help you,' she says, offering an arm. Her face is kind and mumsy, and, because I don't know what to say or do, I focus on the mole above her right eyebrow.

'Come, please,' she says. 'Let's get you and your baby inside.' I step out of the car and turn to lean back in to unclip the belt from Ted's car seat. What am I doing?

'My name is Jessica Howard,' she continues. 'I'm a family liaison officer attached to the Metropolitan Police. But please call me Jess. This is DS Patrick McLennan.' The detective acknowledges me with a look of consolation.

'Mrs Mildenhall.'

'Cate,' I say, forcing myself to say her name. 'I'm Cate with a C. As in Blanchett.' I feel ridiculous saying it. I don't suppose they care how my name is spelt, but it's exactly what Cate always says. *I'm* Cate now it appears, so I said it.

'This is Ted,' I say, looking down at his unsuspecting face.

'We're so sorry for what has happened today, Cate,' Jess says. Her brow furrows with concern. 'I'm here to update you and help in any way we can.'

Jess takes my arm and steers me towards the front door of Cate's house. DS Patrick McLellan lingers back in the driveway, I notice. I grip Ted's car seat, willing him to give me the strength to go through with this as we walk up the black-and-white tessellated tile path and the cream limestone steps to the door.

Cate and Giles live in the kind of home that otherwise I only ever get to see when flicking through the home magazines at the hairdressers. It's a late Georgian villa with tall, shuttered windows and high ceilings in a road off Richmond Hill. The sheer scale of the house is overwhelming, standing there majestically among a plethora of equally magnificent five-star homes. The house must be six times the width of our little terrace in Twickenham. Two neatly clipped bay trees, not a leaf out of place, sit in perfect symmetry in terracotta planters, framing the high-gloss, black front door that could give Number 10 a run for its money.

I hesitate as it dawns on me that I don't even know if I've got the keys to the house. Jessica reads my hesitation as reluctance to enter my empty home.

'You're doing fine, Cate. We're here with you. I'm not going to leave until you feel ready.'

I look up at her and nod slightly to acknowledge what she's said. I place Ted down under the protection of the portico and start to fumble in Cate's Mulberry for the keys. If they're not here, I'll have to say that I forgot that Giles locked up last and I didn't bring mine.

My fingers alight on them. Hallelujah!

Not so good. There are five keys on the keyring. I'd better get this right first time — I can't be seen to not know how to open my own front door. We've not even stepped inside yet and I can already feel this starting to go wrong.

I move Ted closer to the door just to buy some time as I quickly glance at the locks, then at the bunch of keys in my hand. *Come on, Beth, you can do this. Focus.* There are two locks on the door — one a Yale, the other a Chubb. There is only one Yale key, but two Chubbs on the keyring. I spot a dab of red nail polish on one. I'm going with this, guessing that Cate placed it there to differentiate them too. *Are you looking over me?*

I hold my breath until the door clicks open. I step inside on to the highly polished walnut hallway floor. A soft vanilla scent from the reed diffuser on the console table fills the air. I haven't moved an inch when there is an audible beep, followed by another, then another in a deafening rising crescendo. *Oh, God, Cate, why did you have to go and put the alarm on?* My stomach clenches with fear.

To protect my multi-million-pound home, Beth — that's why, you moron!

The beeping gets louder and louder. If I don't hurry, I'll be timed out and the alarm will go off. I might as well throw in the towel now. Saying that Giles always does the alarm won't really cut it. The alarm starts to wail and Ted, in response, cries. I can't bear that I've caused him this distress.

Then inspiration. *I've got one shot at this, but if you've been true to form, I think I can guess what the code is going to be.* I just don't know how many digits it needs. I make a deal with myself: if I get this wrong then I'm going no further. I'll put my hands up and tell the truth. Hopefully, after all the trauma the authorities won't be too harsh on me. Here goes.

I walk over to the alarm panel and purposefully press the number 1, followed by 2, then repeat. I hesitate for a fraction of a second after I've entered four digits but sense the alarm wants more. I enter another 1 followed by 2. I pause. It stops. *Oh, Cate, you little darling.*

'I'm so sorry,' I say turning to Jess. 'I'm . . . all . . . over the place.'

'I think that's very understandable,' Jess says, giving me a sympathetic look. 'May I help you with this little one?' She bends down to pick up Ted in his car seat.

The DS now steps into the hall behind us and carefully closes the door as though it might set the alarm off again. I walk down the cavernous hallway and Jess follows me into Cate's vast kitchen. You could fit the entire ground floor of our house into this room.

'Um . . . tea?' I suggest, wanting something to do while I try to pull myself together.

'Great idea, thank you,' Jess says, putting Ted down on the floor by the central working island, which is the size of a small swimming pool.

I stand looking at the expanse of marble counter worktops to spot the kettle. I try to make it look like I'm composing myself. Cate has had a new kitchen fitted since I was here last. She'd been talking about it and planning for months, but I can't see a kettle anywhere. Surely, she doesn't keep it in a cupboard? What a palaver. This is all too difficult, but I will not be defeated by a bloody kettle. My eyes rest on a row of storage jars over by the sink, one of which is labelled *Tea*. There has to be one nearby. Then I hear Cate singing in my ears.

Quooker, darling. You must get one. No one uses a kettle anymore.

Of course. It's the extra sleek additional tap thing next to the sink. Cate has a boiling water tap and much else besides I note, taking in her new, about as high-end as you can get, kitchen. I walk over and confidently open the cupboard on the wall directly to the right of the sink expecting to see mugs for tea. That was where they were in the old kitchen, but not anymore. It's full of flower vases. I close it again quickly. Great, now I look like I've forgotten where I keep the china. The knot in my throat is starting to tighten again. A wave of nausea wells up inside me as I try to swallow the acrid taste back down. I do the only thing I can think of at this point.

'So sorry . . . you're going to have to excuse me.' I put my hand over my mouth with an audible groan and rush for the loo down the hallway. I deliberately leave the door open. I sink to the floor and open the toilet lid as I allow the bile to fill my throat. Is my body physically trying to expel what I have done? Expunge my sins? I help it along utilising my first and middle fingers, and vomit violently into the toilet bowl.

I splash some cold water over my face and try to regulate my breathing to prepare myself to return to the kitchen. Maybe succeed in making some tea. Look like I own the place and know what I'm doing, even in my tumultuous grief.

I consider whether to continue this dangerous charade, but, as soon as the thought appears, it's quelled. There is a purpose to all this. Ted. Ted and I, we're the survivors from today's tragedy.

Being childless feels like having a blade constantly wedged up against my heart; it stabs and twists within me. If the instant cure for my agony necessitates this monumental lie, then so be it. I'm in it for Ted. There's no guarantee I would be able to adopt him, there's too many complications — not least David — so here we are. I am not a bad person at heart — I'd just like to put that out there. I dab at my watery eyes and walk back into the kitchen.

'I'm sorry you had to hear that,' I say to Jess.

'Oh, Cate, please don't feel you have to apologise.' Jess hands me a glass of water and steers me towards the sofa in one corner of the kitchen. She must have looked around in my absence as she's located a glass. Jess is doing better than me.

'Thank you,' is all I can manage as I slump down in a crumpled heap among Cate's artistically arranged cushions. Jess sits down beside me. The tears fall again and I reach for the tissues that I stuffed up my sleeve. Jess carries on speaking because I can see her mouth open and close, but I can't hear any words properly. Everything in the room looks fragmented as though my vision has now become a kaleidoscope. I think she's repeating what I was told at the roadside. They're gone. My husband and children. All of them. I can't believe she's referring to Charlie and Georgie. I loved them so much. My sister, Beth, has also lost her life. It is a very strange experience being told that you have passed away, I can tell you. I'm the fly on the wall of the life after me.

I glance over at Ted who has miraculously fallen asleep again, still in his car seat. I'm doing this for him, I tell myself. And me.

'Shall I make some tea?' Jess says, interrupting my thoughts. I point towards the hot water tap over by the sink before trying to dry my eyes with a fresh tissue, but the tear tap isn't going to stop flowing anytime soon.

'Ah, you've got one of those,' Jess says, jumping up. 'I wondered where the kettle was. I've always wanted to try one. May I?' She heads over to the kitchen counter. She's already found some mugs. Seeing three mugs set out, I become conscious of the presence of the detective who has been lurking in the background. He's a tall, pinch-faced man with a wrinkly bald head that reminds me of a dried-up piece of used chewing gum. He catches me looking at him and steps forward.

'I'm so sorry to intrude, Cate, but I wonder if I could possibly ask you a few quick questions? It's important and it won't take long,' DS McLellan says, pulling up a kitchen chair to sit close by.

Jess hands me a mug of scalding, strong tea. In my impatience to be doing something, I take a sip and it burns my tongue. Another second to avoid the gaze of the detective who seems to be waiting for me to speak. Is it possible to have G-U-I-L-T-Y emblazoned across your forehead?

'What . . . what happened?' I say.

'We were hoping you might be able to fill us in a little. We understand that you were following behind your husband? Can you tell us about anything you saw?'

'Yes. Yes, there was . . .' I trail off.

'We've had reports of a white van driving erratically. Did you observe anything?'

I nod. I close my eyes to relive the scene. I can see him weaving about.

'Did he hit them? Did that man kill my family through his stupid, lethal driving?' My voice rises; hysterics aren't far away.

I force myself to bite my tongue. I have to be careful not to say any more. Beth would have a rant about dangerous driving, but I have to think like Cate.

'There's no evidence of that as yet, but your husband's vehicle will be fully examined at the compound. Forensic samples have been taken from the scene. We're gradually building up pieces of the jigsaw as to why the vehicle left the road. We're waiting for the senior forensic collision investigator to complete his work, but I promise you, Cate, we'll get to the bottom of this. Can I ask, did you get the number plate of the van?'

'No, sorry, I didn't.' I wonder how I was expected to do that while driving. How was I expected to know that it would become significant?

'No worries,' DS McLellan says. 'We're talking to witnesses and checking CCTV. It all takes time, I'm afraid. Did you see who was driving the Ford Transit? You said "that man"?'

I've been mentally begging for some form of pain relief to blur the scenes that won't leave my head, but now I try to think back to what happened at the beginning of the chain of events. I try to picture the driver's face, but I can't get clarity.

'It was definitely a male,' I tell the DS. 'I only caught a glimpse. He was wearing a beanie hat. I'm sure it was grey.'

'Age? A beard?'

I try to think. 'Um . . . late thirties, maybe fortyish. Sorry I can't be more specific. It was only a fleeting glance.'

I don't mention the grin or wave. I can't risk the scrutiny. *You're a traitor* pounds in my head.

'And any facial hair?'

'Maybe a bit of dark stubble. I'm sorry I'm not being much help. Everything happened so quickly.'

I'm desperate for this conversation to come to an end. My head is spinning and I crave to be alone with Ted, who has woken up and is starting to grizzle. He's my number-one priority. I stand up from the sofa and walk across the kitchen. I crouch down to unclip him from his car seat, grateful for the distraction. I lift him up to rest on my shoulder.

'I'm going to have to deal with Ted. Can we take a break?'

'Yes, of course, Cate. You must see to your baby,' Jess says.

'Tea, bath, bottle, bed.' I try to sound like I know what I'm doing.

'We'll call in again tomorrow. We'll keep you updated and fully informed,' DS McLellan says.

'Is there anyone I can call for you, Cate? I can stay longer if you'd like?' Jess says.

I think for a moment. As much as I'd like to lock myself away with Ted for ever, I know that there's going to be a lot to deal with.

'I'm fine being left alone. But it would be helpful if you could let some immediate family know what's happened. I'm going to struggle to deal with it all tonight.'

'Yes, of course. I'll get on to it straight away,' Jess says.

'There's Giles's parents — Laura and Michael — our mother, Rachel, and . . . David — Beth's husband.' Referring to myself sticks awkwardly on my tongue. I'm going to have to get used to this.

'And the school for tomorrow — Grange Place.' I choke up as, yet again, I think of poor Charlie and Georgie. God, this is painful.

'If I can just take some details.' Jess has her pen poised.

Idiot. I'm now going to have to pass on phone numbers that are either in my phone, which I no longer have, or Cate's, which I do, but haven't yet unlocked and can't risk trying in front of the police. Dumb move.

'I understand that your sister's husband has already been informed,' Jess says.

Realisation hits that David still thinks I'm dead. The thought stabs at my heart. I only meant him to suffer temporarily, but then I had this crazy idea. I want to ask how he reacted. Did he cry? How is he? I don't know where to go with this. How am I going to deal with it all? But I have to. I've made the choice. I have no free hands to wipe away the tears trickling down my face again.

'Our mother, Rachel — Rachel Woods — is in the Swallowfields nursing home in Chiswick. Her speech has been affected by a stroke and she has dementia, so it may be better handled by the staff there; I'm not sure. Talk to them first. It may be a few days before I can see her so that would be helpful, thank you,' I say through my streaming tears.

'No problem. And do you have contact information for your husband's parents?'

I buy myself a few more moments busying myself putting Ted in his high chair. I give him a set of colourful plastic keys to distract him. He puts them up to his mouth to chew.

I need to dig deep. I can't not have my in-laws' details. Then I recall Cate opening a Liberty-print-covered address book given to her by Giles's parents a few Christmases back. I remember her blinking her eyes at me in a way that no one else would notice, but was our childhood code for *vomitsville* as she discovered the contents of the beautifully wrapped and ribboned package. *Where have you put it, Cate?* I remember seeing it intermittently on the console table in the hallway for a while afterwards, probably strategically placed when the Mildenhalls were due to visit, knowing Cate. Where is it now?

'Laura and Michael Mildenhall live in Maida Vale. I'll just get you the exact details, excuse me a moment.' I head back out to the hallway. I have a hunch. I open the drawer to the table and it's there. *Bless you, Cate.* Turning to the letter *M*, the full address and all phone numbers are there too so I write them down on a piece of paper I take from a memo block and head back to the kitchen.

'If you could tell them I'll call tomorrow.' I hand Jess the scrap of paper. As soon as I've done so, I realise that I've done another stupid thing. It's my handwriting on that piece of paper, not Cate's. I can only hope that I'm worrying about something inconsequential on this, the worst day of my life.

* * *

I sit in the nursing chair in Ted's room, cradling him in my arms and drinking in the scent of his purity and innocence. I try to take the imprint as if I can absorb him through osmosis. Ted has, perhaps predictably, taken some time to settle. He's been agitated and gripey, twisting in my arms in a disconcerting fashion, perhaps sensing that his mother is dead and his aunt is trying to soothe him. *It's going to be okay, my gorgeous boy. I've got you now, little one.*

Eventually his breathing deepens, his eyelids flicker and finally lower, tipping over into a sound, peaceful kind of sleep that is a privilege of only the newborn. I watch his face, counting every eyelash and taking in the little white baby spots scattered over his nose. Will I ever sleep peacefully again? Did I make the right call? To take on Cate's life? Sometimes decisions are just made. I'm not even sure that I was the one who made the decision. Wasn't it that Sergeant Radcliffe who presumed I was Cate Mildenhall? I didn't correct him. He was the one who put the marker down. I merely stepped over the line, I can only pray that it's not into the abyss. But that is the little voice in my brain called doubt talking.

I am painfully conscious that I am guilty of a serious crime. I am a liar, an imposter and a child abductor. I falsely hold the title of widow and bereaved mother twice over. But I am also, at long last, a *mother*. Mother to a delightful six-month-old baby. And that, however achieved, I am not ashamed to say, brings me the deepest joy.

CHAPTER 8

Beth

I lurch upright in bed just after six, covered in sweat and gasping for breath as it comes in painful rasps. I've been drowning and have somehow made it to the surface to gulp lungfuls of air. I am alive, I have survived. Then I remember: Cate is dead. And Charlie and Georgie. Giles too. This is a living nightmare. It's real, I realise, as I search out Ted sleeping peacefully in his cot. I'm on a daybed in his nursery where I lay down after he woke for a 3 a.m. feed. I'm going to have to get used to this routine. I already feel exhausted, but lack of sleep is a small price to pay to keep my motherhood prize.

I'm careful not to wake Ted as I creep out of the room. I need some precious moments before he wakes to think and get myself ready to face the day. I know the police will be back and I must prepare myself as Cate. Think like Cate, act like Cate, look like Cate, smell like Cate. First stop — to find some decent scissors to cut my hair shorter. We are identical, Cate and I, but Cate prefers a chic, blunt, Anna Wintour power bob while mine sits just below my shoulders with a few ragged edges where I can't be bothered or afford to go to the hairdressers. Our hair is auburn with a few coppery soft lights.

I find what I'm looking for in the master bedroom en-suite cabinet. I start snipping, but realise I've got to make a half-decent job of this as it could be a while before I can make it to a salon. Popping out to the hairdressers isn't exactly the first port of call on the day after you've tragically lost your husband and children.

'Can you spare a few moments, Cate, while we run through the events of yesterday again?'

'Maybe tomorrow, Detective? I've got an urgent hair appointment right now. Must dash.'

I need to watch a YouTube hairdressing tutorial or something. I haven't yet tried to get into Cate's phone, but have spotted her iPad on the bedside table. Better to attempt to get into that rather than get locked out of her phone. As identical twins, have we got the same fingerprints as we're genetically the same? Can't say I've ever really thought about it before. Guess I'm going to find out.

The answer is an emphatic no. I've tried every finger and my thumb, and the security print is not recognised. I've now got to get the six-digit pin right or I'm stuffed. I'm not sure how many chances I get. Maybe three at most. Cate's favourite sequence of numbers is always one followed by two, but will I strike as lucky with this as the alarm?

'Oh, Cate, you've already become my guardian angel,' I say out loud as the iPad springs to life with 1, 2, 1, 2, 1, 2. I shouldn't be surprised. Maybe a lifetime of being relegated to number two is finally going to reap its rewards. Cate, of course, was always number one. It all started with blowing out the candles on our birthday cake. When we were young, we always used to share the one cake and blow the candles out together. I loved our shared moment.

'One, two, three, blow!' our mother would say and we'd both puff as hard as we could. But Cate would always complain that I blew out more candles than her and it wasn't fair. Our mother's solution was to place two sets of candles on opposite sides of the cake, one for each of us to blow out in unison. We then progressed to Cate demanding her own cake for the following year as she said I spat on her side. Our mother was one to keep the peace, so Cate got her own way. I can remember feeling disappointed. I didn't want two cakes, I wanted only the one to share like always. Looking back, I mark this moment as the start of Cate separating herself away from me.

The first year of two cakes we blew out our candles together, but I succeeded in blowing out mine in record time so the first cheers were for me. Inevitably, once two cakes were established, the goalposts moved again and Cate felt entitled to blow out her candles first.

'I came out first so I'm the oldest. Once I've finished, then you get a turn.'

The following year, a few days before our eleventh birthday, Grandad died so Mum was away in Hastings to be with Grannie. Dad was left in charge.

'I go first, I'm the eldest, Dad,' Cate said.

'No, that's not fair.' I gave Cate a good shove.

'Elizabeth. Stop that now,' Dad said as he struck the match and lit the candles on Cate's cake.

I whined. 'But, Dad, why am I never first?'

'You are. After me, you come first. Always,' Cate said with a satisfied smirk on her face.

This remark was met with hilarity by the birthday-party audience, including Dad. It felt like a slap in the face. My fate was set and Cate's favourite mantra became, 'After me, you come first.' Being born just seventeen minutes after Cate relegated me to the number two spot; a position I have kept for my entire life. Until now, that is.

I watch a short YouTube video on Cate's iPad and divide my hair into sections and hold it back with clips. I snip away, keeping the hair taut and straight between my index and middle fingers. Trying to do the back of my head is the hardest. I can't over-stress about this, though. It's going to have to suffice as there's so much else to do and Ted could wake any minute. Hair clippings go in the bathroom bin and I have a lightning shower, leaving my hair wet so it'll frizz up. Looking dishevelled is my best option and no one is going to expect a day-old widow and bereaved mother to look otherwise.

Adjacent to the bathroom is Cate's walk-in wardrobe. It's about twice the size of David's and my bedroom. Rows and rows of rails are filled with beautiful silk shirts, dresses for every season and occasion, tailored trousers, jackets and coats. Designer label after designer label screams money and privilege. I spot Isabel Marant, Prada, Dolce & Gabbana, Sportmax, Moncler, Missoni, Victoria Beckham. A stark contrast to my Zara and best-of-the-sales wardrobe.

I hardly know where to start. I grab one of the meticulously folded pairs of pale-blue denims from an open shelf and look around for a tee. I find them, dozens of them, immaculately pressed and folded in a uniform shape to fit with precision into the drawers. I grab a white one with a designer motif on the front from the pile and bury my face into it. It smells new and fresh. Something doesn't feel right. Do identical twins smell the same? I doubt it. The most important person I've got to convince I'm Cate is Ted. I need the scent of Cate. I need the laundry basket.

There is no sign of one in the bedroom or walk-in wardrobe. *Silly me.* It's located in the laundry room adjacent to the family bathroom on the first floor. A whole room dedicated to laundry complete with not one but two washing machines and dryers, a large ironing board, trouser press and clothes steamer. No knickers hung on the outdoor clothesline in this household.

I smell the scent of freshly washed clothes still hanging in the air. It's such a painful notion that their owners will not be able to wear them again. The dirty laundry basket offers up two tees and a shirt, plus a couple of bras. I draw the line at Cate's worn panties. I find myself ironing the tee shirts. The heat of the iron releases the smell of Cate. It's like she's in the room with me. Cate's molecules linger in the air.

Please guide me. I'm going to need your help. Oh, Cate!

I'm about to sink into myself when I hear Ted stir. Pulling a tee quickly over my head, I go to collect my baby.

'Good morning, my lovely. Give Mummy a cuddle,' I say, lifting him up out of his cot. Ted eyes me suspiciously.

You look like Mummy, but something's odd.

'Did you have a lovely sleep?' I nuzzle into his neck. 'Come and help me choose a perfume. What shall I wear today to smell like Mummy?'

We go back into the dressing room where I spied a table adorned with perfume bottles. There's a lot of choice — virtually the whole Jo Loves range, copious Jo Malone, Penhaligon's and Chanel, as well as other very expensive-looking bottles with names that I've never heard of.

I know that smells can be very powerful and are one of the strongest memory triggers, but I'm not looking for Ted to recall me as much as to convince him that I am the one and the same mother he's always had. I am genetically and physically the same. I need to smell the same too. I've showered with Cate's shower gel, used her shampoo and hair conditioner — but I've got to be thorough.

'So, which one do you think, Ted?' I pick up and sniff a Chanel bottle. Too strong. There's a bottle of Jo Loves Pomelo, which is nearly empty. Ted gurgles, probably wanting his milk bottle.

'This one?' I pick it up and give it a sniff. 'What are you trying to tell me? I need to smell fruity.' I spritz the fragrance on my wrists and a dab on my neck. I swallow a lump in my throat. It does smell like Cate. No being melancholy in front of Ted; I need to latch on to some positive vibes.

'Thanks for the heads-up, my Teddy Bear. Now for breakfast.' We descend the stairs with me smelling like a grapefruit.

Before we've even reached the bottom step, a key is turned in the door. I freeze. What the hell? A slightly plump woman, about fifty years of age, carrying one of those old-fashioned wicker baskets, steps inside and shuts the door carefully behind her. Who on earth is this?

CHAPTER 9

Beth

The woman puts her basket on the floor and stares up at me.

Who the hell are you? I want to ask, but I freeze on the spot and say nothing. I hold Ted tightly to my chest, fearful that I've been rumbled somehow and that social services have already come to take him away. I take her in, trying to assess the situation. I should be the one in command here. This is *my* house, but I don't want to be wrong-footed and say anything that will put me at a disadvantage. Her black hair tinged with grey is drawn back from her lined face and pinned up in a chignon. She's wearing black trousers, the kind my mother would have called *slacks*. On top she's got a dull lilac tunic with deep front pockets. Her open-toed, cushioned-footbed-style sandals display fading pearly-peach nail polish. She's on her feet all day, it seems. Her face starts to crumple as she rushes towards me.

'Oh, Mrs Mildenhall! It's so tragic. So bad, so bad,' she says, losing her composure with tears welling up in her eyes. 'This can't be true. The children. No. No.' She sobs. 'And Mr Giles? I can't believe it. Oh, dear Lord.' She makes a sign of the cross.

I can't quite place her accent.

'It's true. They're all . . . gone. Car accident. Yesterday,' I say, summoning the memory of Cate from the perfume to choke out the words.

She raises both hands to cover her face and shakes her head.

'How did you know?'

'On the radio this morning. They said a family died. She shakes her head. 'But I never thought . . .' She trails off.

'It was on the news?'

'Yes, Mrs Mildenhall. Reporter man outside told me it was you. Your family.'

'There is a reporter outside?' I ask. That's all I need. Reporters starting to snoop around.

'There are several out there. They want to talk. They gave me cards.' She reaches into her tunic pocket and produces a couple of business cards.

I head for Giles's study, which overlooks the front of the house. I open one of the shutters a fraction. She's right. There's a huddle of journalists out there looking expectantly up at the house, waiting for some action to start. They won't be getting anything from me. I can't take any risks. I'm a grieving widow and mother who will ask for some privacy. I need time to think about how to deal with this.

'Let's go to the back of the house,' I say, returning to the hallway. 'Away from prying eyes. I could do with a coffee.'

I head for the kitchen. The woman picks up her basket and trots obediently behind me. Now my shock has subsided, I'm guessing she's the cleaner. I figure Cate would be doing the school run by this time, explaining why the woman has a key. I wish I knew her name, but I can't exactly ask her. I'll have to think of another way of finding out. My mental checklist of what I've got to find out about without causing suspicion is getting longer by the minute. You don't think of this stuff when you make a decision to impersonate someone and abduct a baby. I don't know whether she's a regular from an agency or whether Cate employs her directly. She clearly knows *me* well enough to be very upset about what has happened. Bless her. I need to get into Cate's phone and laptop. Maybe I can find out more there and go through the bank account to check any regular payments.

'Would you mind making the coffee while I fix Ted his bottle?' I take two mugs out of a soft-close drawer, having now discovered where they live. I also intend to sneak a surreptitious lesson of how the built-in coffee machine works while my new companion makes it. Assuming she knows, of course. Another bad move. Don't make assumptions. Christ, this is difficult. I shouldn't have asked her. Maybe I've already tripped myself up before day one as Cate has hardly started.

'You would like me to have a coffee, madam?' she says, looking incredulously at the two mugs I've placed on the counter.

'Yes, of course. Unless you'd prefer tea? You can take it up with you. Perhaps you wouldn't mind starting upstairs in the bathrooms?'

She stares at me. I've made the wrong assumption here. Another mistake. Maybe she's not the cleaner. I try to instil confidence in my voice. Be Cate. A grieving Cate. I have no choice but to flush this one out — establish who she is.

'Is everything all right?' I ask. 'The police will be at the door soon. They said they'd return this morning. There's stuff we have to go through and . . .' I falter and look at the ground, covering my mouth with my free hand to stop the sobs escaping.

'Of course, madam. Anything you wish.' She rushes forward, touching my elbow in condolence. 'That's what I'm here for. The children's bedrooms? I normally do the bedding on a Monday.' She purses her lips inwards.

'Can we leave that for today? I don't want you to touch their rooms . . . yet.' I bury my wretched face in Ted's shoulder.

'Yes. We leave.' She busies herself with making the coffee.

At least she knows what to do with the state-of-the-art coffee machine. I stand a few feet away, making a mental note of the sequence in which she presses the spaceship control buttons.

* * *

The cleaner is upstairs, and Ted has been fed and his nappy changed. I strap him in his floor rocker and place a baby activity centre over him. He gurgles as he smashes a dinosaur. Time to take a proper look around the kitchen. What I told the cleaner was true — the police will return this morning and I've got to look comfortable in *my own home*. Too many *I haven't a clue where the coffee spoons are kept* incidents and they may start to suspect something.

The kitchen is cavernous with copious floor-to-ceiling cupboards in on-trend navy and white, reflecting light from the shiny, polished countertops and floor. I inspect every drawer and cupboard, making a mental note of each of their contents. The central-island unit complete with breakfast bar and stools is tastefully contrasted in maple and cherrywood. It was one of Cate's agonising decisions.

'What do you think, Beth? Should I go with the lacquered oak or maple and cherry? Or maybe a contrast paint? The designer wants a decision.'

'Why are you asking me? I've only ever been to Ikea. I can do a flatpack if you go that route, though.'

I give the polished wood a stroke. Cate will never see or touch this again.

There's a walk-in larder, complete with shelving units displaying rows and rows of labelled jars, spring-top and screw, filled with everything from spices to pickles, pasta, and every type of rice and lentil imaginable. How does she . . . I mean *did* she have time to do all this stuff? Cate always fancied herself as a bit of a Nigella in the kitchen, but I never realised she was Superwoman.

There's an American-style fridge-freezer about the size of a shed. Not too much in the fridge part, I note, save for some dairy stuff, orange juice and varying jars of sauces and ketchup. There's a separate well-stocked wine fridge — the type with a glass door to impress visitors. There's also what I recognise as a blast chiller.

Somewhere to park your personality overnight, Cate? I mentally quip. I pause, I realise what I've said. She's probably now stored somewhere like this. *Sorry, that was cruel, but I know you'd appreciate the joke.*

There are a couple of pieces of equipment that I can't identify. I lift the lid of what turns out to be a vacuum sealer and then realise that the water-bath contraption sitting next to it is a sous-vide cooker. Watching *MasterChef* has taught me something at least, although I'm not planning on asking the detective how he likes his loin of lamb anytime soon.

'We're going to have fun learning how to use this lot, aren't we?' I say out loud to Ted who ignores me as he's too busy bashing a rattly caterpillar.

Light floods into the kitchen from the floor-to-ceiling bi-folding doors that form the back wall. I'll try to open them now while I'm alone. It promises to be a beautiful day and I could do with some fresh air in here. The garden looks like a series of outdoor rooms. I don't have time to explore all this now; there are other priorities and I feel daunted at the prospect of coping with this lot.

My thoughts are broken by the shrill sound of the front doorbell. Christ, are the police here already? I wanted to spend some bonding time with Ted as well as try to get into Cate's phone. The cleaner calls out.

'I go, Mrs Mildenhall. Mr Ocado man here.' Ten seconds later, a man appears in the kitchen, loaded with shopping bags.

'Hello. Seems busy at the end of your driveway. Where would you like them?' he says jovially, oblivious to the tragedy that has befallen this household.

'Over here, please,' my cleaning lady says, taking charge and pointing to the island before I can take in what's happening.

'Right you are then,' the Ocado man says. 'Were you happy with the substitution? Just the one, a different brand of on-the-vine tomatoes?' He looks at me. I nod confirmation, not really understanding what I've agreed to. Home deliveries are new to me, grabbing bits in Tesco on the go has been more my kind of thing. I busy myself with picking up Ted. The cleaning lady opens a drawer and hands the Ocado man a bunch of bags before ushering him out to the front door. She doesn't immediately return. There are voices in the hallway. I'm curious, so creep closer to listen. I hope that none of the reporters have taken the opportunity to step inside.

My heart sinks as I recognise the voices of Jess and DS McLellan. They are here already. I'm clogged with dread. If I'm going to pull this off, ideally I'd have liked more time to prepare to act like Cate. Practice her face modes: resting bitch, scheming, teasing, mocking, angry, flirtatious. Use her well-trodden phrases: *seriously, darling, not that I'm one to point a finger* and, of course, *after me, you come first.* Nod my head when someone is explaining something or talking to me as a demonstrable sign that I'm listening and taking it all in, when really I've switched off and don't give a shit. It shouldn't be difficult. I've known her all my life after all. Plus, we're similar in far more than appearance. Our voices are — *were* — often indistinguishable when we got together. Cate's laugh is gigglier than mine, but there won't be much cause for hilarity today.

The police never knew Cate so there shouldn't be an immediate risk. Maybe I should see this as an opportunity to practice. There is no point in promising myself this is something I can work on tomorrow. I have to be Cate from every conceivable angle from day one. Warts and all.

'Mrs Mildenhall expecting you,' I catch the cleaning lady say. That's good. I strain to hear more, but don't want to give away that I'm eavesdropping. Then a very useful piece of information emerges.

'I'm Magdalena, the housekeeper.'

Was that Magdalena or did she say Maddalena? I need to do more digging, but that's a useful start. And housekeeper? *You've never mentioned a housekeeper, Cate!* She only ever mentioned a cleaner came every week. I'm guessing Magdalena or Maddalena does a bit more than the hoovering and dusting. That would explain quite a lot.

'Mrs Mildenhall is in the kitchen.' Footsteps echo down the hall, so I dart over to the Ocado shopping and start to take a few items out of the bags with my free hand while still holding Ted securely. Looking like I know what I'm doing. I'm devastated to find I'm clutching two bags of smiley potato faces.

'Thank you, Magdalena,' Jess says as all three appear. *Check*. 'Cate, did you manage to get any rest?' She says this with more than a note of sympathy. I shrug my shoulders and give her an exhausted look. It is how I feel, after all. 'We wanted to see how you were and I'm here to assist in any way I can today.'

She's wearing a navy blazer, which she's unbuttoning. Great — looks like she is intending on staying.

'Your car will be delivered back shortly,' DS McLellan says.

He and Jess hover mid-kitchen. Jess takes a step forward.

'Sorry about the press out there. The media were notified of the accident, but names shouldn't have been released yet.' She tucks her hair behind her ears. 'I've called in to find out how they got your address so soon. I'll help you deal with them anyway; we can talk about that later.'

I nod in acknowledgement and remain silent. Magdalena rushes over to where I stand and relieves me of my unpacking duties. She strokes my arm sensitively. 'I do this, I do this.'

'Thank you, Magdalena.' The sensation of bursting into tears again isn't far away.

'May we sit and chat to go over a few things, Cate?' DS McLellan asks. 'It won't take too long.'

'Yes, of course. We can go into the sitting room. Magdalena, do you mind?' I point to the coffee machine.

'I'll bring in tray,' she says with a nod.

Gripping on to Ted, I reach down to pick up his rocker and activity toy from the floor with my spare hand. I'm not about to leave my precious baby alone for one minute, but Jess comes rushing over.

'Here, allow me,' she says, picking both up in one swift movement and indicating that she'll follow me. Of course, she will. This is *my* house. *Get a grip, Beth.*

The formal sitting room is across the hallway from the kitchen, but also backs onto the garden. You enter through double doors and, like all the rooms in this house, it's vast — acres of walnut flooring covered in expensive rugs, a single one of which would cover my entire lounge floor. An ornately carved silver mirror sits centre stage on a mantel over a contemporary fireplace. Two huge grey sofas engulfed with orange cushions face each other. I'm guessing that Cate is . . . I mean *was* . . . going for the zesty citrus look rather than budget airline. It hurts my soul to refer to my twin in the past tense. The sofas are distanced by a large, low table piled with big, illustrated books, the likes of which I suspect neither Cate nor Giles never even opened.

I indicate for Jess and DS McLellan to sit down. I sit on the opposite sofa, putting Ted back in his rocker by my side. I distract myself by leaning over to rock Ted gently, waiting for the DS to speak. Even though it's probably no more than a few seconds, the silence is painful. It's swallowed my voice and I'm not going to be able to speak. I get a sudden dread that they've come to tell me that they know I'm not Cate and that Ted is not my son. The DS is staring at me, his expression unreadable. He clears his throat. *Brace*.

'Cate, so that we can understand a bit more about the events of yesterday, could you tell us more about the journey your family was taking? Where you were travelling from, that kind of thing.'

'Yes, yes, of course.' My voice comes out in a croak. Will some of the detail be relayed back to David? 'Um, Beth should have been in the Mini with me. At least that was the original plan.'

He leans forward, clasping his hands together in his lap. I tell him about the weekend.

'I was going to drop her back home in Twickenham, but Ted was grizzly so we decided Beth would travel with Giles so I could head straight back here.' Is he asking me this because he suspects I'm not Cate? I can't read him. His face is inscrutable. I plough on. 'Charlie and Georgie were keen to spend more time with Auntie Beth too. They adore her. She's so good with them. I mean *was*, don't I?' I sniff and wipe my eyes. Thinking about what has happened to them pierces my heart.

And something else occurs to me — Cate's death is all my fault. I was the one who pressed her to travel with Giles. If I hadn't done that, she'd still be alive, wouldn't she? I don't dare voice this guilty thought.

'She'd promised to play some games with them in the car.'

I'm praying that they'll buy my explanation and to be honest, it's not a million miles from the truth.

'I see,' DS McLellan says. He unclasps his hands and allows them to rest upon his knees.

'And did your sister get on well with your husband?'

What a strange question. I'm not sure I see where this is leading.

'Yes. They got on fine.'

The DS doesn't say anything. I assume he's waiting for more.

'As well as you'd expect a normal brother and sister-in-law relationship to be. They didn't see a huge amount of each other to be honest, as it was always Beth and I that would get together as Giles would often be working.'

The DS screws his mouth up as though deep in thought. He still doesn't speak.

'Can I ask why you're asking this?'

He contorts his mouth into a different shape. A habit of his I've noticed.

'You may ask . . .' He hesitates. Looks at the ground for a fraction of a second. 'A couple of witnesses say they observed a heated argument going on in the car. Have you any idea why your husband and sister would be arguing?' The DS looks at me intently.

I'm stung, totally floored by this. The conversation is already going in a different direction and not one in my favour.

Probably a domestic tiff, I should say. That wasn't unusual with Cate.

The heat rises up my neck. I hope I don't look flushed in the face. The police catch on to these nervous indicators, don't they? Then a thought comes to me like the dull thud of truth. Thinking back to the traffic on the motorway yesterday afternoon, what would I have wanted to say to Giles if I had been in the car? I take a deep breath, hoping that the words won't dry in my mouth.

'My husband's not a dangerous driver, but he could be a bit erratic sometimes. Beth was a driving instructor and professional driver. A very good one. It meant she could be critical of other people's driving. I've heard Beth complaining he hogs the middle lane. God . . . I feel terrible saying this now.' I cover my forehead with my hand as my face crumples.

I'm treading a fine line here. I don't want to be seen to be blaming my *husband*, but Giles's driving left a lot to be desired and may well have contributed to the accident yesterday. I reach for tissues stuffed up my sleeve, dab my nose and then screw them up into a ball. I tease out an end and rub it between my thumb and forefinger.

'I was driving a few cars behind Giles yesterday and it looked like he was a little close to the vehicles in front of him. I suspect Beth was having a go at him about it. She could get very irate about such things.' I shake my head and tears well up. I look up so that the DS can see my distress. A solitary tear escapes and trickles down towards my nose. 'Particularly with the children in the car.'

I want to ask about the white-van driver mentioned yesterday without deflecting away from my interpretation for the argument. DS McLellan has got to buy this at face value. I can't risk any more probing of why Beth was in the car. Has David been asking for an explanation? DS McLellan bites the inside of his cheek as though he's assimilating all this information. Jess looks at me, concerned.

'There's one more thing, Cate.' The DS pauses for a beat. 'Was your driving-instructor sister normally in the habit of *not* wearing a seat belt?'

Oh, my Christ. *Cate, what the hell were you doing?* I'm fighting for survival here. The words ring in my ears. *You weren't wearing a seat belt.* I can't even begin to imagine why. And now I've made everything a million times worse by over-egging how good a driver Beth was by way of explaining the argument. All I can do is bury my head in my hands and sob. Cry for the loss of my sister and her children, and for the unbelievable mess I've got myself into.

'I can't believe this.' I shake my head in disbelief. 'There must be a reason. Beth would *always* have worn a seat belt. There must have been a fault with it.'

'That is a possibility and is being carefully examined,' DS McLellan says as though he doesn't really believe it. 'We'll let you know the outcome as soon as we get the details.'

'Or maybe she undid it to deal with one of the children in the back? That could be it, couldn't it?' I'm clutching at straws. 'My Charlie. My Georgie. My precious children.' I'm screaming now.

I can tell the DS is thinking something doesn't quite stack up here. I wish to God that I kept my bloody mouth shut. I should stick to sobbing and grieving. Magdalena chooses this moment to walk in and places a tray with coffee and biscotti on the table between us. The interruption thankfully breaks the moment and gives me a bit of a reprieve.

'Can I bring you anything else, Mrs Mildenhall?'

'No, that's plenty. Thank you,' I say, looking up at Magdalena. She's also placed a box of tissues on the tray. I like this woman already; she's thoughtful. I grab a fresh tissue and blow my nose.

'I'll be upstairs if you need me,' Magdalena says as she leaves the room. I reach for another tissue to dab my eyes.

'She seems nice. How long has she worked for you?' Jess says.

I'm so confused and numb by the turn of events this morning, I can't work out if she's asking me a loaded question designed to catch me out or trying to be supportive. Either way I have absolutely no idea what the answer is. Cate has mentioned a cleaner on more than one occasion, but never mentioned employing a housekeeper called Magdalena. Probably because I'd have ribbed her about it if she had; Cate never did like doing much for herself. I've a vague recollection of Georgie mentioning a Mags, perhaps a couple of times, but assumed she was talking about a schoolfriend or a babysitter. I decide to focus on Jess's statement about her being nice and ignore the actual question.

'She's lovely. The children adored her . . .' I say, breaking down again.

'Would it be helpful if I prepared a statement for you to give to the press?' Jess asks. I'm grateful for the change of subject.

'That would be great, thank you. I can't face them. I want to be left alone.'

'Don't worry, then, we'll make a statement for you on your behalf. And sorry again that they've set up camp so quickly — a bit of an admin error on our part, I believe. Heads will roll.' Jess takes a brown sugar lump and stirs it into her coffee. She takes a sip. 'A family tragedy and they all want the exclusive. That's the British press for you, I'm afraid.'

'I won't be talking to any of them.' I know I mean it.

There's a question I'm burning to ask, but don't know how to play. I need to know whether we go and identify the bodies. By *we*, I mean me, as Cate, to identify Giles and the children, but I presume David would have to identify Beth? Beth who miraculously has had a Cate haircut since he last saw her. Do you identify solely the head?

What if they pull the shroud down a bit further? There's something more than her hair that's making my head throb. David *cannot* see the whole of Cate or I am undone. Jess interrupts my thoughts.

'There are a few things I'd like to go through with you, if that's all right?' She puts her coffee cup down. 'To explain some processes and let you know about the help out there for you. You're not alone.'

'Yes, sure.' I look at Jess vacantly as though I'm in a trance. DS McLellan gets to his feet.

'I'm going to leave you in Jess's capable hands now, Cate. As soon as we get more news on the crash vehicle, I'll let you know. We will get to the bottom of this.'

I hope you don't, I think. I go to get up, but he puts a hand up to stop me.

'No need. I can see myself out. Jess?' he says with the intention of her following him into the hallway.

I can hear them chatting with lowered voices by the front door, but due to the colossal proportions of this house I can't make out what they're saying. I'm paranoid. Has the DS decided to leave me alone with Jess so she can gently work on me — get me to give away my true identity? Does he think I'm more likely to let my guard down with a female officer? I try to shake myself out of this neurosis. Why would they even be thinking that Cate's sister has stolen her identity? What they're focusing on is a horrific car accident where four people have lost their lives. They've got to investigate that, I remind myself.

You play stupid games, Beth, you win crap prizes!

Thanks for the reminder, Cate. I feel her presence everywhere. She's infiltrating my brain. Play smart and focus. I've taken a huge gamble, I know that, but the highest wagers can bring the greatest rewards, can't they? I look down at Ted who, I swear, smiles at me.

CHAPTER 10

Beth

I'm finally alone. Well, Magdalena is still in the house, but she's busying herself Lord knows where. She's been very sweet and has checked up on me a couple of times to see if I need anything. I've finally got some solitude. Solitude with my baby.

Before Jess left, she explained that post-mortems will be carried out on all the deceased as requested by the coroner. The fact that *Beth* wasn't wearing her seat belt is of significant interest. We don't have to personally identify the victims as it's already known who they are. The irony. We are free to go and visit them and I will make an appointment to see *my husband and children*. It's going to be traumatic but it's the right thing to do. I'm relieved we don't have to officially identify though. But what will David do? Does he care enough to visit his dead wife? It could still all go wrong.

Jess said funerals can take place once the coroner is satisfied with the post-mortem results. There will be a coroner's inquest too, but that won't happen until the police have finished their investigation. They have to rule out any third-party culpability first and they're still trying to find out how the accident happened, and if the white van was involved. As the wife and mother of the deceased, I am identified as an *interested person*. As I was also a witness, I could be called to give evidence. God, that would be daunting.

'Don't worry,' Jess said. 'I will act as your liaison officer and will be the go-between for you with the coroner. I'll explain all the pre-inquest processes. I can be with you every step of the way.' Jess has given me lots of information about bereavement counselling and support.

One of the leaflets says there are seven stages of grief: shock, denial, guilt, anger, depression, reconstruction and finally acceptance. I think I've fast-forwarded on to stage three: guilt. For persuading Cate to travel with her family and for what I've subsequently done. But I have to hold my resolve. My task is to keep the police looking down the wrong end of the telescope. So far so good.

I need to get into Cate's phone. I retrieve it from her handbag. I try the trusted sequence that hasn't failed yet; one followed by two. It doesn't work. I try three consecutive number ones followed by three twos. Fail. I know Cate runs her empire from her phone and I can't be seen going to an Apple store to get it unlocked. I retrieve the iPad and google *Access iPhone?* Cate has the latest model, of course, while mine is archaic in comparison. I soon discover one of the few benefits of being an identical twin — of course it's activated by facial recognition. I put on my best Cate pout and I'm in.

There are numerous missed phone calls and messages. Three missed calls from Giles's parents, Laura and Michael, one from Swallowfields (Mum's nursing home) and one from what I think is a pet shop about cat food or something on order. That reminds me — I know Cate has got a cat, but I don't remember seeing it.

There are also loads of texts: school notifications, a reminder about a facial appointment, dental-appointment reminders for the whole family, two separate delivery timeslots — one from DHL, one from DPD, and one from a friend, Claudia, about a coffee morning on Tuesday and can we do lunch Thursday? There are about half a dozen clipped messages I don't understand from someone called MS — something to do with people called John and Jane, and several from Ocado thanking me for my order and confirming that Preston in Plum van will be delivering my shopping between 8.30 and 9.30 a.m. with one substitution.

No call from David, I note. *What is he waiting for?* The very least he could do is call his dead wife's sister who has lost two of her children as well as her husband. I can only hope it's because he's dumbstruck with grief, but it looks like I'm going to have to make the first move. I need to know if he's intending to visit the body.

I should ring Giles's parents first, though. Is that what Cate would do? I know she wasn't particularly keen on them and would regale me with tales of their oppressive advice, collective holiday suggestions that Cate avoided like the plague, or gifts she thought in bad taste. But I can't forget that they've lost their only son and two of their grandchildren. They must be hysterical with grief. Ted and I are probably the only close family they've got left. I can't ignore them; it wouldn't be right.

I will call them soon, but David — *what are you planning?* I also want to hear his voice, hear his grief. I'm summoning up the strength to call him when there is an interruption. People at the door.

'I go, I go.' Magdalena calls out to me. I hear voices in the hallway. It can't be the police back already? Magdalena appears in the sitting room doorway and whispers, 'Mr and Mrs Mildenhall senior here.' She looks at me as though this is really bad news and I'm going to want her to get rid of them.

'It's okay, show them in.' I get to my feet. I'm going to be a dutiful daughter-in-law; it doesn't feel right to be anything else. Laura, who is short in stature with a petite frame, rushes in, followed closely by Michael. Neither of them looks like they've slept. Laura's eyes are red and swollen, her face puffy with anguish. She looks bruised with grief. Michael, while a tall man, is stooped, his head bowed, but he looks at me with an expression of such intense pain on his face. He's been crying too. My heart goes out to them both. I am heartbroken at having lost Cate and my niece and nephew, but I can't even begin to comprehend what it must feel like to lose an only child, whatever their age, even though I must behave as if I've lost two.

'My poor darling girl,' Laura says, taking me in her arms in an embrace that I find surprisingly comforting. Before I know it, I'm the one who is sobbing uncontrollably and then we're both clinging to one another for support. I'm taken aback that her first thoughts were for me.

'I'm so sorry. I was about to call you.' I try to compose myself. 'The police were here last night . . . and again this morning. They've only just left. It's been so intense. I hardly know what hour it is.'

I find myself repeatedly running my hands through my hair. I must look a complete mess, but that's no bad thing.

'Has this really happened?' I ask. A concerned look passes between them.

'It's all right, Cate, my love,' Laura says, gently rubbing both my arms as though the action will make the grief evaporate. 'We've come to help and support you; you can't go through this on your own.'

I am genuinely touched by their thoughtfulness.

'There will be a lot to do. Informing where necessary, appointing the undertakers, organising the funeral, church. I can take care of all that if you'd like me too? Keep you informed, of course,' Michael says.

He's trying to control his voice and not let his guard down. I suspect finding comfort in planning and making arrangements to keep himself busy. To make some order of something so tragic. He's even dressed in a pale-grey suit with a shirt and tie. Laura is in a pink, floral cotton skirt teamed with a crisp, white blouse and the obligatory pearls. If I were them, I wouldn't even be able to get out of my pyjamas.

'Thank you,' I say. 'I wouldn't know where to start. I can't think straight.' I reach out an arm for Michael who responds by putting his arm around my shoulders to pull me in close.

'We're family, Cate. We'll get through this together. Somehow. Somehow, we will.' And he kisses me gently on the top of my head. I can't remember the last time, if ever, anyone put me first like this.

* * *

They stay for lunch. A lunch that Magdalena, who is rapidly making herself indispensable, has prepared for us — a quiche with a green salad. Not that any of us have much of an appetite, but I try to eat a few mouthfuls. Laura spends most of the time with Ted on her lap. She clings on to him — her only surviving grandchild. It's painful to witness and comprehend. I bring Laura and Michael up to speed with what happened yesterday, the police concern about the seat belt and the argument seen by witnesses. They listen carefully, but offer no judgement.

I don't know what I was expecting from Laura and Michael, but it wasn't compassion and selflessness. For some reason I thought they'd be angry with me for being the survivor when they've lost their son. The impressions I had of them as a couple were different, but I have to remind myself that the picture was painted by Cate.

For the first time I feel ashamed of my grieving-widow-and-mother act when it's they who have lost so much. But I can't deviate from my course now. I can pinpoint that heavy feeling inside me. I know what it is: guilt. But it's not regret. My mind is stronger than my heart and I'm committed to my path. I can't surrender to the notion that what I've done is wrong based on some unexpected kindness. I'm not going to hand the rest of my life over to apology and guilt. I want my baby. I am Cate.

CHAPTER 11

Beth

My heavy eyelids open and I immediately want to escape the morning light creeping in through the shutters. The room spins and I try to fix my gaze on the abstract art on the wall to steady and compose myself. I bury my head in a pillow and pull the duvet up over me. I need some sort of pain relief to anaesthetise the recurring dream scenes that won't leave my head. I keep seeing the Range Rover leaving the carriageway. I see Charlie and Georgie's faces, panic-stricken, looking at me through the back window as it does a somersault, arms outstretched towards me as though I am the only one that can reach and save them. I fail — of course. The pain of their loss pricks my skin.

And then there is Cate. I think about us as children too. A shared upbringing as two little people, identical in look and voice, but eventually with distinct personalities. Cate cultivated it that way. I never wanted to be separate — not then and not now. To me, we were always two halves of the same person. I never felt whole without Cate. How could she have done this to me? In death as well as life, she's left me.

There it is again, the knot in my throat tightening as I feel the all too familiar prickle of tears welling up at the back of my eyes.

I try to blink them away and wipe the salty trickles with the back of my hand. 'Self-inflicted wound,' Cate would say. She once told me, 'If you sit back and wait for what life will throw at you, Beth, then you'll mostly get covered in shit. I'm not going to let that happen to me.'

I was always the one who took the cautious path, whereas Cate charged at life full speed ahead. She was oblivious to those she knocked aside like skittles when they got in her way. And the biggest skittle of all was me.

Step by step, over the years, Cate gradually ripped away the insulating layers of our twinship. Our mother dressed us identically, normally in stereotypical pink. I found comfort in there being two of everything in our monochromatic wardrobe. The walls of the bedroom we shared were also painted pink. But the year we turned twelve, we moved to a larger, three-bedroom house. Dad asked me what colour I wanted on our bedroom walls.

'Pink!' I replied, as if there were no other option to consider. That was our colour and I saw no reason for us to change. Cate had shrugged. Then, one day a few weeks later, Dad began redecorating the third bedroom, I presumed as a spare room. Mum always said she wanted 'room for visitors'. Paint fumes permeated throughout the house. I watched as two walls were turned bright pillar-box red, the other two chalk white.

'Grannie won't be able to sleep with that colour on the walls,' I said, giggling. Dad put his paintbrush down and wiped his brow on the sleeve of his overalls.

'It's not for Grannie, love.' He chuckled. 'It's for our Catherine. She's moving into this room now we've got more space. You'll have the other room all to yourself, lucky girl.'

'You mean Cate is moving in here without me?' I was horrified.

'Oops. That slipped out,' he said. Dad's face contorted into a mock grimace as he slapped his forehead. 'Sorry, love. I never was very good at keeping secrets.'

I charged into *our* bedroom to challenge Cate about planning to move out without telling me. She was sprawled out on her bed, flicking through a copy of *Just Seventeen*. She claimed it was all a big surprise, letting me have a bedroom to myself. She'd persuaded Mum and Dad to keep quiet about it.

'I thought you'd be thrilled,' she said, looking disappointed. 'You've totally spoiled it. I was even going to buy you a pressie from my own pocket money and leave it in the room for you. Shan't bother now.'

That made me feel bad. I knew I was being ungrateful, but I couldn't work out why I didn't feel ecstatic about the whole thing. Cate buried her head in her magazine and ignored me. I decide to change tack. I could already see injustice in the new arrangement. I went back to Dad.

'This room's bigger. I want it.'

'I beg your pardon, young lady?'

'I want this room. I don't mind being the one to move out of the old room and have the bother,' I said, copying Cate's style with as much conviction as I could muster. It always seemed to work for her getting her own way. Dad raised his bushy eyebrows and pointed his finger at me.

'Those that want don't get. Now run along and stop being a nuisance.'

I skulked back to Cate. All I could think of was to point out that we'd always chosen pink. Our twinship required her to have pink in my mind.

'You won't be happy in there. There's no pink. Dad's painted the walls red.'

'Well, red is pink really, isn't it?' she replied, not looking up. 'Just a deeper, stronger version.'

Even then I was the paler, watered-down version of you.

I force myself to get out of bed and open the shutters. I walk over to the dressing table and flip open a caramel leather jewellery box. I flick through the contents. Nestled at the bottom is a pink-beaded macramé bracelet. I bought it for Cate's thirteenth birthday. She kept it. I kiss it and return it to the box. I open the table drawer to reveal a dozen bottles of nail polish, standing to attention like a row of soldiers. All in graduating shades of red. I'm surprised she has so many as Cate had a penchant for a professional manicure. Have-It-All Cate. I pick one out and give it a shake. It's by Chanel and called *Dragon*. I'm going to paint my fingernails. There should be time for at least one coat before Ted wakes. I splay out my left hand and take the first brushstroke. *I'm being you, Cate.*

Cate would twist our parents around her little finger in a way that I never could. She felt entitled. A deep-rooted feeling that the world revolved around her. And maybe it did. She led for us both. Cate was the favourite; her star shone brighter than mine. The truth was she was my favourite too.

I blow on the polish on my left hand and start painting the right. She had a knack of persuading me to do almost anything. That's one of the reasons I can't get the image of Charlie and Georgie in the back of the car out of my mind. One of the reasons I'm stuck on the detail of Cate not wearing her seat belt. I feel so guilty. I've never told anyone this, but Cate never passed her driving test. Or her theory. I took them for her. That's why, when she said she was tired, I persuaded her to let me drive with Ted.

Swapping identities was a game we played many times at school. We'd switch classes — it could be funny to con teachers and fellow pupils. I got more attention from boys if they thought I was Cate. When it came to attracting the opposite sex, Cate had something special and indefinable that I didn't. It was exhilarating and naughty to pretend to be her.

I never took any exams for her, though. By the time we did our GCSEs, teachers were wise to twin pranks and so we were made to sit in the same room. I passed my driving test with flying colours first time while Cate was still attempting to pass round six of her theory. Another fail and she was so miserable. She passed on the seventh attempt, this time with full marks — and thirty pounds in my back pocket.

Things didn't go too well with the practical driving test either. Cate showed a spectacular lack of ability behind the wheel. After failing three times, she asked me to drive her to the fourth. Mum insured me for her car, so I relished the opportunity to laud my driving skills over her. When we parked up at the test centre, Cate wafted a twenty-pound note in my face.

'Off you go then.'

'You've got to be kidding. No way. Not this time.'

Cate produced a crisp, red fifty-pound note. She knew how to get my attention. I went to take it, but she snatched it away out of my reach.

'Uh-oh! Not so fast. You only get this one on delivery of the goods, missy. Run along now.'

This felt different than before; I knew we'd be breaking the law. As always with Cate, though, I complied. By the time I returned with her pass certificate, she was sitting in the driver's seat of Mum's car.

'One word of this to anyone, ever, and you're dead. Deal?' Cate dangled the fifty-pound note in one hand and offered a pinkie finger to me with the other.

My heart was in my mouth for the entire drive home. Her driving skills improved with experience, but I always worried about her hazard-perception skills. It's a secret we kept between us for over half our lifetime — and one that would ruin my career if it got out.

Looks like I'm being given time for a second coat. As I paint, I stare at a picture of Cate and Giles on their wedding day. Cate's sense of self-entitlement extended to marriage and when oven-ready hedge-fund manager Giles came along, he didn't stand a chance. Cate was panning life for gold and found it the moment she served Giles his champagne in the first-class cabin of the Virgin Atlantic New York-bound flight. I imagine Cate reeled him in, looking radiant in her signature red uniform. Within six months, a Tiffany rock adorned her finger and a year later she walked down the aisle in a stunning Alexander McQueen dress.

As Cate Mildenhall, she led a privileged, romcom montage of a life. Meanwhile, I became plain Beth Brown. I couldn't even compete on the name stakes. Mildenhall sounds like a grand and regal manor. I considered hyphenating to give myself more gravitas, but Cate laughed hysterically when I told her about it.

I've got to stop tormenting myself. The sound of Ted stirring comes through the baby monitor. I enter his nursery and lean over his cot to stroke his head. Darn. I've managed to daub his forehead with a blob of red nail polish. It looks like a drop of blood. I'm going to have to find a way of removing that safely. To my delight, he seems pleased to see me.

'Good morning, little Mr Sunshine. Welcome to Tuesday.' I drape a muslin over my shoulder and lift him up. My heart fills cradling Ted in my arms as if something warm and wholesome has been poured inside my heart. He is truly all I need — all I have ever needed.

Showering will have to wait now Ted is awake. I have absolutely no idea whether Magdalena is going to appear again today. I couldn't exactly ask her working hours, so I'm going to have to see what unfolds. While I'm craving solitude, she could prove useful. I need to go out for a bit to get my hair cut properly. I can't keep it looking like a bird's nest indefinitely to hide my home cut.

I'm also going to call David. Unbelievably the bastard didn't call *Cate* yesterday. Rude. Unsympathetic. Self-absorbed. Thinking of him makes me angry. Right. This can't wait any longer — I'm going to call him now. I don't care that it's still early.

CHAPTER 12

David

My phone rings. Adrianna stirs and rolls over. Yes, Beth only died two days ago and I've spent the nights with another woman in my bed. Our bed. I'm full of self-loathing. I'm behaving off-the-scale bad. But I don't seem capable of stopping myself. I need something to dull the extortionate pain.

I reach to look at the screen. *Cate*. Shit! I should have been the one to phone first. Road to hell and good intentions doesn't quite cover it.

'Sorry, darling, I need to take this.' I grab my phone, leap out of bed and go into the spare room. Tentatively, I press receive.

I hear Cate sigh, but she doesn't say anything. I clear my throat. I should be the first to speak. I don't know what to say. How to deal with this.

'Cate. Oh, Cate, I was going to call you today.' It's silent for a few seconds.

'Been busy, have you?' Her tone is barbed. I don't know what I expected. I plough on.

'I'm so, so sorry for your enormous loss, Cate. Truly. God knows I'm gut-wrenching hurt, but I can't imagine what this is like for you.'

'It's pretty crap.' Cate stifles a sob. The sound takes my breath away. It reminds me of Beth. My wife may be dead, but there is still another person walking this planet looking and sounding like her. It's the strangest, weirdest feeling. I always did feel a bit freaked when they were in a room together. You could only ever tell them apart through their hairstyles. Giles, who didn't even seem to notice that about them sometimes, has, on more than one occasion, walked up to Beth and put his arm around her shoulders.

The first time I visited Beth at her home, she was still living with Cate and her parents. Beth told me she had a sister and they were very close, but I had no idea at that stage she was an identical twin. I rang the doorbell and Beth answered. She greeted me with a big smile on her face, grabbed me by the balls with one hand and yanked me by the shoulder with the other, pulling me towards her before proceeding to stick her tongue down my throat.

When we came up for air, she grinned.

'Hi, gorgeous.'

'Hi,' I replied, thrilled that she seemed so pleased to see me. What happened next has haunted me ever since. She turned and shouted up the stairs. 'Beth, your boyfriend is here.' Cate sauntered down the hallway while Beth descended the stairs. As they passed, I heard Cate say 'After me, you come first, little sis.'

'Ignore her,' Beth said, rolling her eyes while turning me around and pushing me back outside. 'I forgot to mention you were dating number two. Hope that's not going to be a problem?'

It is going to be bloody hard to see number one now.

'Almost my entire family has been wiped out and I've lost Beth. I don't know . . . how I'm going to deal with all this,' Cate says.

We've both lost Beth, I want to say.

'Time, Cate. It's going to take a lot of time.' She doesn't say anything. 'Of course, I'll, um, help. When I can.'

'Yeah, right,' she says, barely audibly.

I hear Cate sniffing, imagine her wiping her nose on her sleeve. Composing herself. Beth does — I mean, did — that.

'David, I need to ask you something.'

Christ. I hope she's not about to ask if I've got anyone with me. I don't want to lie. This is shitty enough as it is.

'Are you going to visit Beth at the undertakers?'

I'm taken aback, but relieved I'm not about to get an inquisition. To be honest, everything has been such a blur I've not thought about it.

'Probably,' I say, not wanting to sound disloyal. I hope it's the right response. 'I never got a chance to say goodbye . . .' I trail off. I've never seen a corpse. I'm not sure I want the first one I see to be my wife.

'You know about the seat belt?' Cate asks.

'The police told me. It doesn't make sense. Beth would be the last person not to wear a seat belt.'

'We'll probably never know exactly what happened, unless the coroner can make some sense of it. But, what I mean is, it might be even more distressing because of the seat belt.'

I'm not following.

'What will be?'

'Seeing Beth. You don't know, she might be . . . damaged.'

I've not thought of that. But I've not thought about visiting up until this moment. The loose floorboard on the stairs creaks. Adrianna is up. I owe it to Beth to pay my respects and say goodbye. It's the one decent thing I can do. Perhaps I could also write her a letter to go in her coffin. Apologise for being such a shit husband. Tell her that I did love her. Atonement.

'I want to see her,' I say, meaning it.

'I'll come with you.'

'Haven't you got enough on your plate?' I don't want to be unkind, but I'd prefer it to be a private moment.

'I have to be there, David. She was my sister. More than that, she was my twin.'

Husband trumps sister, I think. Even a twin. Typical Cate — always did put herself first.

'OK,' I say, not wanting to argue but contemplating getting there early to see Beth alone first. Good plan.

'We can support each other, David,' Cate says with insistence in her voice. 'Beth was so looking forward to seeing you after your weekend apart. She'd gone to the trouble of buying a cute lemon dress in a boutique in the New Forest. Even had her hair done especially. She looked beautiful. It was meant to be a surprise for you.'

Now I feel even more of a waste of oxygen.

CHAPTER 13

Adrianna

While David is on the phone, I take the opportunity for a sneaky peek in a few drawers and cupboards. The kitchen is in duck-egg blue with wooden worktops. A scrubbed pine table sits in the middle where a copy of *Grazia* sits untouched, as if waiting for its owner to return. I flick the switch on the kettle; measure out a few spoonfuls of coffee into the cafetiere. It's like I've landed in someone else's life. Went to sleep and woke up in a different dimension. There are pink coffee cups on a mug tree, a shopper's notepad with *digestives*, *pasta*, *toothpaste* scrawled on it. A mint-and-tea-tree hand cream sits by the sink. I find a contactless credit card in one of the kitchen drawers. It's not yet expired, but I resist the urge to slip it into my borrowed dressing-gown pocket. I don't feel the same way about two of the five £20 notes rolled up with a rubber band that I find stuffed inside an old ice cream tub that also contains loose change, odd keys and a dried-up mascara wand.

A pile of papers is wedged behind the bread bin. This place could do with a tidy-up. I pull a sheet out — it's a payslip belonging to Elizabeth Brown. Beth. I scan it before replacing it, painfully aware that I'm nosing on a dead woman. *Repugnante.* Creepy.

This whole situation is so awkward. I've been plumbing personal depths here. David's clearly remorse-ridden, but it hasn't stopped him insisting I stay. The irony isn't lost on me that it's me, his mistress, if that's what I am, who is here with him now. I'm not sure history will judge us kindly.

But I can't walk out on David. I offered to stay in the spare room, to be in the house for him, but he shook his head.

'What would be the point?'

We did have the decency to change the bedding. I draw the line at sleeping under the same duvet cover that his now-deceased wife slept under.

The thrill of adultery is that it takes place in the shadows. Bring it into the direct sunlight and it can fade. But this is not adultery anymore, because David no longer has a wife. This is new territory for me. What am I doing here? I should walk away, but I'm not sure I want to. David doesn't know he started out as one of my targets. I can't tell him now. Can I?

I put a couple of slices of bread in the toaster as David comes down the stairs.

'God help me — that was difficult.' He puts his phone on the kitchen table. He rubs at something invisible on the side of his face. He tells me it was Beth's twin sister, Cate. David has explained about the car crash and the loss of her family.

'Poor woman,' I say.

David pulls me close to him. 'Thank you for being here. You're special.'

David treats me with such tenderness that my view of the world is beginning to change. If only we could have met before Sol.

I release myself from David's embrace. I pour us coffee and put out plates, butter and marmalade for the toast.

'How long were you and Beth together?'

'Nearly thirteen years married. Two before that.' David takes a sip of his coffee. He looks thoughtful. 'Do you think that marriage, or any long-term relationship for that matter, once someone cheats, lies, is over?'

I know he's thinking of himself, but it doesn't stop my heart skipping a beat. Our relationship has hardly started and I'm the one that's living the lie. I don't know if I can do this. We should start with a clean slate. I consider David's question. I want to tell him I'm a con artist, that a scammer has made his breakfast. A fake girlfriend. I entered this relationship for the money, but he does mean something to me now, too.

'I think it's like an over-inflated tyre,' I say. 'Eventually it'll explode. There's too much pressure.' I'm thinking of Sol. 'Then you're left with nothing but shards. Fragments emotionally so sharp that they leave very deep wounds.' I need to tell David the truth, but can't find the words to explain. Tears prick my eyes.

David squeezes my hand as I start at the beginning, with Sol. Care and concern turning to mental cruelty and controlling behaviour. Lovemaking turning to rape.

'Did you report it to the police?' he asks, when I say the word *rape*.

'We were in a relationship. Who would have believed me?'

'Oh, Adrie. My poor love. You shouldn't have had to deal with it alone.'

'I've dealt with it in my own way — kind of.'

David leaps up from the kitchen table, pulls me to my feet and envelops me in his arms once again. Is now the moment? Can David accept me for who I am? Maybe he is the route to mending my broken heart. I pull away and look up at him. There are dark shadows under his eyes.

'I need to tell you something. About me. Something bad.' David silences me by putting a finger across my lips.

'Shh. No more. There's nothing bad about you. I don't need to hear it.'

But you do, I think. *Or do you?*

'You will continue to stay with me, won't you?' He brushes my fringe out of my eyes. 'Move in. Let's make this permanent.'

'David, I . . .' I'm lost for words. I wasn't expecting this. Not now. It's not exactly appropriate. He rests his hands on my shoulders and looks at me imploringly.

I can envisage our future together. *Have you met Adrianna? She was the scam mistress when his wife was still alive.*

I don't feel comfortable and it won't be long term, but I'm not past putting a rent-free roof over my head for a while. The room in my current lodgings is pokey and I wouldn't have to share a bathroom with the landlady anymore. I nod my agreement. It looks like this Adrianna lives on.

CHAPTER 14

Beth

Well, now I'm in a seriously bad mood. David — typically vague as ever. God, that man can be obtuse. I've not played this well either. I've made things worse by asking whether he was going to visit *Beth*. I should have known he'd probably not even thought of it — and now, of course, he's going to go. Stupid, Stupid. Well, he won't be going alone. I can still control this.

Ted and I have breakfast and after emptying the dishwasher I open two packages delivered yesterday. I need cheering up so might as well see what Cate has bought for me. One is a selection of lululemon workout gear. The other package reveals itself to be from Tory Burch. I've never been able to afford such pleasures. I open a neutral box, but its contents are wrapped in bright orange gloss paper and sealed with a gold Tory monogram sticker. And it's not even Christmas. Inside a magenta geometric-print shoe-box is a pair of exquisite toe-post, flat sandals in a caramel leather with a multi-coloured enamel mosaic badge on the front. They're beautiful and I can't resist slipping them on straight away while still wearing my pyjamas. *Quelle surprise*. They fit.

'You shall go to the ball after all, Cinders,' I say to Ted. There's also a blue tie-dye sweatshirt in the box, which looks absolutely gorgeous. Lucky me. Coincidentally my size too. *Cheers, Cate.*

I hear the key in the front door. Magdalena calls out.

'Hello! Mrs Mildenhall, only me.'

'Morning. We're in the kitchen. Are there still any reporters out there?'

'Most gone after the lady policeman spoke to them. Two left. I'll keep eye on them. Don't you worry,' she says, coming into the kitchen and tapping her nose in a conspiratorial fashion. 'Did you manage to get some sleep, madam?'

I am touched by her concern.

Magdalena agrees to mind Ted for me later so that I can go out. She's telling me about funeral services back in the Philippines (very useful information to learn that my saviour is a Filipina) when I sense an instant change in mood and atmosphere. Magdalena stiffens. I detect a slight straightening in her spine and she inhales sharply. There's a movement in the garden and I follow her gaze to see a man pulling a hose reel across the lawn.

'Mr Max has arrived. Excuse me, Mrs Mildenhall, I must get on with my work. Please let me know when you need me.' She scurries out of the room before I can say anything else. Weird.

Once I hear the vacuum cleaner going, I reach for my phone (it *is mine* now) and start searching for hairdressers. I can't go to my usual hairdresser in St Margaret's — I'm deceased. I know Cate used a celebrity-frequented hair salon in Kensington, but I can't go there. Letting slip that most of your family have just been wiped out so you thought it essential to have a trim is probably not to be advised. Luckily, I know the back streets of west London like a cab driver and think that somewhere like Whitton or Hanworth would be a good bet. For some reason I feel seriously pissed off with Cate today so wonder if I've already moved on to the anger stage. The conversation with David hasn't done anything to lighten my mood either.

As I make my appointment with Donna's Hair Studio for this afternoon, I sense I'm being watched. Max or Mr Max, I'm not sure which, stands in the middle of the lawn staring at me. I presume he's the gardener. Does he need to speak to me about something, or has he heard the tragic news and wants to offer his condolences? I'm still in my pyjamas for God's sake so I raise my hand in acknowledgement. He waves back.

By the time I finish my call, I look up again and he's still in the same position; I feel his eyes linger as if assessing me. I'm a bit creeped out. He's toned and tanned from working outdoors, with muscles that look like he does press-ups for fun. He has the darkest black, tousled hair that caresses his face. I can't decide if he's more of a Heathcliff or a Poldark, or maybe a bit of both. *So, you employ a Diet Coke man as a gardener?* In another time and place, spotting him while out with some girlfriends would spark some speculative, if not crude, ring-a-ding-ding chat, but I don't have time for any pleasantries. If he hasn't yet learned what has befallen my family, he very soon will so that more than excuses any rudeness he may think I'm displaying.

I remove Ted from his high chair, grab my windfall packages and head upstairs. In the dressing room I attempt to neatly fold the blue tie-dye sweatshirt and go to place it on one of the open shelves. I catch sight of another garment in the same fabric. Cate must really like this print. I pull it out to take a look. Strange. It looks identical to the new top that I've opened. Why on earth would Cate want two? Opening it up I spot the issue — there's a two-inch tear across the back. How decadent to be able to replace it like that. I could never afford to spend one hundred and ninety pounds — twice over, I might add — on one garment. Seconds later I remind myself that I can now. There's plenty of money in Cate and Giles's joint current account and Cate has some easy-access savers too, which will be plenty to keep me going until probate is sorted.

* * *

It's mid-afternoon and I've been coiffured. The problem now is I look too perfect for a grieving widow. I showed a selfie of Cate to replicate the cut, but I couldn't persuade the hairdresser to allow me to leave the salon without the blow-dry part of my deal. It was more than her reputation was worth, apparently. She's done a pretty good job. Immaculate Cate is reflected in the mirror. All my life I've looked at Cate and seen a more perfect version of my own image staring back at me. But now I am she.

As soon as I leave the salon, I pop into a convenience store and buy a bottle of water. Back in the car, I pour some into my hand and wet my hair with it, teasing my fingers through and then scrunching it up to look dishevelled.

I head back to my new home in Richmond, back to my son. As I pull into the driveway, Jess is getting out of her car. No sign of DS McLellan, I note. I'm glad as he's the one that asks the probing questions.

Before I get out of the car, I pull on the baseball cap that I wore going out. It was something to hide behind and to cover my atrocious self-cut from any beady-eyed neighbours. This time it's to contain the salon smell lingering in my hair. The hairdresser was swift with the volume mousse and hairspray before I realised what she was doing; I should have been more attentive. I can't afford to be undone by a spritz too many from an unsuspecting hairdresser.

'Hi, Cate,' Jess says. 'How are you feeling today?' I know she's only trying to make conversation, but how does she think I'd be two days after having lost my husband and two children?

'Hanging on, but not great. I needed to get out the house for a bit. Loads to organise. Surprisingly,' I reply tartly.

I take a deep breath to give myself a jolt. *Don't be off with Jess. She's only doing her job.* The combination of grief and guilt renders powerful emotions and I want to punch everyone today. I mustn't let it cloud my judgement and affect my behaviour, otherwise I'll trip up.

'Sorry to call in unannounced, but we've had some information back on the car. May I?' Jess indicates the front door to go inside.

'Of course. I haven't been able to stop thinking about it.'

I get the door keys out of my bag. I won't have any problem with them this time.

'Tradesmen?' Jess says as we pass a van parked in the driveway. The gardener must still be here. He's worked a long day. I thought he'd have gone by now.

'Garden company and general maintenance,' I say, taking in the vehicle for the first time. I passed it earlier, but didn't give it a second glance. The van is black with *The Outdoor Butler* in yellow signwriting on the side. *Gardening. Landscaping. Lawn care. General maintenance & clearance.* There's a large, bright sun motif and the outline of a tree. 'They come regularly,' I add. *Another addition to Cate's apparent staff rota*, I think.

As I turn the key, Ted's cries reach me. My heart lurches. I hasten inside as Magdalena walks out of the kitchen with him.

'My baby boy.' I run to take him with open arms. I plant a kiss on his head. 'Has Mummy been too long?' It's a relief to feel him back in my arms. To my amazement Ted stops crying and starts to settle almost immediately. Top marks, Teddy boy.

'He wants his *mumma*,' Magdalena says, smiling. 'Shall I make the tea?' We follow her back into the kitchen.

Cate's cat chooses this moment to finally appear. It walks over and starts to circle around my ankles, brushing his purring body against me. Magdalena must have been putting food down for it because I haven't thought to.

'Hey, puss-puss. I had a tabby as a child. What's its name?' Jess asks, bending down and reaching out a coaxing hand.

Probably an innocent question, but I have absolutely no idea what sex the cat is, never mind its name. *Breathe, Beth.* I must see the positives here. Ted has been soothed by me and the cat clearly recognises me as one of its providers. All good signals for Jess in case she has any suspicions. *Dig deep. You must know the cat's name sunken somewhere in your befuddled brain.* I could say anything, but Magdalena is within earshot. This is another reminder of how fragile my situation is.

I hear Cate in my brain. *Wriggle out of this one, smart arse.*

Not helpful — tell me its name, Cate. Except it's Magdalena that comes to my rescue.

'You already been fed, Cedric. Greedy boy.'

Relief floods as I escape the noose, but immediately start to worry that Magdalena deliberately helped me out. Now I'm being paranoid.

'You said you had some news, Jess?' I say as Magdalena warms the pot for the tea.

* * *

After Jess has left, I go into the back garden to take in some air. The early-evening sun is weak and pale, but it's still warm. Magdalena is bathing Ted for me. I would have preferred to do it myself as bonding time, but I'm still going over what Jess told me in my head.

The car forensics haven't found fault with the seat belt. Which means that Cate deliberately unfastened it. Why? I don't understand. I can only imagine it was to help either Charlie or Georgie in the back.

Unless Cate was trying to reach something, but what could have been so important? I suspect this was why Cate and Giles were arguing too. Giles would have been furious if Cate unclipped her seat belt. There's also no indication that the white van made contact with Giles's car. It had been parked up on the slip road for a while before it joined the motorway. False number plates, so they've not been able to trace it. Typical. The inference is that the van's erratic driving may have caused Giles to brake sharply and lose control of his vehicle. The van driver will get away with this.

I've never felt so torn. I want to probe, fight for justice for Cate and the children, but in doing so I increase my chances of exposing myself for who I really am. I can't take that risk. I'm going to fail Cate, but maybe she failed me first? Maybe it had something to do with the fact that growing up, Cate sucked all the oxygen out of the room leaving me with little to breathe or flourish. Cate left me devoid of oxygen; maybe I will leave her devoid of justice.

The calm and solitude of the garden is comforting. I step out onto a vast deck area that encompasses a large L-shaped rattan sofa, reclining chairs and a glass-topped dining table and chairs to seat ten. There's also a built-in barbecue and pizza oven on a patio next to the deck. The garden is impossibly huge and adjoins others equally as sizeable. A high, original wall with some trailing jasmine runs along one side of the garden as well as the rear, a new fence separates the garden from the neighbour on the other side. There's a large well-manicured lawn, tended flower beds festooned with rose bushes, immaculate paved pathways edged with lavender and a summer house that I would have been happy to move into. The rear of the garden has a play area with a climbing frame, large sand pit and Wendy house. Tucked into the far eastern corner is a series of sheds, which I presume must house the lawnmower and all the gardening tools.

I take in gulps of air scented with lavender and jasmine. It's intoxicating. I've not had the opportunity to explore the garden properly up until now, so I take the perimeter path.

As I reach the turn at the top end of the garden near to the summer house, I sense a presence behind me. I jump like a startled fawn and turn to see the gardener. I had no idea he would still be here this late.

'Hell-o,' he says, imbuing the two syllables with emphasis. Misgiving starts to root itself in the pit of my stomach. He moves a little closer, too close, his eyes burning into me. I can see that they are golden-brown flecked with green. They are fixed on me. This is seriously awkward. My heart flutters like a trapped bird in my chest.

'I've been waiting for you all day,' he says.

His voice is elegantly raspy with a deep, rich tone, both velvet and honey. He looks like a character from a trashy romance novel with his mop of dark, silken curls and his torso rippling beneath a white T-shirt stained from a day's toil in the garden. He's devilishly handsome, but looking into his eyes is making me feel uncomfortable.

He breaks into a cocksure smile, which I find disarming. He looks so at ease. His whole face is beaming, but I can't work out if it's with menace or actual joy at seeing me. Alarm bells start to buzz in my head like a swarm of bees. Something is so very off here. Why would he have been waiting for me *all* day? He scans my face expectantly, waiting for a reply. I don't have one. I swallow what feels like a mouthful of glass.

'I-I . . .' I open my mouth but can't draw air.

His face turns mutinous. Clearly this wasn't the response he was expecting. I manage to step sideways and put my arm up against the wall of the summer house to steady myself. Also, to buy myself a bit of time to think of an adequate response. Perhaps I'll pretend to be feeling faint. My brain is frantically trying to assess the situation, which I fear is leading me down a path that I most definitely do not want to go.

He mirrors my sidestep and stands in front of me again.

The first of the row of sheds is behind him. Something blue catches my eye. It's a piece of fabric caught on the side of the shed; it flutters limply in the gentle evening breeze. I recognise the print

— it's the tie-dye from Cate's torn sweatshirt. Cate has leaned up against that shed.

He reaches out and takes my wrist. I freeze. He slowly guides it up to his mouth and kisses the back of my hand. Then, more forcefully, he plunges my middle and index fingers into his mouth, circles his tongue around them and starts sucking hard. I'm gripped by a fear that starts in my abdomen and spreads through the rest of my body.

'What are you . . . ?' I manage to blurt out a protest, instinctively pulling my hand away as though I've been scalded. I rack my brain for his name. What did Magdalena call him? 'Max. No. Please. I've lost my children, my husband. I can't.'

'Well, this is going to make life easier for *us*, then, isn't it.' Max sneers, leaning forward to push my back up against the summer house and propping his arm up behind me. He lowers his face towards mine as though he's about to kiss me. I seize the opportunity and duck down beneath his raised arm. I race across the freshly mown lawn, which is slippery underfoot, causing me to stumble. I gather myself up, looking behind me in case he is following.

'Maybe tomorrow then, Lady Jane?' He calls out to me. I reach the open doors to the kitchen and forcefully close them. Not fucking likely.

CHAPTER 15

Beth

I sit at Giles's desk in his study going through papers and making lists of so much stuff that needs to be done. He certainly left everything very organised. There's even a super-sharp letter opener on the desk to slice open the envelopes. I feel like the King. I bet he doesn't struggle to concentrate, though. I haven't been able to stop thinking about what happened in the garden yesterday.

Talk about leaving me a trail of breadcrumbs. What the hell have you been up to? What Max said is drilled into my brain. *Well, this is going to make life easier for* us *then, isn't it?*

Are you seriously telling me, Cate, that you've been involved with this man? Your so-called bloody garden butler. This man who comes to your home, God knows how frequently, seems to be expecting quite a bit more than his pay cheque. You have got to be kidding me.

I can't do this. I can't. This could ruin everything. I don't know what to do. Surely, he can't be serious? Max must appreciate that having lost my husband and two children, I can't carry on as though nothing has happened.

Whatever I thought was going on in Cate's life, I never saw this one coming. Even in death she has the capacity to surprise me. How on earth did she get herself into this? As soon as I pose the question, I already know the answer. On the surface, Cate was the perfect wife, mother and hostess. But she got bored, as Cate has been bored with others all her life. Cate would pick up people like precious gems, but would soon let them drop out of her basket if they no longer interested her or proved useful. Is Max her latest shiny stone?

I think back to the messages on Cate's phone that I skipped through because they didn't make any sense. Did I delete them? I scroll through. They're still here. In fact, there's a whole string of conversation between Cate and MS from the day of the accident.

Sunday 11.08
MS: *Missed you. John Thomas even more so. What time you back? X*

    11.11
    Cate: *Probably mid-afternoon. Clearing up now. Exhausting! Tell JT that Lady Jane needs a break. Naughty! X*

11.12
MS: *Shall I come tomorrow? X*

    11.15
    Cate: *No. Maybe Tuesday. Got to be careful. X*

11.16
MS: *I want to see you! X*

    11.22
    Cate: *Seriously NO! Defo NOT possible. X*

11.24
MS: *It's not me — it's John Thomas. You'll have to tell him yourself.* X

11.31
Cate: *Only when Lady J is good and ready.* X

11.58
MS: *JT waiting. You left yet?* X

12.10
Cate: *Locking up now. On the road in a few mins.* X

12.11
MS: *Thought I might catch a glimpse of LJ.* X

12.12
Cate: *Stop it. You CANNOT come to the house at the weekend.*

12.13
MS: *Don't worry! I'm a man with a plan.* X

12.46
MS: *Ready & waiting!* X

2.12
MS: *Why the long face?*

2.51
MS: *You home yet?*

3.44

MS: *Lady Jane?*

4.36

MS: *Tell me you're not pissed off with me. I only
wanted to show you my Max Verstappen alter-
ego impression. Cool, huh? X*

5.01

MS: *Are you ghosting me, Lady J?*

5.37

MS: *It was only a sneaky peek! You looked beautiful btw. I get the msg. Til Tues. X*

A bead of sweat trickles down my back. Cate's mobile rings,
making me jump. I'm relieved to see it's not Max. It's Feline
Furries. I think they've left a message before. It must be something
for Cedric. I pick up.

'Mrs Mildenhall?'

'Yes, speaking.'

'Hello. It's Bill here from the Feline Furries Breeders. Your
kittens are ready for collection. Worming up to date so good to
go. When would be a good time? Tomorrow possible?'

Kittens? Oh, blimey. This is all I need.

'Um. Look, I'm so sorry, but I'm not going to be able to do
tomorrow. You see—'

'No worries, Mrs Mildenhall. Everything is all paid for, so
thinking about it we can deliver to you. If I'm quick, I can catch
Sarah now with the van. She's making another delivery. If I've
missed her, I'll call you back to let you know. Bye now.' And he
rings off.

This is a nightmare. I'm learning how to cope with a baby — I wasn't expecting to have kittens thrown into the mix. But they were meant for Charlie and Georgie — how can I not take them? I have to do this for the children.

I turn my attention back to the thread of texts between MS and Cate. I presume that MS is Max. God help me if there were to be another one. Clearly there was a relationship of some kind going on. And what is John Thomas and Lady Jane all about? Silly pet names? *Cate . . . really?* John Thomas is ringing a bell, but maybe I'm thinking of *The Waltons* from when Mum used to watch all the repeats when we were children. I google it. *Oh, I get it, Cate. Very funny. You're playing Lady Chatterley. At least that confirms that MS is Max. The closest thing you'll get to a gamekeeper around here, I suppose.*

I check the times the texts were sent. Cate was messaging Max while we were still at the cottage and she was on her phone as she locked up. Something's bothering me. Or are pieces of the puzzle starting to fall into place? I go over the texts again.

I'm a man with a plan. Why the long face? It was only a sneaky peek. You looked beautiful.

Max wanted to see Cate that afternoon. Even though she said no. This man is obsessed with Cate, which means he's now obsessed with me.

I keep replaying the motorway scene leading up to the accident in my mind. The more I do, the more physically sick I feel. It's combined with fear. Genuine palpable fear that feels like a fist squeezing the blood out of my heart. What did the white van look like? It wasn't the black *The Garden Butler* van, but did it have any markings? And the man inside? I'm trying to recall his face; it's a blur. I can only recall the beanie hat. Maybe Max has got another van for rubbish clearance or something? He smiled and waved at me, then sped on. That's what that was about. *Why the long face* was referring to me. He was showing off. Max referenced a racing driver in his texts. His driving antics were a strutting cockerel displaying his feathers.

If it were Max, then he thought I was Cate. And he doesn't seem to care that Giles and two of Cate's children are dead. As far as he's concerned, he's got a clear run and it's business as usual.

Looking back, Cate did seem tired and distracted. I thought she was exhausted from looking after a new baby, but now, knowing the full scope of help Cate had, I wonder whether it was about Max. Didn't she say she had something to tell me in the car? What was she about to reveal? I need to tread carefully and buy myself some time. I compose a text.

> 11.33
> Cate: *Hi. Sorry about yesterday, but I'm distraught.*
> *Need to take a break.*
> *Funerals coming up. Loads to organise. Giles's parents here frequently.*
> *Hope you understand.*

I press send with a prayer that I'm doing the right thing. Within minutes, Cate's phone lights up with a reply.

> 11.35
> MS: *Okay, Lady Jane.*
> *You're the boss.*
> *I'm not going anywhere.*
> *Will be looking out for you.*
> *JT at the ready! X*

My flesh crawls. I can't deny Max's attractiveness, but every nerve and sinew in my body screams danger.

CHAPTER 16

David

The door to the funeral parlour slams shut behind me. Enough to wake the dead. You'd think they'd have a soft-close door in a place like this. I should be more careful, I know. It's the nerves. I'm shitting myself to be honest. Didn't sleep a wink last night. It's not every day you have a meet with your deceased wife and I'm not sure what to expect. Do bodies change colour after a few days? Will Beth already be in the coffin I selected online? Am I supposed to touch her? I want to do the right thing.

I've brought Beth's favourite outfit with me for her final journey. And a photograph from our wedding day. I bottled writing a note. Such things never have been my forte and I couldn't find the right words. But I'm pleased I thought about the pic.

I ring the bell on the reception desk. The place isn't quite what I was expecting. A white high-gloss reception desk is centre stage with a glass vase of tall cream roses perched on top. Tranquil pictures of blue seas and treetops adorn the walls. I could be in an insurance office or a hotel reception. Or maybe I'm the one that's at heaven's door? I'm making sick jokes — proves I'm nervous. Footsteps echo down the corridor. I'm here early to see Beth alone. I don't want Cate with me. She can go in after me or we can go in together later, whatever she prefers. She may not even need to know I've already seen her — I'll play that one by ear.

A man in a grey suit appears. 'May I help you, sir?'

'David Brown. You should be expecting me.'

'Roger Tupper,' the man says, extending his hand. 'On behalf of Tupper and Sons, please accept our sincerest condolences, Mr Brown.'

I give him the bag of clothes I've brought.

'We're nearly ready for you. Come this way, sir, through to the family room. Your wife's sister has been waiting for you.'

Crap. Well, that's scuppered that plan. I check my watch — I'm more than half an hour early. How long has she been here? The undertaker opens an oak door. Cate sits in a green pleather armchair, focusing on the contents of a mug resting in her lap. She looks up, draws in a breath. 'David.'

'Can I offer you any refreshment?' Roger Tupper says.

'Er, no thank you.' The thought of consuming anything right now makes me feel sick.

'Please take a seat, sir. We'll call you in very shortly.'

Cate stands up and stares at me. I mean fully stares at me. There's a tear in her eye. I feel bad for having tried to dupe her. I do the only thing I can think of and open my arms wide. She puts her mug down on a side table and steps towards me. We embrace. I'm taken back by how much she feels like Beth. It's like I have the ghost of my wife in my arms. A wave of emotional turbulence swells within me. I've never hugged Cate properly before and, other than the snog on the doorstep way back, only kissed her on the cheek. Identical twins for you, I guess. She smells different, though. I gulp in air.

'You don't have to come in with me, you know,' I say. 'Maybe I should go first.' Cate doesn't take the hint.

'I want to see her, David.'

There's no time for any further discussion as the undertaker reappears.

'Beth is in the visitation room now. Please come whenever you wish.'

Cate withdraws from my arms and follows him out the door, leaving me to trail behind. I'm beginning to understand how Beth used to feel being around Cate.

Roger Tupper respectfully closes the door behind us and we're left alone. The silence is eerie. An open coffin rests on a table. Cate positions herself by the head end, leaving me to stand below her. I look at my shoes, preparing myself.

'Oh, Beth,' Cate says, stifling a sob.

I force myself to look at Beth. My dead wife. She looks serene and peaceful, eyes closed, lips slightly parted. Like she's asleep. I can't believe this is Beth. She looks more like a waxwork model out of Madam Tussauds. There's some visible bruising on her face and forehead, which have been touched up with make-up. This will be my last enduring memory of her. I'm beginning to wish I didn't come. She's wearing a gown with a high ruffle collar. Maybe to cover damage from the accident. I'm not sure I want to know. She'd hate the gown, so I'm glad I bought her some clothes. I finally got something right.

I'm so sorry, Beth. Sorry for what I did to you. How I behaved. You didn't deserve it. I can't say any of this out loud because of Cate.

None of this was meant to happen. I'm tormented because of how distant we became. And doubly worse is that this tragedy has got me off the hook. I didn't know how I was going to explain about the missing IVF money. I knew Beth would kill me when she found out, but I was shown the destruct button and I pressed it. I pressed it willingly. I pressed it hard. I saw it as a form of detonation. Or maybe a fast-forward button. Why not throw my life upside down and watch the fallout? I never imagined things could get worse.

Safe journey, my darling. You're at peace now. At least I won't be able to hurt you anymore.

I reach out and touch Beth's hair.

'New haircut,' Cate says. 'She looked so pretty. Beth was hoping you'd like it.'

'Makes her look even more like you. If that's even possible.'

I run my fingers down Beth's cheek and allow them to rest on her neck. She's stone-cold to the touch. I don't know what I was expecting. I move my fingers around her neckline. My last caress. Cate flinches.

'Sorry. I'm finding this difficult. Seeing Giles and the children was excruciatingly painful too.' She reaches over and takes my hand away from Beth. She gives it a squeeze. 'I can't believe this is the last time I'll ever see my twin. I've lost my whole family. I don't know how I'm going to get through this.'

I can't help feeling exasperated even though I know I shouldn't. This is the final time I will see my wife. Cate was the one who insisted on coming.

'Know she loved you,' Cate says tearily. She tightens her grip on my hand. 'Shall we say our final goodbyes? Together. Like this.'

The warmth of her touch transfers to me. What the hell is wrong with me? Cate has lost four members of her family. I've failed one twin. I can't argue with another.

CHAPTER 17

Beth

Jaime and Cersei are playing in the kitchen, a game of hide-and-seek around the central island. Jaime crouches around one corner with his back legs jiggling, poised and ready to pounce, waiting to take Cersei unawares. Cersei on the other hand — she's definitely the smarter of the two — has doubled back and stalks Jaime from behind. The kittens keep us all entertained; particularly Ted. He will sit happily in his rocker or high chair for ages watching them. His eyes are open wide as he giggles and chortles, waving his little arms and legs as though he wants to join them in play. My heart melts.

I thought taking in the kittens was going to be a nightmare, even though I couldn't have it any other way, but the light relief they've brought is immeasurable. They are part of our little family. It's proved to be a particular blessing for Ted as the house must be much quieter than before. Magdalena thinks they are adorable too. She cried when she first saw them, knowing that Charlie and Georgie selected one each.

Ted and I discussed what to call them one evening at bathtime. Jaime is pitch-black with two white front paws, while Cersei is a smoky blue-grey. We debated Ebony and Smoke, or Shadow and

Storm, but concurred that they were too cliché. We settled on Jaime and Cersei, because I like the fact the characters are twin brother and sister. Even though they were pretty evil — particularly Cersei. I've promised to let Ted watch *Game of Thrones* to understand their heritage when he's old enough. He told me that was fine. We often talk like that, Ted and I. Or at least I talk out loud to Ted if there's no one around and I respond for him too. We're quite a team. It's become such a habit that I still hear his voice in my head if we've got company.

Ted and I love that Magdalena calls Jaime 'Jammy'.

'It's pronounced Jay-mee.' I say.

'Jammy,' Magdalena repeats, laughing to herself. 'Shersee,' she says for Cersei. We all chuckle and decide to roll with it.

We keep the kitchen doors to the garden closed most of the time as the kittens aren't yet old enough to venture outdoors alone. That suits me fine. Easier to shut Max out too.

I've bought myself a bit of time, but I have no idea when he is going to start to put pressure on me again. I get an emoji or a stream of kisses most days. I rarely reply.

At least I was telling the truth about being busy. Laura and Michael have been here frequently. There's an immense amount to organise with a triple funeral to be held at St Bartholomew's in Richmond followed by a burial in the cemetery at Kew.

I've decided to proceed slowly to extricate myself and hopefully draw a line under Max. I'll give it a few weeks and then tell him not to come anymore. Pay him off if he's on a contract if I have to. He's been appearing a couple of times a week and keeps the garden immaculate. Max doesn't seem to come at regular times, unlike Magdalena, so I never quite know when he's going to appear.

Magdalena works here full time and doesn't stop from the moment she arrives until her departure time, normally about 6 p.m. I've finally worked out her schedule. Six days a week in total, with Wednesday and Saturday afternoons off. The only day Cate had to fend for herself was Sunday, and she had Giles at home then too.

I've decided to take Ted to visit Mum in her care home this afternoon. Max arrived about half an hour ago so it's a good excuse to get out of the house. I've been putting it off. I know I should have visited sooner, but Mum is the last person I ever want to deceive. And the most challenging. I have no choice, though. I've needed the time to get myself more Cate-ready. The staff have told Mum about *Beth*, Giles and the children. I'm told she cried for a while, but then joined in the afternoon activities and later seemed quite relaxed. Mum's short-term memory isn't good and she frequently wants to pack her suitcase to go on holiday to the Isle of Wight with Dad, who passed away ten years ago.

'Robert is coming to get me,' she insists. 'We're on the two o'clock ferry. We'll be in Ventnor in time for tea,' she used to say, pre-stroke.

Conversation is difficult since the stroke. It's robbed Mum of much of her vocabulary and she gets frustrated that she can't express herself. The words 'yes', 'bus' and 'railway' get strung together on repeat, clearly making perfect sense to her. The intervals between her lucidity and dementia have been shrinking, so you never know which face of Rachel Woods you are going to get each day.

'Now Mummy needs to get ready for our little outing,' I say to Ted, taking him into the dressing room with me. 'Better not turn up in sweats, huh?'

Cate has several baby rocker chairs dotted around the house, so I've placed one in here so Ted can advise me on my choice of outfit. We're only going as far as Chiswick and I don't suppose the old folk there are expecting a fashion parade, but I've got to be Cate. Nothing less will do.

Everything about Cate signalled money. From her hair (check), to the diamond on her finger (check), the gleaming bracelet adorning her wrist (check) to the cut of her clothes.

It's too warm a day for jeans. Maybe a skirt or summer dress. I scout the rails and feel the lustrous fabric of Cate's clothes, all evenly spaced out on wooden or padded hangers like a luxury boutique. I think of my crammed wardrobe at home — a mish-mash of wire and plastic dry-cleaner hangers. I pull out a white, cotton broderie-anglaise skirt with little green daisies. I hold it up for Ted to see.

Too complicated. What would you wear with it?

Good point, Teddy. I decide a dress might be an easier option. I pull out a floaty chiffon number in the palest beige. It's very pretty.

We're not going to a wedding, Ted is telling me. Next, I pull out a navy Ralph Lauren poplin midi-dress with short sleeves and a contrasting white rope belt. Ted bounces his approval. *That's the one. Not too over the top. Crisp and smart-casual. Good colour choice too. Appropriate.*

'You're good at this Ted,' I tell him appreciatively. I slip the dress on. I like it. I find a pair of navy, suede open-toed espadrille wedges from the shoe section of the dressing room. Mirror check. A slick of red lipstick and a summer basket-weave handbag complete the look. Cate is staring back at me. Check.

* * *

Roadworks on the A316 over the Chiswick Bridge slow the traffic. I don't mind. Ted has fallen asleep and the longer we can be away from the house the better. Swallowfields is set in an area between the Hogarth roundabout and the river. It's spacious with communal areas as well as private rooms looking out on a beautiful garden with walkways and plenty of seating. I'm hoping to be able to sit outside with Mum today if she fancies it, to take advantage of the sunshine. The staff are wonderful and caring. Cate and I were so relieved when a place came up for Mum.

Once parked I transfer Ted to his stroller, fastening him in securely, and place a little sun hat on his head. We report to Reception to check in. Mum is in one of the residents' lounges, we're told, and someone will be with us shortly. Within minutes, one of Mum's regular carers, Sally, appears. She's about mid-forties with shoulder-length dark brown hair that is always so tightly tied back that I wonder if she does it as a DIY facelift. A pair of glasses on a chain hang around her neck. I guess you can't be putting them down in here too often, otherwise you'd never find them again.

'Cate. Oh, Cate,' Sally says, coming through the security doors. She has genuine tears in her eyes. 'We are all devasted to hear what happened. I'm so sorry for your loss. Poor love.'

'Thank you. It's really tough,' I reply with a lip tremble. Sally steps forward with her arms outstretched and I can tell from her caring nature that she wants to give me a hug. I allow myself to fall into her and momentarily rest my head on her shoulder.

'Everyone has been so kind,' I say, pulling away from her embrace. 'It's difficult to know how to carry on, but I have to, don't I? I still have a son and I have to keep going for him. He's my only world now.' I reach out for the top of Ted's head.

'You're amazing, Cate. You truly are and you'll find an inner strength you didn't know you had. The world will right itself again one day — it always does,' Sally says, stroking my arm. I've noticed this stroking business more and more. Nobody really knows what to say to me. Losing a husband and two children at the same time is so inexorably painful that people find it difficult to know how to react. It's a soothing response mechanism — maybe just as much for the stroker as the stroked. *Would I be stroking you, Cate, if you survived?*

'How's Mum been?' I say to pull myself together and move the conversation on. Sally lets out a little sigh.

'She's been very up and down, to be honest. A difficult few days after we broke the news, but then she went back in time again and I think was trying to tell us how she was expecting twins. It's obviously been on her mind.'

Sally uses her pass to open the double security doors and holds them open for Ted and I to go through.

'I feel bad about not having visited. I wanted to, but I've been so overwhelmed.' I can't help but sniff. 'I didn't want to make things worse, wasn't sure I'd cope.'

'Don't beat yourself up about that. You must look after yourself and your baby right now. Everyone understands. We're here to take care of your mum.'

'I hope Mum won't be too cross with me.'

'Confusion and distress are to be expected as the disease progresses, but it's been worse recently and exacerbated of course by communication being so difficult. But she's comfortable, Cate — I can assure you of that.'

We follow Sally to the main residents' lounge. Mum is sat in a high-backed armchair by the French windows to the garden.

'Look who's here to see you, Rachel. It's your daughter, Cate,' Sally says.

'Hi, Mum.' I plant a kiss on her cheek. 'I've brought Ted to see you. It's such a lovely afternoon. We could take a walk in the garden. What do you think?'

Mum looks up at me quizzically. She frowns. My heart quickens.

'Bus. Bus. Railway.'

Sally gives me the nod that she'll leave us together and goes to attend to another resident struggling to retrieve a dropped newspaper.

I get Mum outside and we stroll super slow, side by side, pushing Ted in his buggy. Mum has her arm linked through mine for security as she likes to be guided. There's a free bench in the shade of a cherry tree. I make Mum comfortable and sit down beside her. Her skin is sallow with dry, flaky patches and red thread veins cluster on her cheeks. Her once-lustrous chestnut hair is heavily streaked with grey and hangs lankly around her face. Where has our beautiful mother gone? I can only feel sadness. Mum is only seventy-four and this awful disease has robbed her of so much.

I take her hand and put it in mine. The back of it is marked with liver spots and the veins are looking raised. I give it a squeeze and start to stroke it. My turn to be the stroker.

'I'll always be here for you, Mum. Ted too. We love you.' She turns and looks at me.

'Yes. Bus. Bus. Bus.'

'This is nice, Mum, isn't it?' I point up at the near-cloudless blue sky. 'Look, as blue as your favourite delphiniums. Not often we get days like this.' I continue the idle chatter while stretching out my legs and inclining my feet upwards to reach the puddle of sunshine filtering through the shade of the tree canopy. My peeping toes glint in the sun. Mum takes a sharp intake of breath and lets out an audible gasp.

'Yes, yes, yes. Railway.' She screams, turning towards me and grabbing me by the shoulders.

'Whatever is it, Mum? Are you okay?'

Mum's eyes bulge with excitement.

'Yes. Be . . . Be . . .B-Beff!'

Mum yanks at the neckline of my dress, indicating for me to pull it down. *No way. You cannot take the pin out of that grenade.* I move her hand away with care. Guilt starts to blossom like rampant weeds growing across my chest. My heart pounds. I'm not here to cause her anguish.

'Shh, shh. It's all okay, Mum. Let's enjoy the sunshine. What's on the menu for supper this evening? Maybe it's your favourite fish pie,' I continue, trying to distract her. Mum isn't having any of it.

'Railway. Be . . . Beff. Beff. Beff.' She screams this on repeat.

'Beth's gone, Mum. She's not here.' I grit my teeth. I don't want to say *dead* in front of her. I keep my voice measured. 'I'm Cate. I'm here with Ted, see.' I indicate his buggy, as though that proves everything. I need to calm Mum down. She leaps to her feet and clutches her head while still trying to get the words out. Frustrated with me that I'm not understanding. But I understand perfectly well.

'Yes. Yes. Bus. Be . . . Be . . . Beff. Beth!' She points her index finger at me with her eyes bulging out their sockets. We've started to attract attention. Inquisitive faces turn in our direction to see what all the commotion is about. Mum gets more and more agitated.

'Please, Mum. Sit back down. Would you like a cuddle with Ted? Shall we walk around the garden again?'

Mum continues to point at me while struggling to speak at the highest pitch possible to let the whole garden know her discovery. At this moment, the truth is hanging between us like a stained sheet on a washing line. A wave of shame washes over me again, but I refuse to engage with it. Shaming myself won't get me where I intend to go.

Sally appears in the French windows and shades her eyes from the sun as she looks across in our direction. 'Is everything okay?' she's saying.

I shake my head back at her. *No, it's not all right. Yes, I need help here. I've fucked up. I've fucked up big time.*

Sally turns and says something to someone inside before heading across the lawn towards us at speed. She's closely followed by Rahul, one of the male nurses.

'Rachel. There you are, my lovely. What's going on here? Time to take you in for a cup of afternoon tea. Cate would love a cup too, I'm sure,' Sally says as she and Rahul frame Mum and steer her back towards the residents' lounge.

'Bus. Bus. Beff. Beff,' Mum continues to say, glancing back at me. She's looking confused and I can see the fight being squashed out of her. I feel terrible. I fuss over Ted for a couple of minutes to allow them to settle Mum before we return indoors.

'Sorry that had to happen, Cate. That's all you need right now, I'm sure,' Sally says, coming over to help me manoeuvre Ted's stroller over the French window's step.

'She wants me to be Beth, I think.' I might as well face it head-on in case Mum starts up about *Beff* again.

'It's only to be expected, unfortunately. Sadly, there will come a time when your mum doesn't remember Beth at all. Or maybe not recognise you, I'm afraid.' Sally gives my arm a consolatory stroke.

I look down at Mum who's sitting back in her chair with a floral teacup and saucer in her hands. A custard-cream biscuit is perched on the edge of the saucer. She's staring out at the garden again, lost in space and thought. The anguish has gone out of her, but what is left behind seems far worse. Mum looks all hollowed out and disconnected.

On the drive back home, I contemplate my afterlife living in hell for being grateful for Mum's condition right now. She did, however, have a moment of perfect clarity this afternoon. Mothers always know. She isn't fooled. She knows what I've done.

'That makes two of you,' I tell Ted. 'But lucky for me, neither of you are in a position to snitch.'

I've got to be sharper on the details. I've told myself before — the devil is in the detail. You think you've thought of everything, then it's the minutest, stupidest of things that risk exposing me. As soon as we get home, I'm going to be painting my toenails red. I'm sick of bloody pink.

CHAPTER 18

Beth

Can you begin to imagine what it's like to attend your own funeral? Beyond weird, that's what. Today's the day. The day we get to say goodbye to Beth. To me. There's a gaping hole in my stomach at the thought as I park up at the South West Middlesex Crematorium.

I'm going to have to really stretch myself today to pull this one off smoothly. Turning off the ignition, I allow my eyes a really slow blink and then extend them wide to prepare myself to meet David again. I'm sick with nerves at the prospect. If only he knew the truth. Will he cry, I wonder? Will he show any emotion at all? There's a small bit of me that's glad if he's hurting. I want him to suffer. I wonder what stage of grief David's at? He'd better not be at acceptance already.

I've also got a bone to pick with him. I distinctly remember telling him that I wanted to be buried. We discussed it. Back in the day when we communicated with each other.

'I don't want to end up in a jar,' I told him. 'You'll stick me on a shelf in the garden shed and forget about me!'

'I wouldn't. I'm never going to let you out of my sight. Keep you close,' he said with a deep, infectious laugh.

'Then you'd better jolly well lay me to rest in a nice plot with a beautiful headstone and visit me every day with flowers.'

'Gotcha.' David hugged me close.

He's forgotten. In less than half an hour I'm to be incinerated.

David greets me outside the chapel. He plants a staccato kiss on both cheeks like a bird pecking for worms. He's wearing a new dark grey suit, white shirt, black tie. I can smell his aftershave. Eau Sauvage — I bought it for him last Christmas.

'Cate. Hi. A tough day for both of us.' I nod. Already tears prick my eyes and a lump forms in the back of my throat. 'Thanks for coming.' What a stupid thing to say. Does he seriously think I wouldn't turn up for my own sister's funeral? 'How've you been?' He takes my hand and cradles it between both of his.

'Devastated. Distraught. Bereft. Numb. How many more adjectives would you like?'

'I only meant — I hope you're okay. Will be okay.'

David's gaze doesn't leave my face. He's waiting for me to say something, but all I can think of is *when did you turn from Mr 'I love you' to Mr 'I can't do this anymore'?* A cold trickle of unease runs down my spine. Is he scrutinising my face because he recognises something? Am I really going to be able to pull this off? I flick my hair like Cate would.

'Like you said. It's going to be tough.'

David releases me and strokes my arm instead. I'm not sure I'm going to be able to get through this. I want him to continue to hold my hand, to support me. But he turns away to greet other mourners.

* * *

Well, that was one of the crappiest funerals I have ever been to. And it's my own. My remorse at how David must be feeling turns to anger. He could have arranged a church service somewhere first and have a cortège move on to the crematorium for the final bit. We never attended church, but I'd have appreciated a bit more of an event. No hymns or a WH Auden poem in sight. Is David seriously in that much of a rush to get rid of me?

In we filed to Take That's 'Shine'. Yes, I know I'm a Gary Barlow fan and I've seen them in concert three times, but really? Anyway, it's Mark Owen that sings 'Shine' so David didn't even get that right. We took our seats, still warm from the previous occupants who could be heard chattering and offering condolences on the other side of the exit door.

At funerals, I always imagine each congregation member carrying their own memories of the deceased in with them. All those individual fragments put together by everyone to make the person whole again. So, while everyone was supposed to be thinking of me, I was remembering Cate. The other half of my whole.

Except there really wasn't much time for any of that. A brief eulogy from a colleague at the driving school (did I really have so few close friends?) and a few words from David. Solemnity he did well, but no tears.

Sitting there, I realised David didn't consult me about the service at all. He certainly had the opportunity when we visited the undertakers. I should have been asked to give the eulogy or a reading at the very least. I'm the identical twin after all, weird as it would have been for the congregation to feel like Beth was giving her own tribute. No pun intended. I've been so caught up in my own mess and looking after Ted that I didn't pay any attention to the planning for *my* funeral. I vowed there and then that I must put things right by Cate, otherwise she will seriously end up housed in a cannister at the back of David's wardrobe and be given to an unsuspecting charity shop at some future date.

All too soon, the ejector button was pressed and my coffin was swept away behind the nondescript blue velour curtain. *Bye, Cate.*

We're now in a function room above a pub in Twickenham. Platters of dried-up tuna-and-cucumber, coronation chicken, and egg-and-cress sandwiches are scattered on white-paper-covered tables around the room. Bowls of crisps and some rather unappetising-looking sausage rolls complete the lunch offering. Cheapskate.

Laura and Michael have been good enough to come; they're here to support me, they said. They're caught up chatting with David's aunt and uncle, but Laura keeps glancing over at me to make sure I'm all right. She really is quite a remarkable woman, considering what she has been going through herself.

I take a sip from a rather warm pinot grigio. David works the room, shaking hands, acknowledging condolences, accepting thanks for the 'anything we can do', promising to keep in touch. Disconnection from it all spirals through me. I look at what I have given up — my husband. It's such a bittersweet feeling. I genuinely believe that being Ted's mother has saved my life, but I now must act as though the man standing on the other side of the room is not my husband. Inside, though, I want to scream — *David, it's me.*

David senses my eyes on him as he looks over. He saunters up to me with a glass of red wine in his hand. My heart does a somersault.

CHAPTER 19

David

I caught a glimpse of myself in the mirror this morning. I didn't recognise the reflection. I asked myself *was that really me? Reflections can deceive, can't they? Are eyes windows to the soul? If so, then mine is beyond dark.*

The moral tightrope I've been walking is fraying by the minute; it's not that wide now. I'm waiting for it to snap completely and throw me into the abyss. I live with a tight pain in my chest. I'll suffocate and it's what I deserve. Contrary to popular belief, the worst of situations doesn't always bring out the best in people. It certainly hasn't in me. I'm ashamed but don't seem capable of behaving differently. I've needed Adrianna and I've come to accept my sin as a survival strategy. It's as if keeping her close helps release the yawning pain of Beth's loss I feel. A loss deep down in the marrow of my bones.

Cate's gaze has been scorching me all afternoon; it's unyielding. I admit I've been avoiding her but it's bloody hard coming face to face with your wife's double when you know that her ashes are cooling down and being sieved into an urn. When I look at Cate, every single hair on my arms and the back of my neck stands up. But it's time to face the music.

'Hi, Cate. We got through it — huh?' She runs her fingertip lightly across the edge of her eyelid as if removing a stray eyelash. 'This is bad enough for me, but I can't even begin to imagine what it's like for you,' I add. I mean this, sincerely. Losing Beth is like a wound that won't heal. Cate has it four times over.

She looks up.

'Not exactly much to get through, was there?' Her eyes bore into me.

'Sorry? You referring to the service? It was traditional, I believe.'

'I'm sure,' Cate says tartly. 'Christmas trees look bare without their baubles too, David.'

Ah — the service didn't meet with Cate's approval. Personally, I don't think Beth would have wanted the horse-drawn-hearse-type send-off. I decide it's best to say nothing. Voices shrill and babbling drifts around us, but Cate seems impervious, like stone. I'm learning that grief leaves you stranded, though. Like being left alone on a desert island. I know how Cate must feel. It's as if grief has suffocated all emotion out of her. Grief follows its own journey with every individual, I guess, and she's still to get through Giles's and the children's funeral in a few days. I need to cut her some slack, given her situation, but there's still something unnerving about her. Can't put my finger on it.

The air is jangling with unspoken recriminations. She looks at me then glances away, as if she's going to say something and stops herself. Her head movement is so like Beth's. I never noticed before how similar their mannerisms were. Cate takes a sip of her wine and eyeballs me again. She squares her shoulders.

'So, what was keeping you busy all weekend that you didn't call Beth? Not even a text, if I'm right.'

And then it occurs to me that she's sore with me. On Beth's behalf. They wouldn't have spent that weekend together and not discussed Beth's suspicions.

'I'm not sure this is the time or place, Cate.' I try to keep my voice low. 'But for the record, I did call. Not until early Sunday afternoon, I grant you, but I was only doing as instructed.' Cate's nostrils flare. I plough on like a guilty man trying to justify myself. 'We agreed to give each other space. I thought that included communication. She never called me either.'

'What time on the Sunday afternoon?' Cate is curt.

'Sometime after twelve thirty, I suppose. I called repeatedly then.'

'Yeah, right.'

Cate continues to sip her wine as though it were vinegar, looking like she's going to spit it out at me.

'You assumed a break meant no communication? You could have sent Beth a message at least. You knew she was hurting. Was a golf weekend seriously that distracting?'

'She distinctly said don't try to reach me. I took her at her word.' I realise I'm digging myself a deeper hole.

'Seriously, David.' A citric expression of distaste is painted on Cate's face. 'Whatever happened to "for better, for worse" — "to love and to cherish"?'

She lets her words hang. I have no choice but to examine the floorboards.

'What are you going to do with her now?' Cate says eventually.

My self-protection reflex wants to grab for the safety rail. I don't understand what she's talking about. I can't quell the hideous anxiety that Cate is about to lob one of her cluster bombs. Beth certainly had to deal with them. Could she possibly know about Adrianna?

'Do with her?' I take a gulp of my wine.

'With Beth's ashes. You need to scatter them in a special place.'

'Oh, her ashes.' I'm relieved, let off the hook. 'I haven't thought about that yet. It's all been a bit rough, you know? The funeral director said I can collect them in a week or so. They'll call me. I must plan something.'

'Can we scatter them together? It's important to me as her twin.' Cate reaches out and touches me on the arm. 'Especially as I wasn't involved in her funeral.'

The colour rises in my cheeks.

'I would have involved you more, but I figured you've got enough to deal with.'

'It's always nice to be asked, David,' she says acidly.

'Any ideas where?' I want to move on from yet another of my cock-ups.

Cate screws up her face, deep in thought.

'We had happy memories of Sunday-afternoon picnics in Richmond Park with our parents. You'd have to get permission.'

'Sounds perfect. I'll sort it and call you when I've collected the ashes. Just you and me as we were the closest to her.'

'Make sure you do. I'll be waiting for the call.'

It's going to be majorly weird. Scattering your wife's ashes with her doppelganger.

CHAPTER 20

Beth

Within an hour or so, mourners are offering their final condolences and the room is emptying. Laura and Michael give me a big hug and say they'll come and visit Ted and me tomorrow. In less than a week they'll be burying their son and grandchildren; *my* husband and children. I've had enough of my very own funeral day and decide to make my excuses too. I say goodbye to David, reiterating that he's to call me very soon. He's full of promises, as usual. I'll certainly be calling him if he doesn't.

I walk out into the fresh air, grateful for the change of scene. I plan to take a stroll and then call an Uber. Clouds are swelling up like billowing bruises, dirty yellow, grey and black skirting across the sky. It's an oppressively muggy day with a storm brewing.

I take out my phone, which was on silent. FFS. There's a string of messages from Max. Talk about on a day like no other. The untimely reminder of his existence fills me with dread. He's not going to go away. I probably shouldn't, but I read them.

11.43
MS: *Hey, Lady Jane!*

11.44
MS: *'We fucked a flame into being'*

11.48
MS: *'All hopes of eternity and all gain from the past he would have given to have her there . . .'*

12.02
MS: *'She was always waiting, it seemed to be her forte'*

12.07
MS: *'We've got to live, no matter how many skies have fallen'*

12.22
MS: *'A woman has to live her life, or live to repent not having lived it'*

Is this something I'm supposed to decipher? What on earth am I supposed to make of this? Is he seriously telling me I've got to live my life and forget about grieving? There's more.

12.47
MS: *'But that is how men are! Ungrateful and never satisfied.'*

1.22
MS: *'Me? Oh, intellectually I believe in having a good heart, a chirpy penis . . .'*

Oh, for goodness' sake. Creep or what? I'm not sure I want to read much more of this. I skim to the last text at the bottom, sent about twenty minutes ago.

3.03
MS: *I'll be waiting for you, Lady J! xx*

This guy really is something else. What is he on? How does he make all this stuff up? Then I notice he's used quotation marks. I google 'We fucked a flame into being'. I'm being dense. He's reciting from Lady Chatterley's Lover. I forgot that was their thing. I'm not in the mood. More googling and, against my better judgement, I send a reply.

3.34
CM: *'I only want one thing of men and that is, that they should leave me alone.'*

I receive an instant reply.

3.35
MS: *Clever girl. We're back in the game. Xx*

God, give me strength. I'm bombarded with more messages. I put my phone back on silent and away out of sight in my bag.

I pass a newsagent and on impulse, I walk in. I do something I haven't done in the best part of twenty years — I buy a packet of cigarettes. I'm compelled to draw in on something distasteful and then exhale; to expunge my sins with a foul taste in my mouth. If it makes me nauseous, then it serves me right. I lean in a doorway to an old-fashioned mansion block of flats, like a guilty teenager. I light the cigarette and inhale deeply. After a few drags, my chest feels like hardened concrete. I attempt to steady myself and breathe evenly and slowly, but I can't take in air properly. It's like I'm being held underwater. This is drowning.

Except it's not the cigarette that has caused my lungs to collapse in this way. It's the sight of David. My husband walking down the opposite side of the road, hand in hand with a young woman. Sharing smiles lit with unspoken intimacies. They look like a couple. They look happy. In love, even. Her hair is dark, long and lustrous like a cascading waterfall. And she is so, so beautiful. And it's the day of my funeral.

CHAPTER 21

Adrianna

David doesn't let go of my hand until he pushes open the door to the wine bar. He says he needs a drink and it's started to rain. Typically, neither of us has an umbrella.

'Can't think of a better place to shelter. What are you having?' He strides up to the copper-topped bar.

'Red, I think.'

'I'll get a bottle, then.'

David orders a bottle of Chilean Cabernet Sauvignon and a charcuterie-and-cheese platter. Says he was too nervous to eat anything at the funeral. We take our bulbous wine glasses and sit side by side on a burgundy leather banquette. David likes to keep me close. It's kind of endearing, but a bit irritating too at times, if I'm honest. He pours the wine and makes a show of swilling it around. He sniffs it before clinking my glass, then takes a sip.

'Cheers. Good stuff, this.'

'*Saúde!*'

'To us too. How do you say that?'

'*Para nós também.*'

'I love your accent, my little Brazil nut. It's sexy.' David kisses me on the cheek before taking another swig. 'Appropriate that we're drinking South American wine.'

'Chile is a long way from Brazil.'

'What was it like there, growing up as a child?'

I don't want to talk about my childhood. I'd rather know more about the funeral. I'm intrigued — and nosey. Other than telling me he's not eaten, he seems to be avoiding the subject.

I know this is kind of unusual — drinking with the widower on the day he's said goodbye to his wife — but it seems disrespectful of me to not mention her at all. I ignore David's question about Brazil.

'I think we should make a toast.'

'No need. I've ordered some food,' he says, chuckling at his own joke. I continue to ignore him.

'To Beth. *Que ela descanse em paz.* May she rest in peace.'

'Yes, that.' David taps my glass again. He drinks the rest of his wine in one and pours himself another. I can see where this is going. He must have had a shit-awful day, but I don't want to be shut out. If this is going to work between us then he needs to open up so I can play the role of the supportive girlfriend. That's what I should be doing, surely?

'Would you like to tell me how everything went.'

'She died, coffin arrived, we gave a tribute, played some music. Beth's been cremated, she's gone.' David rests his hand on my knee and caresses it by circling his thumb.

'I'm sure there was more to it than that.' As I chide him, the food arrives. David pours more wine and orders another bottle. I haven't even finished my first glass. I decide to press him a little more about the day.

'Was Beth's sister there? Must have been tough for her too.'

'Cate? Course. She looked beautiful.' He looks off into the distance. 'Tough for me — like looking at Beth. She's still a cold fish, though.' He takes another gulp of wine. 'She wants us to scatter the ashes together. Said I would. Must do that, I suppose.

Plan something. Me and Cate . . .' He trails off, then turns back to me and asks, 'Can we go home now?' just as the second bottle of wine arrives.

'I think you'd better eat first, don't you?'

David stuffs a slice of salami and a triangle of artfully cut cheese into his mouth. 'Want some?' He pushes the plate towards me.

'No, thanks. I ate earlier as I wasn't sure how long you'd be.'

We sit in silence. I'll have to quell my curiosity about the funeral, but I don't want to just sit here and watch him drink. I wonder what to say next. I don't know David well enough to know what subject to broach.

'I was thinking about tidying up those planter pots in the garden and repotting a few. Would that be okay?' I rest my fingers on his arm.

'Sure. Do what you like.' David continues to gaze into space. I have a thought.

'Do you fancy going to the cinema? It might help take your mind off the day.'

He turns to look at me with an expression like I've suggested we take an ice bath. He shakes his head.

I'm not getting anywhere other than feeling exasperated. David clearly doesn't want to talk. He's studiously peering into the depths of his yet-again-full wine glass. I need to get him to talk to me — about anything. Maybe I'm expecting too much today, but I want a purpose here —otherwise there's no point. He calls me, insists I meet him, then pulls up the drawbridge. This boy has a lot to learn. I consider leaving him to it as his phone rings. I can see on the screen *Cate Mildenhall*. Interesting. I wonder why she's calling so soon after the funeral? David stares at the screen.

'Don't you think you'd better answer it?'

'S'pose so,' he says, taking another gulp from his glass. It's one too many; the ringing stops.

'David, it could be important.'

'I don't want to be constantly reminded of Beth.'

'As an identical twin, that's going to be hard to avoid.'

'Yeah — tell me about it.' His phone rings again. It's Cate. I nudge him to let him know that I think he should pick up. He answers it with his mouth full.

'Hi.' He swallows, but doesn't get the chance to say any more. I can hear Cate crying. She's screaming in between sobs. David turns to me with a grimace as he moves the phone away from his ear. Poor woman — she's devasted, hysterical. Who can blame her? It must have just hit her — David said she was cold and distant at the funeral. I think she's in delayed shock, more like.

Still bawling, Cate says, 'David . . . I don't think I can do this.' And then she hangs up. David gives me a resigned look.

'Aren't you going to call her back?' He shakes his head.

'I can't deal with this today.'

The rain spits meanly against the windows. The promised storm arrives with a lightning crack, closely followed by a deep rumble of thunder. I don't fancy walking home yet. Maybe I will help David drink that second bottle of wine. He pours us both another glass, and sits back and closes his eyes, lost in thought. What's he thinking? I know what I'm thinking. If I'm going to be part of this drama, then I need to know what role I'm really playing. I sense Cate is turning to David. I need to be honest with myself — am I feeling a bit jealous? Maybe. I may need to involve myself a little more. I lean my head on David's shoulder.

'When is the funeral for Cate's husband and children?'

'A few days away. It's a full church service and burial. I expect half of west London will turn out.' David's eyes remain closed.

'It's such a tragedy. There's still snippets in the papers. Maybe I'll go along to pay my respects.'

'I'll have to go. Be there to support Cate. She'll have Giles's parents too. Bad for them,' David says, not responding to or questioning my suggestion I'll attend.

David slumps back further in the seat; he still hasn't opened his eyes. I hope he's not going to fall asleep here. The weather comes to my rescue. There's a bright white flash that seems to extend from outside to inside, and for a nanosecond everything feels suspended. A deep rumble of thunder follows. The couple seated at the table in the window strain their necks skyward. I can see the tail of a flash of forked lightning from behind the roof on the building opposite; it's immediately followed by another thunder crash. David sits upright, startled.

'Typical her,' he says.

'Who?'

'Beth, of course,' David says over another deafening thunder crack. He raises his glass towards the window. 'I hear you. I get it.'

'I don't understand.'

'Can't you hear her? She's making a lot of noise.' David theatrically points both index fingers in the air and waves them about like a conductor. He's definitely had too much to drink.

'What on earth are you talking about?'

David downs the last gulp of his wine. 'Beth is mad at me. She's playing her exit symphony.'

I'm beginning to know how she feels.

CHAPTER 22

Beth

I'm trying to come to terms seeing David with another woman. I can't believe I was right all along. I suspected David might be up to something, but I never truly acknowledged it to myself. I so wanted to believe his denials. Fool. It's been going on all around me and I didn't have a clue. Cate included. Talk about being blindsided.

Loneliness has taken up residence — I have no one to talk to. I've declined and ignored all Cate's friends' invitations to come over or take me out. Particularly the one called Claudia. Cate needs time and has become a recluse while she's healing. There's no other way — it's too risky. Many of them have started to drop by the wayside already. Even the supposed best mate Claudia signed off with a text last week.

> *I can sense you need some time, babes — won't keep pestering you. Know that I'm here. I'll wait for you to get in touch. Xx*

Not that I'm complaining, but you know what? If I really was Cate, how about a bestie ignoring all that and turning up with a bit of unconditional love and support? Cate could be suicidal for all she knows. Great friends you have, Cate.

Ted is on the changing mat and as I reach for the Sudocrem, I see Magdalena out the window striding across the lawn. She's heading towards Max who is kneeling with a trowel in hand and a garden-refuse bag parked beside him, weeding a flower bed. Strange because she tends to avoid him. Does she know what went on between him and Cate? What a sordid mess.

Max doesn't seem to have heard Magdalena approaching. She's standing right behind him now. She takes a step to the side so she is in view. He scrambles to his feet, pulling earbuds out as he does so. Magdalena reaches into her pocketed blue tunic (a favoured garment of hers — she owns several in different colours) and takes out what appears to be some folded banknotes. I paid her yesterday in cash. I'm ashamed to say she had to remind me — I'm still catching up with all this stuff. I'm not exactly used to paying staff. I checked Cate's banking app and she regularly took out six hundred pounds in cash on a weekly basis, so I've had to guess that it's the right amount for Magdalena. She extends her hand out to Max. A smirk spreads across his face as he takes the bundle and places it in his trouser pocket. There's a short exchange of some kind, but I can't hear what's being said. Magdalena hurries back across the lawn.

'What was that was all about, Ted?' I pull a little pair of red shorts over his nappy. Should I be concerned? Probably, but I've too many other things to worry about — like Laura and Michael visiting again this afternoon. Oh — and the small matter of another funeral to get through. I'm burying *my* husband and children.

CHAPTER 23

Adrianna

I mingle among the crowds in a churchyard waiting for a funeral cortège. A funeral for people I have never met; a father and his two children killed in a tragic road accident. I don't have to remind myself it's the same accident that killed David's wife. *Que Deus abençoe a todos eles.* God bless them all.

I know it's an odd thing to do, but the last few weeks have been unbelievably strange. I find myself catapulted into another life — a life not mine. Or maybe that's because it's not one I deserve. David says otherwise. How would he react if he knew what I was up to when we first met? The cheating, scheming me. As far as he is concerned, our relationship has slid comfortably into place and I'm going along with it because I do kind of like him and there is the added bonus of free rent. *Obrigada!* Maybe I should commit to a relationship again, but I can't dispel the ghost of Sol talking in my head. He sits jagged and misshapen in the corner of my mind, taunting me. *Men may desire you, Adrianna, but they will never love you.*

David is the complete opposite to Sol. He's loving and kind, with a warm and rich laugh. A man I have inadvertently stolen from another woman. A dead woman. I'm painfully aware that we're seriously breaking the unwritten rules, but David insists there's no turning back.

'We may be judged, but we're not going to get locked up,' he says.

I don't feel comfortable, though, and I'm not sure I'll stick around long term. Cate is turning to David for comfort and support even if he doesn't realise it. David may be loving in some ways, but he's not always emotionally intuitive or communicative. I'm here to get a better handle on what I'm dealing with. I want to see David interact with Cate from a distance and get a feel for the dynamics. Am I jealous? *Não*. Well, maybe a little. I need the facts. I told David I might come along, but he barely seemed to register, so let's see what unfolds.

I'm not going inside the church for the service. I'm used to being incognito so I blend in with the crowds and school-mum mourners who are already gathering in their hundreds. There has been such an outpouring of emotion at what has befallen the family.

Clouds have started to bunch and settle, blocking out the sun and sucking away the day's heat. I slip in with the crowd gathered closest to the church door. People are saying that the church is already full, but I have no intention of going inside. It's not my place. There's a low, insect-like buzzing hum of muted conversations. People clearly delighted to see each other but in check for the solemnity of the situation. There's a lot of *mwah-mwah* air-kissing going on, followed by hushed chat about the shock of it all.

Where were you when you heard the news? We saw the children only the week before. Such an unbelievable tragedy. We must do something about an appropriate school memorial. I'll get a fundraiser going . . .

A woman with a wasp waist, and what I can only imagine is a surgically enhanced backside, comes and stands directly in front of me. Her gold-chained shoulder-strap Chanel bag brushes my arm. She turns to look at me. Two espresso-coloured mutant slugs have chosen her face to take up residence somewhere in the region of where her lips used to be. I'm not sure what fate has befallen her eyes as a pair of giant sunglasses covers half her face.

'So sorry. Are you queuing to get into the church?' she asks.

'No. Please go ahead. I'm not planning on going in. Just paying my respects.'

'Me too. Mind if I wait here, then?' She squeezes herself in next to me. 'I'm Camilla, by the way.' She offers me her shocking pink talons weighted down with some seriously sparkly carats. She raises her sunglasses to perch on her head.

'Adrianna.' I'm fixated by her eyes, which are pulled up tight in the corners.

'I can't process this. Believe it. Can you? He's got some explaining to do. Taking young children. Tragic.'

'Sorry, who?'

'God, of course,' she says, indicating the church. 'Not even a life. I don't get it. How do you know the Mildenhalls?' Camilla continues, not waiting for my view on the behaviour of Him upstairs.

'I worked as a teaching assistant at the children's nursery.' I pray that Camilla doesn't know history that I don't.

'Which one?'

'The Montessori. How do you know the family?' I don't want to dwell on the subject.

Before Camilla can answer, the crowd becomes hushed as if a blanket of snow has fallen, muffling all sound.

The hearses pull up. There are three in total, followed by a funeral limousine carrying the principal mourners. The church bell starts to toll and is the only sound now audible as, one by one, the coffins are skilfully unloaded by the pallbearers. Mourners, mainly dressed in black, bow their heads; all eyes downturn and mouths pinch. The churchyard becomes a thoroughfare for grief as the crowd parts to allow the procession to solemnly make its way to the church entrance. The pallbearers walk as if in rhythm to the bell toll. A mechanical, heartless sound, as if chiming out the reminder of what has been lost.

I underestimated the impact the sight of three coffins was going to have on me. Tears prick the back of my eyes and a lump swells in my throat. You can hear escaped sobs from the crowd and Camilla puts a hand on my arm as if to steady herself; she's feeling it too. The quiet convivial atmosphere has changed and is now palpably full of anguish and sorrow. *Isso é de partir o coração.* This is heartbreaking.

The first two coffins are made of willow and I am shocked to see how small they are. I'm beginning to understand what Camilla meant. The lead and smallest of the three has a garland of lemon flowers and variegated ivy interwoven around the circumference of the casket. A beautiful double-end spray of yellow roses sits on top. The second willow coffin has a blue lilac, sweet pea and lavender garland with a spray of purple iris seated above.

It's hard not to be affected. My heart is going to break and I didn't even know them. I'm an intruder. I have no right to be a spectator here, but I've done worse. The third and final coffin is the father's. It's solid oak and takes six pallbearers to hold it steady. A beautiful, large spray of white bud roses and greenery is balanced on top. I can smell the floral lushness as they pass.

The priest has met the family at the gate and walks with them behind the coffins. A very smart-looking woman with porcelain skin, wearing a sharply tailored black trouser suit with a crisp white blouse, is flanked by an older couple. She must be Cate, David's sister-in-law. She keeps focused on the coffins ahead. Her face impenetrable. She must be feeling stabbed through the heart. I can't comprehend how she is managing to hold herself together. She's carrying three individual red roses clasped in her right hand, which glints with high-gloss red nail polish.

The church bell continues to toll its ear-piercing rhythm, calling for the dead as the procession is swallowed up by the church. Orders of Service have been distributed among the mourners outside and speakers have been set up so we can follow and listen to the service getting underway inside. A moment of silence slices through the air as the bell stops.

'Blessed are those that have died in the Lord; let them rest from their labours for their good deeds go with them.'

An organ pipes up and we clear our throats to commence singing the first hymn, 'Abide with Me'. I sense we are all grateful to have something to do. A channel for the emotion.

* * *

We've been standing outside the church for nearly an hour. Turns out it's a full Catholic service with a requiem mass. The priest is now giving his final commendation and there is only one more hymn to sing. Camilla taps me on the shoulder and whispers.

'Are you planning on going to the burial service?'

'Wasn't intending to. I don't have transport.'

'I've got wheels. Happy to give you a lift?'

'I'm not sure it's appropriate. I don't know them that well.'

'Don't worry about that. I've heard that all are welcome. It's a huge cemetery. Bet that most of this lot follow on. Come with me?' Camilla encourages me as though we're about to embark on something fun. I'm not sure it's the right thing to do, but this will give me more of an opportunity to see David and Cate together. I allow myself to be persuaded.

'Let's get away now. It'll be easier to park,' Camilla says, gently tugging at my sleeve.

I feel a bit like a naughty schoolgirl bunking off early as we tiptoe through the throng as everyone starts to sing, 'Lord of all Hopefulness'.

* * *

It turns out Camilla doesn't know the family either. She does have a daughter at the same school, though, but not in the same class as either of Cate's children. Her claim to fame is she once lined up next to Cate in the Friday after-school ice-cream-van queue. They've waved at each other a few times since. Camilla's link, however tenuous, is rather more legitimate than my own. I decide to stick to my classroom-assistant story if anyone asks. Best not to mention that I'm actually shagging Cate's dead twin's husband. Camilla may decide to abandon me on the South Circular otherwise.

I see David in his dark navy suit among the principal mourners at the graveside. He is standing next to Cate, but they're not touching each other. The older couple, I understand to be Giles's parents, are on her other side; she turns to look at them. This is uncomfortable. Camilla was wrong about everyone heading to the graveyard — the crowds aren't here and I feel conspicuous. David still hasn't spotted me, but he's bound to look up eventually. What will he make of me being here? It's a very private occasion for family and inner-circle friends. I should have stuck to my original plan and not been swayed by Camilla. I don't know what the hell I was thinking. It was not my intention to be a voyeur and place myself among this most intimate and sorrowful gathering. I have made a big mistake, all in the name of research.

I've left it too late to leave now and I'm kicking myself. If I walk away, it will be too obvious. Instead, I do that ridiculous thing where you mentally shrink into yourself in the hope that you become invisible.

The grass in the graveyard has that freshly mown smell, but is still quite squishy underfoot from last week's rain. The air lingers with musty earth that is piled up high along one border of each grave. When we first arrived, I was horrified to see such monstrous and deep holes in the ground. Two graves, three coffins. The two children are to be buried in the same grave. I presume that the space in the other grave will be for Cate herself when the time comes. I'm not sure I'd want to see my own grave dug.

All thoughts of trying to sidle away are quashed as it's clear that the committal is about to start. A hush descends; the only sound is from the gentle breeze making the pages of the priest's bible dance. Cate holds the hands of her in-laws; I'm glad it's not David. Their heads are bowed, motionless. The priest steps forward and starts to read a prayer. Tears stream down Cate's face, all composure gone. She must be thinking of the children. And her husband. It's painful to watch.

'. . . *In sure and certain hope of the resurrection to eternal life through our Lord Jesus Christ, we commend to Almighty God our brother Giles, his son Charles and daughter, Georgiana, and we commit their bodies to the ground.*

'Earth to earth, ashes to ashes, dust to dust.

'The Lord bless them and keep them.'

One by one the coffins are lowered into the deep chasms dug into the earth. The priest sprinkles holy water on the coffins once they are interred, blessing each in turn. Cate is handed her three red roses and throws them in the graves, one for each loss I presume. She bends down and picks up a handful of earth, examines it in her hand for a second. Cate steps forward and stands perilously close to the grave edge with her arm outstretched. I think we all take a sharp intake of breath. David, on reflex, moves closer to steady her by putting his arm on her shoulder.

Cate allows her fingers to slowly unfurl and a trickle of soil starts to land on the coffin below. You can hear it splatter on the lid like tearful raindrops. At this precise moment, the people in front of me who have protected me from view change alignment. As the last of the soil grains fall from her hand, Cate looks up abruptly and stares straight at me. It's unnerving. I glance around to see what's caught her attention, but I can't dispel the thought that it's me. *Merda!* Shit. She opens her hand again, fingers outstretched to grasp a handful of nothingness before snapping them shut. Her eyes continue to hold my gaze as she dramatically snatches her arm back by her side as though she is claiming the distance between us.

CHAPTER 24

Beth

I'm in the kitchen chopping vegetables to make some purées for Ted. Parsnip, carrot, broccoli and sweet potatoes. I seem to be mastering my knife skills today. There's something very satisfying about slicing vigorously. Once cooked, I think I'm going to enjoy pulping them to oblivion in the food processor even more. She was there. David's whore, piece of chum, had the audacity to show up at my family's funeral. David really is a despicable, arse-end of a scumbag. Why the necessity to bring her along?

'Maybe we should add some tomatoes. Even better — beet-root. It'll make a very satisfying blood-red colour. What you think, Ted?' I brandish my knife from a very safe distance. Ted chortles at me. He's thoroughly enjoying strengthening his legs in a bouncer contraption that Michael helped me put up in the door frame. *Boing, boing* he goes.

I knew it was her — you never forget a face like that. Did David feel a stab of guilt? Because he came and stood very close to me; he reached out and touched me, as though proximity to the wife look-a-like was a cure for his betrayal.

My new life as Cate necessitates me having to live through Beth's *afterlife* and watch my husband move on with his widower status. It's a bitterly unique position. Maybe, like grief, seeing David in his new relationship isn't something I can get over; it's something I'm going to have to learn to live with. But you don't get new beginnings if you're not prepared to give up what you had. There's always the possibility of screwing it up for him, though.

David was driven away through what he saw as irrational behaviour. Maybe I was, irrational that is, but I bet he can't even pinpoint what sent me over the edge. He never was in tune with how important a baby was to me. It was when Cate detonated her bombshell that she was pregnant again. I didn't even know she wanted a third child. Cate dropped it casually into the conversation as if she was ordering an extra topping on her pizza.

'I'm not sure we'll be able to get away for the autumn half-term break this year, honey. I probably can't fly as it's only a few weeks from when the new baby arrives. Let's look at the spring break instead?'

This was not inconsequential news. This was a mammoth atom bomb. I cried. They were not happy tears for her but ugly, dark green tears of incredulous jealousy. Why did Cate need another baby? It should be my turn.

I clung on to the thought that our elusive happy ending could be a cycle away. My infertility started to fill every corner of my mind. My life became just work and IVF. I'd take the day off after a transfer and stay in bed. I'd sing and talk to it. And then I'd bleed. My intended life evaporating away. Again.

'I'm so sorry, Mrs Brown. Not this time,' I'd be told as if I was just unlucky not to draw a winner for the tombola. Cate was the one with the golden ticket.

'But look at us now, Ted. Who'd have believed it?'

Consequently I will nurse my PTB (Post Traumatic Betrayal), but I will endeavour to get some semblance of the truth and find out who she is. The pain of knowing David has been unfaithful has to stand to one side. Because the big black hole, where my heart used to be, has been filled by my son. My beautiful boy. I can't promise, though, that I haven't inherited the manual on how to take the pin out of the grenade. I'm sure Cate left it in the kitchen drawer somewhere.

I can still see David and his girlfriend walking down the road hand in hand in my head as I pile the vegetables in the blender and watch them whizz around being pulverised. It's satisfying. I shake my head to snap myself out of it. What I really need to be focusing on is the important execution of another kind. Of a plan that I've had for a while, but I need to figure out how to do it. I'm going to reunite Cate with her children. Or maybe Giles? Or maybe I could split her between the two? I am determined to return Cate to her rightful place with her family — tuck her in with them, so to speak, so they can all be together. It's the right thing to do. I've got to get my hands on the ashes first, though, and that's not going to be easy. In fact, it's downright difficult, not to say extremely risky, but I'm compelled to do it.

I remove Ted from his bouncer and sit him in his high chair, ready to aeroplane spoon-feed him chicken-and-vegetable purée. A movement in the garden startles me. It's only a pigeon landing on the lawn. Silly. I'm permanently on edge in case it's Max, but he's away on holiday so I can relax.

'Here it comes. Open wide.' Ted obediently opens his mouth and as I think he's swallowing he blows a food raspberry and grins at me.

'Not helpful, young man. Now let's run through the options, shall we?'

I wipe around his mouth with the edge of the spoon.

'What do you think, buddy? How about we invite David to the house first before we go and scatter the ashes, distract him somehow and then make the switch?'

How are you going to distract him for long enough?

'Good point. Maybe get him to change your nappy.'

Very funny. It's a serious question.

'I could ply him with coffee so he'll need to visit the loo. We could do it then.'

That's your master plan, is it? What if David leaves them in the car? What if he doesn't need to pee? What if he suggests you meet in Richmond Park? It will be too late to do a switch by then and you'll be stuffed.

'Okay, smart arse. What do you suggest?'

You're going to have to retrieve the ashes yourself. It's the only sure way.

'Break into my old house, you mean? That's seriously weird. Although at least I know my way around the place. What if I get caught?'

You won't. I'll be with you. Babies don't get arrested.

No, but they do get taken into care, I think. I obviously don't voice this to Ted.

I've had an idea. An elderly neighbour keeps a spare key in case of emergencies. We'll show up and ask to borrow it. I'll say David asked me to sort through a few things. I'll introduce myself as Beth's twin and Ted will be a great distraction. She loves children. I doubt David will find out — he rarely spoke to her. And if he does, I'll say that I knew about the key from Beth and I had the sudden urge to look at and touch a few of her things. It's a bonded-twin thing.

'We'd better get the substitute sorted. Any ideas?'

Magdalena glides into the kitchen carrying a dustpan and brush, and the hoover. She makes me smile. She never walks; it's like she's permanently got roller skates attached to her feet.

'I'll put this away, Mrs Mildenhall. I'm finished today. Is there anything else you like me to do?'

'We're all good, thank you, Magdalena. Have a lovely evening. See you tomorrow.'

'Thank you,' she says, making a little curtsy bob.

'Magdalena, you are a treasure.' Ted and I glance at each other conspiratorially. We have a solution.

CHAPTER 25

Beth

I stand outside my old home in Twickenham. It is tired and small compared to the house in Richmond I've been living in for the past couple of months. The front garden looks smaller than I remembered — a postage-stamp-sized concrete-covered rectangle with a single, forlorn, empty flowerpot. No sweeping drive and immaculate path here. The wheelie bin is left hanging around instead of being neatly put away against the wall in the corner. I resist the urge to put it back in its rightful place. Magdalena is rubbing off on me.

The paint on the front door is starting to peel. Farrow and Ball Castle Gray. I remember David and I agonising over the colour choice, buying half a dozen trial-sized pots and painting little squares on the front door before we made our decision. Back in the days when we agreed on everything or one of us would easily acquiesce because that's what you do when you love each other. We chose this shade together.

I'm now looking at a faded, peeling, flaky front door. Strange how I never noticed the state it was in before.

'We have to get the key first,' I say out loud to Ted. 'Two doors up.'

155

We knock on Mrs Crowley's door and stand back. I don't want to alarm her so have placed my little decoy accomplice in his buggy in front of me. I've washed and straightened my hair into a sleek bob, and raided Cate's wardrobe for a pair of white capri pants and a long, vibrant red-white-and-blue geometric-print silk blouse. Something I would never have worn. In my previous life, stripes were an adventure.

The chain on the front door rattles; the door opens a fraction as Mrs Crowley peers out.

'Hello. Sheila Crowley? So sorry to disturb you. Let me introduce myself. I'm Cate Mildenhall, Beth Brown's twin sister.' Her face immediately softens.

'Oh, my goodness. Yes. One moment.' The chain is slid back and Mrs Crowley opens the door wide. She looks older than I remembered. Her grey hair is now almost pure white. Have I been living in a time warp and years rather than weeks have slipped by?

'I'm so sorry about your sister. You must be devastated. Tragic.' Sheila Crowley covers her mouth with her hands in disbelief. 'I've still not got over the shock of hearing the news. And you have suffered such a personal loss, my dear. My heart goes out to you. God bless your husband and the children.' She shakes her head.

'Thank you, Mrs Crowley, I really appreciate it. I have to stay strong for this little one.' I use the stroking Ted's head technique. Poor child will lose what little hair he has if I keep this up.

'Oh, who's this then?' Mrs Crowley bends over to greet Ted, grateful for the distraction as much as I am. 'Please call me Sheila.'

'This is Ted. 'He's over eight months old now.'

'I've got a great-granddaughter the same age. Amelia. She's such a poppet.'

I bite my tongue as I'm on the verge of letting slip *eight months already? She's Sam's daughter, isn't she?* I can't relax for a moment.

It's unbelievably easy to give yourself away. Blurt out something that you wouldn't know. *Stay sharp.*

'Sheila, I've come to borrow the key to number forty-four. Hopefully David remembered to mention that I would call? I'm going to collect a few of Beth's things.'

'David didn't, actually, but no matter. I can see that he's been rather busy of late,' Sheila replies somewhat tartly as she rubs her hands on her apron. 'Let me find it for you. Do come in.'

'I won't because of the buggy and we've got to get back soon.' I want to hurry things along a bit. 'But it's been lovely to meet you. Beth always spoke very fondly of you. Said you were a wonderful neighbour.' Sheila beams.

'Let me grab that key.'

* * *

Five minutes later, Ted and I stand outside the door to number 44. My marital home. Deep breath. The key is rather stiff in the lock as we had a new one cut to give to Sheila. It's hardly been used. I don't think it's going to turn. I wiggle it a bit, but it gives way abruptly and turns with a sharp click. I push the buggy into the hallway rather than leave it outside so we don't draw attention to the house. It's super freaky to be standing inside after all these weeks. When I left on that Friday back in June, I had no idea what was about to unfurl. Life can certainly turn on a sixpence.

'Where shall we look first, Ted?' I unstrap him to carry him around. 'Front room, I think.'

The only sound I can hear is my own heart echoing in my eardrums. I can't believe I'm here, looking to steal Cate's remains from *my* own home. Creeping around as though I shouldn't be here. Life really has become a game of consequences.

'A game we're going to see to its conclusion, aren't we, my sweet? And with you on my side, darling boy, I will surely win.'

I can't see any sign of Cate's ashes in the front room. I'm not sure what I was expecting exactly. They've certainly not been placed centre stage on the Victorian mantelpiece. I run my finger across the top, expecting to sweep up a dust trail. There isn't one. Looking around the room, everything is neat and tidy. The seats to our sagging sofa have been plumped up and the black-and-cream scatter cushions are lined up in a neat, angled, overlap formation. Maybe David has hired a cleaner? I look in the cupboards built into the recesses either side of the fireplace. All the usual rubbish — nothing there.

'Let me show you the kitchen.'

We look around. I immediately spot a vase of pink and orange gerberas sitting on the window ledge. Odd. Did David buy those or has someone bought them for him? Nothing of consequence left on the worktops. We look in all the kitchen cupboards, and the old pantry in case David has stored me with the rice. No sign. We check the understairs cupboard that houses the loo. That would be seriously disrespectful, but I still have to check.

A noise startles me momentarily. It's only a floorboard creaking. This old house has a way of talking to you sometimes. Maybe it's pleased to see me back.

'Must be upstairs.'

Have we covered the ground floor already?

'Yes, Ted, we have. This is a very normal-size house. Not everyone is as lucky as you to live in such a fabulous mansion. I hope you learn to appreciate it.'

Upstairs, we head straight for the main bedroom and first port of call is David's wardrobe. 'Let's look in here. What do you think, Ted?' I can smell David as soon as I slide back the mirrored door. His aftershave, his body, his being. My husband. My fingers lightly caress a row of David's work shirts in a sweeping motion, as though scaling the keys on a piano. I can't resist. Making sure I've got Ted in a firm grip in one arm, I grab an armful of shirt sleeves and bury my face in them. I drink in the scent of him.

'Oh. David, my love.'

Ted starts to wriggle. He's getting bored.

I squat down, still with Ted in my arms, to check the wardrobe floor among David's shoes and gym bag. Nothing. We look around the room. It looks different somehow, but I can't pinpoint why. Our king-size bed with my favourite White Company bedding still takes centre stage. But it has a new, multi-coloured-checkerboard velvet cushion on it. The room feels different. It smells different too. There's an unfamiliar scent. Roses? Stale particles of a floral perfume, not mine, floating like scum in the oppressive air. I rush over to my wardrobe and slide the door open at such full tilt that it shudders in its tracks. *The seven years' bad luck can be yours, David, if the mirrored glass breaks.*

There are women's clothes in the wardrobe and they're not mine. *You're a fucking scumbag.*

Christ, I didn't say that out loud, did I? No, I can't have done, but you bet I'm thinking it. I've been cleared out already. Despicable bastard. He could have had the courtesy to at least scatter me first. Why the big rush? I know she exists. But somehow, I didn't expect this. Seeing someone is bad enough, but David's moved her in. Why am I so surprised? I stare at her clothes. *I'm not liking you too much right now, either, whatever your name is.*

I'm seriously close to doing that jealous-rage-revenge thing you see in films — find a pair of scissors and slash and cut holes in all her clothes. It wouldn't be difficult. I happen to know there's a sharp pair in the kitchen utensil drawer. Or even better, use a Stanley knife from the toolbox. I summon all my strength to resist. Walk away. Stay calm. Ted is with me and I can't have him witnessing his mother totally lose the plot. I've chosen my path and it's the right one.

Gently this time, I slide the wardrobe door closed. I will walk out with my dignity and not waste time persevering with someone I can no longer trust. I hold on to my baby a little bit tighter. My strength giver, my moral compass.

'They're not in here, Ted.' Even David wouldn't have the audacity to sleep in the same room as both of us.

I'm praying that David hasn't kept the urn rolling around in the boot of his car. I peer into the bathroom. There's a new aqua-green toothbrush in the holder by the sink, nestling in comfortably with David's blue one. Shared toothpaste, I note. How cosy. I can't see where the ashes would be in here, so we check out the spare bedroom at the back of the house. I don't see it at first. Everything looks the same as I left it all those weeks ago except for a suitcase I don't recognise, propped up against the wall underneath the window.

It's Ted who draws my attention to the solitary chest of drawers in the room. He's spotted a small, ginger teddy bear holding a red velvet heart that David gave me one Valentine's Day about a decade ago. He gives an excited gurgle and twists himself in my arms to reach out to touch it. It's propped up against an inconspicuous-looking brown rectangular cardboard box, about a foot in height. My heart gives a little flutter. This must be it.

I sit Ted down on the floor by my feet and give him the bear to play with. He immediately starts to suck on it. I pick up the box and open the flap. Inside is a dark green opaque cannister about the size of an old-fashioned screw-top sweetie jar. I pull it out of the box. It has a white paper label stuck to it.

Cremated remains of the late
Elizabeth Jane Brown.

Its coolness chills my hands. It's lighter than I expected, but then it's only made of a cheap plastic resin. I wasn't worth the expense of a stone jar or brass urn. I think I'd rather have been in one of those biodegradable cardboard ones.

I unscrew the lid. It's lined with a paper bag, which holds the ashes. I take the large zip-seal freezer bag with my replacement ashes out of my handbag. I've brought another empty bag to tip the actual ashes into. I carefully unfold the paper bag.

'Hello, Cate. How's it going? Thanks for the gift of the baby. I promise I will treasure him for ever,' I say, barely audibly as I don't want Ted to overhear. He's convinced I am his mother now. Which I am.

I tip Cate's ashes into the empty freezer bag and do the switch. They are both a mid-grey, but the texture is different to what I was expecting. Cate is more like beach sand than the wood-ash substance I imagined. I've absolutely no idea where I'd get hold of grey sand, though, so this is going to have to do. I doubt very much if David will have examined them, so I'll take the risk that he won't notice the difference. Job done. With Cate secured away in my oversized handbag, I give it an affectionate pat.

'After me, you come first. Look who's blowing out the candles now, sis.'

CHAPTER 26

Adrianna

She's here. She's come to the house. Has a key and let herself her in — David's sister-in-law, Cate. I happened to look out the main-bedroom window to check the weather as I was planning to go out and get something to cook for supper. Cate was there with the baby in the buggy. Standing motionless on the pavement by the little wrought-iron gate with this blank expression on her face, staring at the front door.

I darted out of sight, but when I checked a few moments later she was walking on. I thought that was it, that maybe she wanted to call in on David, but realised he was out at work.

I changed and was brushing my hair when I heard a key turn in the front door. I assumed it was David, so I rushed out onto the landing and peered over the banisters, thinking maybe he was feeling unwell or needed something. I was about to call out when the wheels of the buggy came into view and I realised who it was.

What the . . . ? I'm edging away from the stairs, trying to process what's going on. Maybe she's come to sort through Beth's stuff? David would have warned me, though, and there's no way he'd have agreed to it without him being here. Then I remember the look she gave me at the graveside. Maybe Cate knows about me somehow and has come to have a go at me. I'm going to be forced to face her and explain why I've been sleeping with her dead sister's husband.

I'm contemplating how best to handle the situation when I hear her speak. At first, I think she is in the house with someone else. By this time, I'm pinned up against the far wall on the landing out of sight of the stairs so I can't catch everything, only snippets.

I soon realise that I am only hearing one voice. Cate is talking to the baby and having an imaginary conversation. Sweet, I guess. But then I panic when I hear, 'Must be upstairs.'

Merda! Merda! I have to make a split-second decision as the distinctly audible third and fifth stairs creak. David pointed them out to me not long after I moved in.

'You can't creep out in the night and leave me,' he said light-heartedly. 'The stairs will give you away.'

Should I pretend to come out the bathroom and act surprised? I dismiss it as too dangerous — she is carrying a baby and I might scare her. So, I dash into our bedroom and look for a hiding place. Not exactly many options. The wardrobes are the obvious choice, but the sliding doors will make a noise and Cate is too close now. I can't slide under the bed either — my reflection will show in the mirrored doors and then this weird situation will become even more bizarre. With a nanosecond to spare, I dash into the space between the open door and large chest of drawers against the wall, grabbing David's dressing gown from the hook on the back of the door as I go. I crouch down, curling myself up as small as possible, and pull the gown over me. Hopefully, at a glance, I will look like a pile of washing.

Cate goes over to David's wardrobe first and slides open the doors. She is chattering away to the baby all the time. It is quite endearing and, knowing what she's been through, who wouldn't be desperately sorry for her. In grief, there are no timescales or judgements and so whatever Cate is up to is all part of her personal path. I can deal with that. Only, it's best that we don't meet yet.

'Let's look in here. What do you think, Ted?'

She is looking for something, but what the hell does she think she is going to find in David's wardrobe? Part of me wishes that I braved facing her. At least then maybe I could have helped her find whatever it is she is searching for. I can only presume it is something of Beth's that means so much to her.

I know at this point that Cate must have her back to me, so I risk peering out from underneath the dressing gown to see what she is up to. I can partially see her reflection in the mirrored wardrobe on the opposite wall. But that's when things start to get mysterious. Creepy, even. Cate says and does something that makes my stomach clench. She gathers up a handful of David's shirt sleeves and buries her face in them as though she were drinking in his scent. Trying to feel and absorb David as though he is familiar and precious to her. He's not the one who died. Her husband did. I can't fathom. Then I hear her whisper.

'Oh, David, my love.'

It was barely audible, but I am pretty sure that was what Cate just said. I'm doubting what I heard, but then she says it again. Louder this time. 'Oh, David, my love.' Her words hang in the air like puncture wounds to my heart. Were David and Cate having an affair? Was something going on between them when the accident happened? But why would David have been so anxious to move me in if he had Cate on the back burner? Unless I was being used as a cover-up? I can't believe that. I really don't think David is that good an actor. He's the type who wears his heart on his sleeve.

I think she is about to leave when she rushes over to the other wardrobe and pushes it aside so violently that I think the glass will smash. The coat hangers are dragged along the rail as my clothes are examined and then discarded. I don't dare risk moving or taking another peek. I certainly don't want to face Cate now. I sense jealousy. Fierce jealousy, from what I observed. Or is it anger on her deceased sister's behalf? No, it is the green-eyed monster. Got to be. Why the odd behaviour with the shirts otherwise? Cate is in love with David.

Cate leaves the room and there is a pause; maybe she's taking a quick look in the bathroom? I'm pretty sure she's now in the spare bedroom. I don't know what Cate hopes to find in there; it's such a sparse room. She's taking such an age that my back aches in my crouched position. I decide to risk it and stand up to stretch my legs and back. This has also enabled me to edge closer to the door opening so that I can hear better.

'Hello, Cate. How's it going?' she says, and something about treasure. She definitely said Cate. I can't even begin to explain how confused I am. Is this supposed to be the baby talking to her? Or is she saying hello to herself? I'm beginning to question whether I've heard anything right. Bewildered doesn't even cover it.

I shuffle back to my hiding place. After what seems an indeterminate age, there's a movement on the stairs. A few moments later, I hear the front door click shut. She's gone. I dash over to the bedroom window and peer out, taking extra care not to be seen. Cate is walking down the road pushing the buggy. She crosses over, stops by a red Mini and starts to unclip the baby to put him in the car. She holds him in her arms, cuddling him, before carefully placing him in his car seat. This was a planned, purposeful visit.

I wait until Cate drives off before going into the spare room to see if I can work out what she's been up to. Everything looks the same, but the smell of a citrus perfume lingers. Invisible evidence that Cate has spent time in here. The cover on the bed is untouched. My suitcase stands exactly in the same position. I check the bedside-table drawers. Full of typical bits and bobs.

Detritus that you never get around to clearing out: a comb, a couple of paperback books, tissues, a tape measure, some safety pins, pens, hand cream, an old pot of pink nail polish that has separated and congealed. Nothing unusual, although one drawer has a few loose photos of David and Beth, plus a framed wedding picture. Was Cate looking for a photograph? But why the need to be so surreptitious about it?

I take in the chest of drawers on the far wall. The little Valentine teddy is still propped up against the box that houses the urn with Beth's ashes. I walk over and pick it up. Its ears are damp. *Que nojo.* Yuck. Sucked and dribbled on. Cate must have given it to the baby to play with. But what necessitated the distraction?

I pick up the box. It has weight to it. Cate's not stolen the ashes. But then why should she? She's scattering them with David in Richmond Park on Saturday. Absolutely nothing makes sense.

* * *

David's home and I've cooked a special dinner. I intend to introduce Cate into the conversation. Probe a bit to see how things unfold. To test his reaction to the mention of her. Then I'll determine how much I should tell him. I've prepared *moqueca de peixe* — a Brazilian fish stew with coconut milk — and chocolate fondants for dessert. David pours himself another glass of chilled Chablis.

'Wow. This is delicious. Much better than I'm used to. Don't let me get fat.' David smiles, leaning over to give me a peck on the cheek.

'Didn't Beth cook?' I say, keen to get the conversation underway.

'She wasn't keen. Quick oven or one-pot stuff. Beth would often have to work into the early evenings with students learning to drive after school or college, so we had to keep it simple.'

David takes a sip of his wine.

'My mum taught me when I was little — family meals were important. It's a shame if Beth's didn't. What about her sister? Does she cook?'

David nods. He doesn't seem unduly bothered by the mention of Cate. Maybe he doesn't realise she's in love with him?

'Cate is more of a cook. I think she did a cordon-bleu course or something at one point. Probably why Beth hated it. They were funny those two — a bit of a love-hate relationship. What one excelled in, the other avoided.'

This is my cue. I swallow my mouthful.

'Talking of Cate. I saw someone down the street today that looked remarkably like her. I don't suppose it could have been her around here, could it?'

'Cate? Nah, I very much doubt it.'

'I was wondering, would she have a key to the house? Perhaps she'd want to collect a few of Beth's things. Some mementos. Photos or something.'

'Cate rarely came here to my knowledge. She always complained that parking was too difficult.' David stuffs a piece of fish in his mouth. 'Beth never mentioned she'd given Cate a key. The only spares I know of belong to Beth's mum and I'm pretty sure she took that back. And Sheila a few doors down keeps a spare for us in case of emergencies.'

So that's why Cate disappeared for a while. I take a sip of wine, wondering how to further direct the conversation.

'I know I've only seen Cate once, at the funeral, but she looked so like her. She was with a baby too. So loved-up with it. Chattering away in conversation like it could understand everything she was saying. It was so cute.'

'Definitely wasn't Cate then.' David lets out a snort.

'Why do you say that?'

'Cold Cate. That's why. I don't mean to sound unkind. She's been through a hell of a lot, but shall we say I've never observed her to be the warmest of mothers. Sad really, given Beth was the one so desperate to have a baby. Are the fondants ready?'

So desperate to have a baby. What if? No. Can it be? *Eu tenho sido tão estúpido.* I've been so stupid. Realisation floods in like the sluice gates have been opened. *De jeito nenhum.* No fucking way. It explains an awful lot. In fact, it could explain everything. But that's a crazy thought, isn't it? Maybe Cate is so traumatised that her twin psyche is making her act out being her sister? But she was so loved-up with the baby. 'Cold Cate', David said. I don't know what to think, but I still can't dispel the notion that David's wife is very much alive. And if that's the case, then I have stolen her husband. But she has stolen a baby.

CHAPTER 27

Beth

My head is down the toilet bowl. I've been sick and I've not even finished breakfast. I've been feeling groggy since I got up. I had a decent night as Ted regularly sleeps through to morning now — my little angel. However, the more sleep we're both getting, the more tired I seem to feel of late. But it's not the grogginess that brought up this mess I'm staring at, though.

The post dropped on the mat with a plop while Ted and I were in the kitchen having breakfast. There's a mound of daily admin to deal with as I'm having to send off death certificates, liaise with the solicitor's office about Giles's will, notify insurance companies, and so much more. It's exhausting, but Laura and Michael have been helping me with it all, for which I'll be eternally grateful.

I went to collect today's additions as Magdalena isn't around today. I've given her the morning off — she more than deserves it. There was the usual pile and I carried the bundle into the kitchen. I was shuffling through the various white and buff envelopes to see if anything needed my prompt attention. Laura and Michael are coming around shortly to collect Ted for a day out, so I wanted to see what would be easier for me to pass on to them. Michael always asks if there's anything he can help with. I think it gives

169

them an anchor in this tumultuous time, a tether to Ted and me, and I am very happy to have them on board. They are my son's grandparents after all and, as much as I want him all to myself, I think it's important he has a relationship with them.

Then something slipped from the pile as if making a break for freedom as it skidded across the polished floor. A postcard. All the way from Turkey. It was one of those with multiple images on the front — a sandy beach with alluring turquoise sea, a rugged coastline, archaeological ruins of an amphitheatre, a skyline at sunset with minarets silhouetted against the orange sky. I turned it over.

> *Missing me, Lady Jane? I'm counting the days!*
> *You and me next year. Where shall we go?*
> *I'm hungry for you, my love.*
> *MS & JT xx*

And that's when the bile rose up my throat. I had to drop the post and dash for the toilet bowl, making it here with zero seconds to spare. Thankfully Ted is still safely secured in his high chair. I rinse my mouth out and return to the kitchen.

The nausea doesn't want to subside. I gulp down a glass of cold water to try to steady my nerves. I've been an idiot to think he's taken the hint to leave us alone. Max has been thinking about me on holiday. Soon he'll be coming back for me. I check the postmark. It's dated nearly three weeks ago.

Bloody hell, Cate. I can't deal with the fucked-up side of your life. Why couldn't you have been satisfied with your lot? A dull, rich husband, a wonderful home and three gorgeous children. So typical of you to stir Max into your bland life like an extra dose of chilli sauce.

The sick feeling in the pit of my stomach will not go away. David is coming this afternoon. We're going to Richmond Park to scatter *Beth's ashes*. I feel like curling up into a ball instead.

* * *

It's still oppressively warm around the edges by the time David and I reach Richmond Park's gates. The detergent-blue sky is giving way to a heat-haze cover that is now fuzzing the edges of the horizon. It's a violently hot July day. The type where you can feel the heat of the pavement through the soles of your shoes. I'm glad I settled on the Veja trainers to wear with my tailored white shorts rather than the espadrilles I toyed with. The thin soles would have glued me to the pavement.

I had expected David by 3 p.m. That's what we agreed. He didn't turn up until nearly four o'clock.

'Sorry I'm late,' he said when he arrived. 'Time just ran away with me.'

Too busy shagging and playing house with your new bitch, weren't you? Good of you to prise yourself away and spare the time to come and scatter your wife's remains.

I should have voiced my thoughts out loud. Cate would have done. But there's still too much of Beth inside me that can't deal with confrontation, so I bit my tongue. Luckily, I've agreed with Laura and Michael that Ted is going to spend the night with them in Maida Vale. But David doesn't know that. Ted's very first sleepover.

The breeze blows hot air over us like a hairdryer. Maybe walking to the park wasn't such a good idea. The problem with auburn hair is that it comes with a pale, peachy skin that lends itself to burning. I've foolishly worn a sleeveless, tie-at-the-waist pink linen shirt and I can already feel my shoulders and arms burning even though I've applied sunscreen. The smell of it reminds me of the days when David would say, 'Roll over, baby,' and massage it into my back, working up my spine and finishing with kisses on my neck. It only serves to remind me that I am no longer the recipient of David's kisses.

'Which way do you suggest?' David asks once we're inside the park.

'Straight ahead. Then we'll do a right. I know a lovely place beyond a small pond. It's screened by lots of bracken. It should be pretty private.'

'It's hard to imagine living with this right on your doorstep. You're so lucky,' David says, indicating the expanse of beautiful parkland.

'Yes. Lucky me.' *Insensitive bastard.*

As we cross the road, David touches my arm to get my attention and points across the grass to a herd of grazing fallow deer.

'Beth always loved to see the deer whenever we drove through the park. She'd always look out for them like an excited kid. Bless her.'

To my intense surprise, David's voice starts to crack. He does care. Now I love him and feel sorry for him, when a few moments ago I was feeling angry and pissed off. How the hell does he do it?

Flocks of birds circle overhead as we find the path I'm looking for. Swifts, swallows and martins are swooping, swirling and chattering in their volumes, catching flies on the wing. The lush green fern fronds framing the path tickle my legs.

'I think a storm might be coming,' David says, pointing to the horizon where clouds are beginning to gather and tumble. In the distance, the cocktail-coloured sky is losing its picture-postcard hue as it begins to darken to a gravel grey. The clouds fluff up like angry pillows. 'That's why there are so many birds. They must be feeding on thunderflies.'

'We'd better get a move on, then. We don't want to be scattering poor Beth in the rain,' I say. Great. Now we're probably going to get soaked in the process, thanks to David being an hour late. This should have been over and done with by now. 'This way, it's not far.'

Five minutes later, we're standing side by side in a small clearing away from the path among the ferns with a view of the pond. Typically, David hasn't sought permission to scatter the ashes. He didn't think it was important. I allow myself a wry smile. We've timed it right as a family have just recently packed away their picnic and are beating a hasty retreat, perhaps sensing the approaching change in the weather.

We are alone. David stands motionless with his hands in his navy chino shorts pockets, looking out at the distance. I'm not quite sure what he's doing. Trying to compose himself or doesn't know how to begin? I wish I could read his thoughts. I feel smug that David doesn't realise how utterly futile this exercise is. But I allow him his moment.

'Go on then,' I say eventually, with an eye on the looming clouds.

David takes a sharp intake of breath and removes a black rucksack that he's been carrying. He crouches down to unzip it, gingerly takes out a tea towel that has been neatly folded over into a package and starts to unwrap it. David passes me two champagne glasses to hold. He pulls out a bottle of Taittinger and stands it on the ground next to the rucksack. I am to be toasted. I am impressed and touched for the briefest of moments before it occurs to me that this is probably somebody else's influence. *She* has suggested this. The irony of the situation is overwhelming.

Then comes the green urn. David stands up and tentatively unscrews the lid. He avoids looking directly inside as though the contents may sizzle and spit at him. He glances over at me. I nod encouragement.

'Together?' he says. I move closer and rest my hand on the urn. We start to move in a circular motion as David shakes the cannister, gradually scattering the contents. We are careful to keep downwind. Some disperse among the ferns, but others clump in stubborn little piles. *Typical Beth*, I bet he's thinking. David surprises me again by starting to speak.

'Dearest Beth. We miss your presence and will forever treasure your memory. We will always love you and will never forget you. Goodbye, my love.'

'Amen,' I say.

David removes the foil from the champagne bottle top and gently teases the wire fastening. He cups the bottle between his hands, using both thumbs to ceremoniously prise it open with an invigorating pop. The cork rockets sky-high before plummeting back down to earth and is swallowed up by the undergrowth. David pours me a glass and hands it to me with a thoughtful look on his face. He pours himself one.

'To our darling Beth. Dearly beloved wife and sister. May you rest in peace,' I say, raising my glass.

'Amen to that.' David raises his to mirror mine. We turn to face each other and clink our flutes. The wind starts to pick up, efficiently dispersing the remainder of the contents of the Hoover.

We've almost finished our champagne when the first drops of rain fall. A large plop lands with decisive accuracy in David's glass. I giggle. I'm sure it's the champagne on an empty stomach. I was too nervous about seeing David to eat lunch. We both look skyward as a deep rumble of thunder reverberates around the park — roaring the promise of a deluge.

'We're going to have to run.' David reaches to grab my champagne glass.

'Oi! Not so fast,' I reply, laughing as I down the last swig and hand him the flute.

David packs everything away with speedy efficiency. He slings his rucksack over his shoulder and turns to go. I stand still with my arms outstretched, looking up at the now-molten silver-black sky.

'Do you think that's Beth sending us a message?' I start to giggle again. 'What do you want to tell me, sis?'

'She's telling us to get a move on.' David grasps my hand and gives it a tug. I allow my hand to slip into his; it feels so familiar. I entwine my fingers with David's and hold on tight. A flicker of surprise crosses his face, but he doesn't let go. We start to run as the heavens open. David pulls me along as we stumble back through the ferns to the path. The heated air quickly becomes shot through with the smell of damp grass. Our clothes and hair are already drenched.

'Wait. Wait a sec. Shoelace,' I say, darting under the shelter of an oak tree. I squat down and re-tie my laces. David stands over me. I look up at him and reach out my hands to be pulled up. He responds and I bounce up, toppling into him.

'Oops. Too much champagne,' I say with a hiccup.

David puts both hands on my shoulders to steady me. My hands grace his waistline. I look up into his eyes and he returns my gaze. For a fraction of a second I imagine we're lost together in eternity. I want this moment to last for ever.

CHAPTER 28

Beth

Once back at the house, I fetch towels and David meanders into the kitchen. By the time I return he's crouched on the floor playing with the kittens. He looks like an excited kid. It tugs at my heart to think what a great dad he *should* have been.

'So, who do we have here, then?' David strokes Jaime while Cersei attempts to climb up his back. She gives a successful mew as she reaches his shoulder and starts to purr contentedly in his ear.

'Meet Cersei and Jaime — the latest additions to the family.'

God, that was awful. I didn't mean it to sound like two kittens have conveniently replaced two dead children.

'I thought you had just the one cat. Where's he got to?'

'Cedric. He's around somewhere. Out mousing, I suspect. Will probably present me with something disgusting later to show that he's still top cat.'

'How long have you had them?' David pulls himself up from the floor with Cersei still carefully balanced on his shoulder.

'They arrived literally a few days after Charlie and Georgie . . . died,' I say, faltering. 'They chose them. They were to be their kittens.' My voice cracks and tears start to prick the back of my eyes.

'Oh, Cate, no. I'm so sorry.' David carefully prises Cersei off his shoulder. He winces as she tries to hang on with her claws, but he manages to place her gently back on the floor.

The tears start to fall. David steps forward and draws me towards him in a comforting bear hug.

'Bless you, Cate. It's so tough. You're doing really well. Honestly you are. Time. We all need time.'

A riptide of selfishness is pulling me. At this moment, I want it all. I want David and I want my baby. My heart's breaking. My face crumples. I completely lose my composure and cling to David tightly. All the grief I've been holding swamps me; my sobbing body shudders with convulsions. The whole sordid situation is tearing at my head, my heart, my entire being.

I muster the strength and draw away from David, looking up to meet his eyes. He brushes away my tears with the back of his hand. He tucks my hair behind my left ear before curling his fingers behind my neck. He hesitates for an instant before leaning in to kiss me.

We break away, him perhaps questioning where that came from. I know, I'm kissing my husband — the man who has another woman waiting back at home for him. I want to think that for David, this is perhaps him saying sorry and goodbye to me, Beth. For the part he played out so badly, for the betrayal.

'Forgive me, Cate? I shouldn't have done that.' David purses his lips, looking embarrassed.

I deliberately don't reply, but feign as though my legs are threatening to buckle under me. David holds on to me and guides me to the sofa in the corner of the kitchen. I sink into it, but don't let go, pulling him down on top of me. I fix my gaze on him and open my mouth in a shallow pant. The shape and firmness of his body pins me down as he gives the gift of another kiss. This time it's much more powerful and sexual. The type of kiss that melts your bones, the kind David hasn't given me in a long time. Is this how he's kissing his new girlfriend? Well, I'm going to take some of it for myself. I'm going to leave my scent on him.

His mouth closes in on mine and it becomes an open doorway to another time, a different place. Back to when we first met and were so hungry for each other. I'm conscious of trying to act differently than I normally would during lovemaking. David may momentarily be lost in a moment of make-believe where he's with Beth, but I can't *be* Beth for him. I'm Cate.

I undo the belt on David's shorts and unzip his fly. He does want me. I pull my shorts down with my knickers, but they drag against my skin as they're damp from the rain. No matter — this can't wait. I arch into David as he starts to undo the buttons on my shirt. Realisation dawns that this has to be out of bounds.

'Best not. I still do a night feed,' I whisper. David complies and moves his hand away. I can't take the risk.

I'm electrified by my proximity to David again. After everything. David keeps looking at me nervously as though he's expecting me to tell him to stop. There's no going back now. My body is primed and aching for him. As David enters me, a sonic boom of emotion engulfs me, enough to shatter glass. It's electrifying and, oh, how I've missed this. This isn't the baby-making love that became our routine. This isn't the sex by appointment only that I dictated and allowed to become the norm.

As our tryst reaches its culmination, relief floods over me. It's like a cooling balm soothing my body. My only regret is that I can't allow this to happen again as much as I want it to. The stakes are too high. I can't have David and Ted; it wouldn't work. David wouldn't allow himself to be part of it.

David stands up and looks at me sheepishly.

'Cate. I don't know what to say. That was unexpected.' He's pulling his shorts on. 'I don't know what came over me. I hope you don't think—'

'It's fine. Honestly fine,' I say, sitting up and pulling myself together. 'It's been an emotional day. Things happen. Beth never had a chance to say goodbye. She'd have wanted to, so I did it for her. I have it on good authority — it's a twin thing. She'd understand.'

I hope I've not said too much. Maybe he's thinking of the first time he met Cate. She snogged him then. David kisses me on the cheek and leaves.

I'm left reflecting how close that came to game over. You see, I have a tattoo. And so did Cate. A tattoo with a theme, but slightly different. And hers was on the other shoulder. It was the one thing that, for those that knew us, distinguished us apart. Decisive and irrevocable proof.

I go to the mirror in the hallway, lower my shirt and twist to look at mine. Even in death, Cate's message lives on. She was always the superior twin and I allowed that to be emblazoned on me for all eternity. Because charismatic and commanding Cate orchestrated it that way.

Prior to our eighteenth birthday, Cate and I were plotting to get tattoos. We knew Mum and Dad wouldn't approve, but we didn't care. Like smoking, that was part of the attraction. It would be presented as a *fait accompli*.

We discussed various options for designs. Our favourite animals? Except Cate's was a lion and mine a zebra, and I wanted them to be the same. Also, I didn't like the idea of Cate's lioness being able to hunt and eat my zebra. We looked online, we considered a whole range of symbols and motifs, but could never find anything we both agreed on. They were to be identical — like us. About a week before our actual birthday, I suggested the number two. I liked the shape and fluidity of the number, and it was a signifier that we were a pair. We both had necklaces as children with a number two charm on, a childhood gift. This would be a permanent extension of our twin code.

'Brilliant. Why didn't I think of that?' Cate said looking pleased.

We booked into a tattoo parlour in Hounslow for consecutive appointments. I knew Cate would want to go first, but I was fine with that. I would be by her side being supportive. We were both excited and stayed up well into the early hours, giggling about it conspiratorially. I was happy.

On the day of the appointment, a Saturday, Cate didn't appear at breakfast.

'Where's Cate?' I asked Mum anxiously.

'She's still in bed. Complaining about a dodgy kebab from her night out with Craig or something.'

I tore up the stairs and flung open her bedroom door. Normally I would have been reprimanded for not having knocked. She said nothing. Cate lay groaning in bed and was rasping as though she was finding it hard to breathe.

'Bucket.' Cate gasped, pointing at the grubby blue bucket that Dad used for washing the windows. It was sitting on the carpet by the side of her bed. I picked it up and thrust it at her. She stuck her head in it and started making retching noises.

'You've got to get up. The first appointment is at eleven. We can't be late.'

'Sorry, Bethy. No way. Not today.' She plonked the bucket on the floor and sank back into the pillows, clutching her stomach. 'I feel like shit.'

'What the hell is wrong with you?'

'Food poisoning. Must be. I really didn't have that much to drink. We stopped off at the kebab shop. Big mistake. That or someone spiked my drink.' She curled up into a ball, moaning in agony.

'Bloody typical. What am I supposed to do now?'

'You go. Don't waste the appointment. Make me one for next Saturday if you can. And I promise I'll stay in Friday night. You can guard over me.'

'Promise me you're not stalling. You are going through with this, aren't you?'

'I swear on Mum's life I will be getting mine next Saturday. I'm so jealous you'll be getting yours first. Why did this have to happen?'

Gullible me bought it, so off I went to get my tattoo. When I returned, Cate was getting ready for another date with Craig, having made a remarkable recovery.

'Let me see?' Cate said.

'I thought you were dying?' I feared she was trying to dupe me.

'All passed through. Both ends. Seriously disgusting. Sorry if there's still a stink in the bathroom, by the way. You wouldn't have wanted to be here,' Cate said, wrinkling up her nose. 'Come on. Aren't you going to show me? What's it like? Does it hurt?'

I was too eager to show it off to care for long. I was brave. Cate gasped like she was seriously impressed at the italic number two on my left shoulder.

'Promise you'll hide it from Mum and Dad until I get mine? They'll stop me otherwise. We'll still do the big unveiling together as planned.'

I offered to accompany Cate to the tattoo parlour the following Saturday, but she was adamant she'd go alone.

'You were super brave, so I've got to be,' she said.

I was on edge until Cate returned. She did eventually about five o'clock. I was sitting at the bottom of the stairs ready to pounce.

'I did it,' she whispered excitedly as she came through the front door.

'Show me, show me?' I tried to pull at her T-shirt.

'Wait. And shush. Mum will hear.' Cate pushed my arm away. 'Let's do it later. Big reveal to Mum and Dad. We'll put our dressing gowns on so it'll be easier to do. I need to get ready first as I promised to meet Craig. Give me an hour, okay?'

'All right,' I said, disappointed. Eventually Cate appeared in my bedroom. All made up and ready to go out, but with her dressing gown on.

'What are you wearing underneath? Will it be visible?' I asked.

'My black camisole. You ready?'

'Sure am.' I was sat ready and waiting in my gown for nearly two hours.

Mum was cooking supper when we entered the kitchen. The smell of greasy onions filled the room. Dad sat at the kitchen table with a beer bottle parked in front of him. He was reading out newspaper snippets to Mum. Something they often did. Dad peered out over his *Daily Express*.

'What's up, girls? Bedtime already?'

Mum stopped stirring and turned around to look at us. A frown formed across her brow.

'We have something to show you both,' Cate said with an entitled air. 'We're adults now and have the right to express ourselves. Ready, Beth? One, two, three!'

We turned around and dropped our gowns in unison, thrusting out our shoulders. For what seemed like an age, no one said anything. When I peeked, Mum had covered her face with her hands. Then Dad spoke.

'Look like a pair of bloody bruises. Idiots. I could have drawn them on with Biro. Saved you the money.'

'Oh, my God, girls. What the hell have you done? Your beautiful skin. Why?' Mum said in disbelief. Her head was moving continually from left to right between us like she did when watching Wimbledon on TV. Taking it all in. She paused and her mouth dropped open. Mum's gaze settled on Cate's shoulder.

'Oh, Cate. No. That's too much.' Mum shook her head before starting to cry.

I was waiting to see if Cate was going to say anything else. Waiting for her to take the lead. I didn't understand why Mum only referred to Cate — we both had a tattoo. Then I looked across and saw it. An intricate and beautiful number one was tattooed on her right shoulder.

Cate shot me a gloating, triumphant smile.

'After me, you come first. They were out of number twos.'

Cate pulled her gown off and threw it defiantly over the back of a kitchen chair.

'I don't want any dinner, thanks. Gotta date. Gotta dash.' She flounced out of the kitchen and we heard the front door close.

I should have known better. I had eighteen years to learn. I finally saw right inside Cate that day, into the runny, yellow yolk of her. That was Cate's ultimate salvo in her battle for supremacy. It created a doorway for resentment in me. Something I would feel towards her for the rest of her life.

I loved but hated her in equal measures. Is it terrible to say that? The truth is, loathing Cate was easier than not liking myself. We were the egg with the double yolk after all. That's the problem with being an identical twin. Whenever I looked at my sister, I only ever saw myself reflected — faults and all. And God knows there were enough of those. Cate was the self-appointed superstar who felt entitled to be number one. She commanded attention and, more often than not, got it. That's what confidence and self-belief get you. I was put in my place — my role was to follow behind. All I could do was learn to hold on to my grudges like little pets.

I drag my finger over the shape of my *two*. This damn tattoo is yet another thing I've got to confront and deal with. I pull my shirt back over my shoulder and head upstairs. With Ted away for the night, I think I'll allow myself the luxury of a bath. Light a few candles. Wash away David. Turns out I was number two in his life as well.

CHAPTER 29

David

Adrianna's gone for a run and I've promised to fix Sunday brunch. Even I'm capable of smashing up some avocado on toast and grilling some bacon. Not that such a simple gesture can appease my guilt. I'm looking at the larder. Is it lemon juice or vinegar I'm supposed to mix in to stop the avocado turning brown?

My innards are squeezing tight. Talk about an avalanche of self-inflicted pain. Will I ever learn? I'm such an idiot. Shagging Beth's crazy twin. What was I thinking? I'm hopelessly in love with Adrianna, but it's like my mind isn't receiving the transmissions my heart is making. I swear if it wasn't for the rain, it never would have happened.

Truth was, I didn't even want to be there. I dreaded performing the ritual and wanted to put it off, but knew I had to face the inevitable. I wasn't ready to say goodbye to Beth either if I'm being honest with myself, but I couldn't refuse Cate. She was so upset with me about the funeral and her lack of involvement. I procrastinated for as long as I could before realising I had come up with something to say. It took me half an hour to write four short sentences including *Dear Beth*.

Adrianna has been so kind and thoughtful. Concerned about me and constantly asking about Cate. She cares. She even went to the trouble of buying a bottle of champagne for me to take to make a toast. She packed my rucksack, told me everything was going to be okay and pushed me out the door. I probably never would have gone otherwise. And now I've done this to her. I don't deserve Adrianna. I really don't.

I have to deal with what I've done. Being in self-denial about it is as good a strategy as any. Block it out. I've done it before. I won't give Adrianna any reason to suspect anything, but I'm not sure I can trust Cate.

I turn the streaky bacon over under the grill as Adrianna's key turns in the front door. I've laid the table and found some paper napkins. I've folded them to make it look nice and welcoming. *Act normal.*

'Perfect timing. I'll be serving up in a minute.' Adrianna appears in the kitchen doorway. 'Coffee?' I give her a peck on the cheek. She's panting so I know better than to attempt a full-blown kiss.

'Glass of water first. *Por favor.*'

I put it down on the table for her as she leans on the back of a kitchen chair, stretching out.

'Good run?'

'*Sim.* Yes. Had to dodge a lot of Sunday-morning dog-walkers, though.'

She pulls out the chair and slips off her trainer socks to fold them into a neat ball as I place her brunch plate in front of her.

'*Obrigada.*'

Adrianna picks up the bottle of ketchup I've taken out the fridge and laughs. She places it back on the table and grinds pepper on her avocado instead.

'Can I ask you something?' she says, putting down her knife and fork. 'What would have happened if Beth hadn't been with the family in the crash?'

Is Adrianna asking if I'd still be seeing her? I pause for a beat as my mouth is full and I'm not sure how to react.

'I mean, if Cate had been killed but, miraculously, the baby had survived? What would have happened to the baby?'

'Wow, that's a loaded question,' I say, recovering. 'Beth would have wanted to adopt Ted, but I'm not sure how easy that would have been. She'd been a bit unstable — and Giles's parents would have had a say.'

'But you'd have tried to adopt the baby with Beth, then?'

I give Adrianna a pensive look.

'I don't think I would have, no. In fact, definitely not. I'd have put my foot down. I'd met you by then. Taking on someone else's baby, even a relative of Beth's, wouldn't have been the answer to heal the rift between us. Not at that stage.'

Is Adrianna feeling broody? Maybe we'll have our own family one day. I could let her know I would be up for it in time. How shall I phrase it? But Adrianna interrupts my thoughts.

'How are you feeling after yesterday? You've not said much.'

There it is. I must try to normalise this situation. It's no surprise she's asking, but there have been a lot of questions about Cate, and now Beth, come to think of it, ever since Adrianna saw the woman in the street who looked like her.

'It was tough. I'm relieved it's over. I have to look forward now. I'm glad you're here with me.' I reach over and squeeze her hand. Adrianna eyes me brightly.

'And Cate. How was she?'

I stuff avocado and bacon into my mouth to buy some time. I will choose my words carefully.

'She was very upset. She's lost so much.' I shovel in another mouthful.

'You are *gentil*, kind of you to care for her. You were gone a while. I was beginning to wonder if everything was okay.'

Don't panic. Adrianna has no way of knowing — she can't possibly. Can she? No. I'm being paranoid. It's not to be repeated. I won't be showing the normal signs of adultery: late nights at work, sneaking out of the room to read texts and take calls, inadvertently leaving restaurant receipts in jeans pockets. I've learned my lesson. I must preserve what I have with Adrianna. I will not lose her.

'We got caught in the storm — had to shelter for a while, that's all. How's your food?' I add, hoping we can change the subject. I get a thumbs-up, but it's followed by another question.

'Were Beth and Cate completely identical?'

I decide to comply as I don't want to arouse suspicion by keeping on trying to divert the conversation. 'Sure were. Different hairstyles, but the same colour, height, build, eyes — all of it. Even sounded the same.'

'Did they ever pretend they were each other? You know, for fun?'

'As kids. Yes. Beth used to tell me a few stories.' Now is not the time to tell Adrianna about the first time I met Cate.

'Did they ever wear a perfume that smelled citrusy?'

Christ. Did she smell Cate on me yesterday? I'm not sure what she's angling at here or where this conversation is going.

'What's this all about?' I stand up and move to the back of Adrianna's chair, leaning over to cradle my arms around her. I drop my nose to the top of her head and inhale deeply. Sweet rose.

'Nothing. I'm curious. That's all. It's not always easy being the one after. Especially after, well — you know.'

'It's you I love. Think I have done from the moment you enticed me with that cupcake.' I turn her head and lift her chin up to kiss her irresistibly soft pink mouth.

I wanted to kiss her the very first day we met. Adrianna came into the store about a phone and then coincidently we bumped into each other on Richmond Green during my lunch break the same day. I was brooding about my marriage. Adrianna happened to come and sit on the same bench, clutching a box from a local bakery. She was wearing a short, pleated tartan skirt and over-the-knee black suede boots. I couldn't take my eyes off the glimpse of olive-skinned thigh on show. God, she was sensual.

She lifted a buttercream-frosted cupcake out of the box and took a bite — Nigella-fashion. She sidled along the bench and offered me one. I couldn't resist — either the cake or her. We must have chatted, and I'll admit flirted, for nearly an hour before she leapt up saying she had to leave.

'I don't even know your name,' I said. I was disappointed she had to go.

She stood so close to me that our knees were almost touching. Then she leaned forward and I thought she was about to kiss me, but instead she turned her head and whispered in my ear, 'Adrianna,' rolling the '*dr*'. It was so sexy. Then she turned and walked away.

'You have my card — please call if you need anything.' I shouted out to her, desperate to see her again. She turned to me, taking a few paces backwards, and raised her eyebrows with a flirtatious glint in her eyes. 'Sure,' she said.

I waited four days before I received a text message with a single cupcake emoji. I called her straight away and I've been kissing Adrianna ever since.

I stroke her hair to soothe me like I'm stroking a cat, but the thrashing in my chest won't subside. Guilt and paranoia. I can't quell it. My nostrils smell the scent of rose, but another fragrance steals inside my head. It makes the hair on my arms prickle and stand up. Like a whispered proposition, it's settled in as an uninvited guest and taken up residence. Grapefruit.

CHAPTER 30

Beth

A surge of overwhelming love for Ted and disbelief that he is mine is always with me. *My son.* In the beginning my nerves were frayed with exhaustion, being in constant fear of being discovered. I was convinced the police suspected me, but it was my own guilt persuading me. They had zero reason to believe I switched places with my sister. Why would they? They were merely doing their job and investigating the cause of a fatal and tragic accident. We are all awaiting the coroner's report, but things have gone quiet. For now.

I've got Cate's ashes safely stored to reunite with her family and I've physically said my goodbye to David. That little incident was over two weeks ago now and I've not heard from him since. Why am I not surprised?

I've started to breathe again — live a little. The tiredness never seems to go away, but then I am learning to adjust to being a mother.

I'm in my happy place, being with Ted. He's such a sweet little boy and we've bonded in a way that I couldn't have thought imaginable. We walk around the park to ground ourselves, Ted and I. Sometimes we go for a coffee afterwards at a café on the hill and Ted's allowed a small biscuit as a treat.

Today we're heading for the park again. It's a paradise on earth that I've never experienced so regularly. We drink it all in. Ted delights at seeing the deer and we often spot both fallow and red. He loves seeing the birds and we've seen squirrels and even spotted a grass snake on our last visit. I pointed it out to Ted as it slithered away from the path to disappear among the bracken. We might even stop for lunch at Pembroke Lodge if we can get a table. A white van skims past at speed as we're crossing the road near the Richmond Gate entrance. I instinctively pull the buggy back and am thankful that I waited a moment in the central reservation. The idiot. What is it with white van drivers?

We meander through the grounds of Pembroke Lodge for a while. The golden August sunlight bathes the gardens in an iridescent glow. The wisteria at the front of the lodge has faded, but the rhododendrons and azaleas are still blooming in places. We go inside to the Butler's Pantry and buy a small sandwich platter and a bottle of water. We say no to the delicious pastries. These days I only have to look at them to pile on the pounds. I wheel Ted outside to see if we can secure a table for the two of us. I love the sweeping views to the east of the Thames Valley from here. The terrace is filling up, but I spot a table in the corner in the shade and we race over to it. I put the bottle of water down to mark it as taken. I turn to face Ted and unclip his harness to seat him on my lap. I put on his sun hat and lift him up.

'Come on, my lovely. Let's see what I've got for you. You must be getting hungry?'

As I turn around, a barrel of a man with a near bald head and comb-over is placing his rather large derriere on a chair at our table. His football shirt stretches out close to ripping point across his inflated stomach.

'Excuse me . . .' I say. The man looks up as though he didn't know we were there. His eyes almost disappear in the puffed-up rise of his cheeks.

'You got a problem, love?'

The vein throbbing in his neck acts as a warning beacon. I say nothing, deciding to avoid confrontation.

'Come on, Ted. Let's go back inside.'

I'm holding Ted in one arm and negotiating wheeling the buggy with the other when a man stands up as we pass his table. He looks at me with a half-smile and clears his throat.

'We have a spare chair. You'd be most welcome,' he says, indicating a vacant seat. 'We'll be off shortly.'

He's tall and slim, but with broad shoulders. His dark blond hair is worn slightly long — a tad dishevelled. Very Richmond, I think, with his faded blue jeans trendily ripped at the knee. The outline from his white polo shirt hints at a toned torso. I'm guessing he's early forties. I'm wary after what's happened, but a small girl, no more than three years old, is sat next to him clutching a white bunny with long, floppy ears. I decide to chance it. It's a warm day and I want to sit outside.

'That's so kind.'

'I hope he got his money back in full.' The man looks over at the usurper.

'Sorry?'

'From the charm school. Rude doesn't cover it. Now say hello, Abigail.' He lifts the child onto his lap. The girl buries her head into his chest, her golden mop of curls hiding the boldest, deepest blue eyes. Like her father's. She thrusts out an arm and waves the cuddly bunny at us by way of greeting.

'Hello there, Abigail. It's very kind of you to let us join your table. This is Ted and my name is Cate. Cate with a C as in Blanchett,' I say directing my gaze back at the chivalrous stranger. Inwardly I cringe. I can't believe I came out with that. I don't have to play act in front of this man.

'Pleased to meet you, Cate with a C.' He holds out his right hand with a look of mirth lighting up his tanned face. 'Harry. Harry Snow. No relation to Jon.'

I blush.

'We've got a Jaime and Cersei at home,' I say, catching on to his *Game of Thrones* vibe. Grateful to be able to say something to hide my embarrassment. 'Haven't we, Ted? Kittens. Do you like kittens, Abigail?' She lifts her head up from her father's chest and nods excitedly, making her ringlets bounce up and down like springs. Abigail has the most astonishing head of hair for a toddler. I can't take my eyes off her.

'Your daughter has sensational hair. Has she inherited those beautiful curls from her mum?'

'She has, yes. Nicole had the most gorgeous, bouncy curls too.'

'Did she have a haircut?'

'No. Um. Nicole passed away when Abbie was eighteen months old.'

I'm dumbstruck. A flush rises up my neck to my cheeks. I fiddle with my necklace. Something I do when I'm nervous. This poor man. His loss is genuine. And this beautiful little girl will never know her mother. What am I supposed to say? *I can top that. I lost my husband* and *two children in a car accident a couple of months ago.*

'Oh, how devastating.' My hand instinctively goes up to cover my mouth. I wait a beat. 'I'm so sorry for your loss. What happened?' Then I think that's rude to ask. I'm not handling this at all well. I wish the proverbial big black hole will swallow me up.

'We're learning to live with it. Slowly. One day at a time.' I notice Harry cuddles Abigail a bit tighter. 'Nicole hadn't long since gone back to work. She'd started cycling in.' He pauses and takes a sip of his fizzy water. 'She got hit by a refuse truck that turned left without indicating. The driver didn't see her. She died the next day.'

Tears start to well in my eyes. I think of how cruel life can be — a child losing her mother. I am so desperately sorry for a man I have only just met. I think of Cate. I think of Charlie and Georgie. I summon the courage. I tell Harry about the car accident. About Giles and the children. And my sister, Beth. He listens in silence, shaking his head. When I've finished, our eyes meet. We're the ones left behind; the veterans of emotionally draining tragedies. Each playing out on different stages — cast members who are never quite sure whether we're the survivors or the victims.

'I thought I recognised you,' Harry says. 'When you first walked out on the terrace. I couldn't quite place you, though. I saw you in the press.'

I nod. 'The story ran for a couple of weeks. I kept quiet at home, but *friends* must have supplied the pictures.' I couldn't bear to read any of it.

We stay chatting for another half an hour. Harry is kind and the conversation is easy. He tells me about being a sculptor and his Putney studio. It's the first time I've relaxed in months. But Ted is due a nappy change and I'd rather do that at home. Reluctantly, I bring our encounter to a close.

'It's been lovely to meet you, Harry. You too, Abigail. And Mr Bunny.'

'Do you live locally?' Harry blurts out the question.

'Yes. A few streets away from Richmond Gate.'

Harry stands.

'Well, if you fancy doing this again sometime, Cate? Abbie and I tend to make a habit of this on Tuesdays. Lunch here. We'll be here again for the next few weeks — until she starts nursery in September anyway. It's not often you meet someone who understands what it's like. What you go through.'

A rush of intense pleasure overwhelms me. 'Until next Tuesday then. Bye, Abbie. Lovely to meet you.'

* * *

'Well, that was unexpected, wasn't it, Ted? Making new friends,' I say once we're back on the exit path from Pembroke Lodge. A light-headed sensation takes over. Perhaps a little drunk with happiness.

As we walk our way along the path that circumvents the car park outside the Lodge, an overwhelming sense of unease unexpectedly rests itself on my shoulder, displacing what went before. Are we being watched? Followed? Did we leave something behind? I stop abruptly and turn around. There's a loved-up young couple about twenty yards back walking with their arms draped around each other, a fraught mum struggling to get a screaming toddler into the back of a Volkswagen Golf, and a woman pushing an elderly man in a wheelchair across the gravel towards the Lodge's entrance.

'I'm imagining things, Ted.' I try to shake off the feeling of disquiet. My brain is playing games with me.

You don't deserve to feel relaxed, my inner turmoil voice replies. *Or enjoy the company of strangers. I'm going to set you on edge. It's what you deserve. How could you even begin to imagine otherwise?*

I try to pull myself together. I have to learn to extinguish the guilt and suffering nestled within the embers of my self-directed anguish. I'm in danger of reigniting the flames otherwise; it's only going to lead to devastation and destruction. *Do not burn.*

Once back at the house, I take Ted upstairs for a change. Magdalena comes rushing into the nursery. She looks disconcerted, agitated even.

'Mrs Mildenhall. I have a message for you.' Magdalena closes her eyes as though trying to remember word for word. 'He said to tell you that tomorrow he collects his bonus.'

'I'm sorry. Who? What are we talking about?' Perplexed, I try to pin down a wriggling Ted on his changing mat.

'Mr Max. He said to make sure I told you exactly.'

My heart sinks and the room becomes airless. 'Max? Was he here?'

'Yes, Mrs Mildenhall. He called at front door,' she says as though considering it highly inappropriate.

All the oxygen has been sucked away. Do I have the strength for this? My bubble has been well and truly burst.

CHAPTER 31

Beth

My stomach plummets like an untethered lift hurtling down a shaft. Max is parking up in the driveway in his van. He's early — it's barely 8 a.m. yet.

'How are we going to deal with Max, huh?' I say to Ted in his nursery. 'Any ideas?'

Saying his name out loud — Max — the feeling of it on my tongue, on my lips, makes me feel nauseous. My heartbeat quickens. Seeing him again feels like a physical illness racking my body. There's such emotional turmoil going on in my stomach. Max gets out the van and preens himself, running his right hand several times through his mop of dark curls. By the way he holds himself, I can tell he's buzzing like an old fridge. He looks toned and bronzed — his Turkey tan, I presume. Khaki cargo shorts and a pale lemon tee accentuate his glow. He reaches back into the van and retrieves his phone. His thumbs skim over it at speed. On cue, my phone lights up.

I'm here Lady J! xx

The message is finished with the lip-smacking emoji. Just so creepy. Does he seriously expect me to fling open the front door and rush out to greet him with open arms? I don't open it up in the app so he can't tell I've read it.

'We need to avoid the garden this morning, I'm afraid, Ted. You come up with a master plan yet? I'm going to need you to, buddy. Relying on you.'

Working on it, Mummy.

Magdalena arrives at eight thirty, letting herself in the front door as usual. I've been waiting upstairs with Ted. It's easier to spot me on the ground floor from the garden. I think we'll be shadowing Magdalena around the house this morning. Safety in numbers. It's Wednesday so she'll leave at lunchtime, but Max will have gone by then too as he's arrived early. He must have plenty of other jobs to catch up on having been away.

'Morning, Mrs Mildenhall.' Magdalena closes the front door as though it were made of glass. She lovingly takes care of everything she touches as though it will repay her with kindness. 'How's Mr Ted?' She chortles, giving him a little squeeze on the cheek. We traipse behind Magdalena into the kitchen.

'Can I get you anything? Tea or coffee?' I say as I strap Ted into his high chair.

'Maybe later, thank you. *I'm good for now*,' Magdalena says, looking pleased with herself that she's mastering English idioms, even ones borrowed from America. 'Are you okay, Mrs Mildenhall? You look little unwell,' she continues, before hastily adding, 'I hope you don't mind me saying so?'

I'm deliberately keeping it casual rather than making myself up as Cate often did. Normally I've been mirroring what Cate would do, but I'm allowing an exception today. I don't want Max to think I've made any effort for him so I'm slopping in sweatshorts, a couple of layered loose vests and flip-flops. Zero make-up and I haven't yet showered or washed my hair.

'A little tired. We're being lazy this morning. Not had breakfast yet. Hopefully we won't get in your way.'

Ted chooses this moment to let rip and fill his nappy. The look of surprise on his face makes Magdalena and I both laugh.

'Oh, Ted. Honestly. Not in front of the ladies.' I pretend to chide him. Magdalena laughs even more.

There's a movement in the garden. The smile on Magdalena's face disappears and the jovial atmosphere evaporates.

'I'd better go and sort out this young man's bottom,' I say, wrinkling my nose at Ted as I lift him from his high chair. 'Never a dull moment with you around, my little precious one.'

A shadowy figure appears by the glass doors. As hard as I try not to, I'm forced to look up. It will be too obvious otherwise. God, I feel sick. I don't know how to deal with this. Max is standing on the other side of the locked door. He is smiling, but the smile doesn't reach his eyes — there's something cold about them. They're fixed so firmly on mine, it hurts. He watches me intently, expectantly, and, to my horror, with something that I can only conclude is naked desire written on his features. The urge to run away is strong yet I'm frozen, rooted to the spot.

The seconds tick by. Max's full lips tighten as though he's eaten something distasteful. His expression changes. A deep frown spreads across his forehead, his jaw appears to clench and there's a twitch on his cheek that extends to his eye. I don't know how to read him.

I have left my response too late, I should have acknowledged him earlier. Smiled at him coquettishly perhaps, even though all I feel is utter revulsion. *What the hell have you been up to, Cate? You always did enjoy punishing me for my existence, but leaving me with this? I bet you're laughing at me now, aren't you?*

I strain a smile I do not feel and point to Ted's nappy. I stick my tongue out and wrinkle my nose to signify a smelly emergency. Max's face relaxes and the smile starts to return. He nods at me in acknowledgement, gives me a thumbs-up. Good, he's understood.

I race out the kitchen door for the seclusion of upstairs with the kittens in hot pursuit as Ted's nappy starts to leak.

'Mammoth delivery, mate. You timed that one well, buddy.'

All part of the routine, Mummy. And the master plan, of course. Oh, God, give me strength. Please go away and leave us be.

* * *

I watch Max leave around lunchtime, backing his van out the driveway. I've hidden away upstairs all morning so haven't had to face him again. I'm now free to change for the garden and gather together the bits we need to enjoy a couple of hours of afternoon sunshine.

I spent most of the morning watching Max from the safety of partially closed shutters at the back of the house. I could see him, but he couldn't see me. He has an unconscious habit of fingering his lower lip as if lost in thought. It works wonders in drawing attention to his full red mouth.

He works painstakingly hard — I'll give him that. Following his absence, there's plenty of gardening and maintenance to catch up on. He tended to the plants with such precision and care, caressing them almost. Does he talk to them? Occasionally I could see his lips moving. Or perhaps he was singing to himself as he worked? Either way the garden is looking immaculate again, the clippings and dead-heads removed and everything put away neatly in the sheds.

I also observed Magdalena hand him another envelope. She placed it on the corner of the wall by the lavender flower bed, then turned and left without speaking to him. Max picked it up, pulled out and counted what looked like twenty-pound notes. I don't know what the hell is going on, but it looks to me like Magdalena is being exploited somehow. I need to find a way of talking to her about it as well as dealing with Max. Period. Time to get him out of our lives.

Finally alone, we make our way to the garden. I sit Ted on a rug and place his little white sun hat on, securing it in place by a strap that dangles underneath his chubby chin. He's surrounded by toys and cushions, and the kittens frolicking nearby. I make myself comfortable on a large, cushioned sunbed — the type you see lined up with precision around turquoise swimming pools in holiday brochures. I could do with a snooze, but mustn't fall asleep as Ted is at the crawling stage. It's important to stay alert.

I'm aware of a movement behind me, but before I can turn around everything has gone dark. A pair of hands cover my eyes and thumbs caress my ears.

'Now you wouldn't be avoiding me, would you, Lady Jane?'

Max leaps around in front of me and in one fell swoop straddles me. I'm an idiot. Max would know that Magdalena doesn't work Wednesday afternoons. Of course he's come back. He pins me down with his inner thighs pressed hard up against my legs. He smiles at me, watching intently for a response.

'Hi, there,' is the best I can manage.

'Well, this is all rather serendipitous, isn't it? All alone on a beautiful afternoon.'

I'm struck mute. How the hell am I going to deal with this and get him off me? He scrutinises my face, tipping his head to one side in curiosity. The silence hangs heavy between us.

Max is unquestionably handsome; his dark curly hair frames his tanned face. Maybe he'll grow on me. I could try. Instinctively I recoil. Any developing feelings I have for this man are akin to the mould that develops on a mildewed bathroom ceiling or the nasty stuff you find at the back of your fridge. My physical response spells it out for me in case I'm not getting the message loud enough. My stomach clenches; bile touches the back of my throat and tongue. I fight the sensation and in doing so involuntarily belch.

'My, my. What's going on here?' Max says. He strokes my hair and then cups my face in his hands. 'You're trembling. Cate, my sweet Ca-te.' Did I imagine it or did he over-emphasise the way he said *Cate*?

'I'm sorry, Max. I've not been feeling at all well. In fact, I still don't.'

I put my hands around both his wrists with the intention of gently moving them away. I've explained I'm not well. Surely, he can understand? Whatever was going on between him and Cate, after the events of that day in June, things have changed. Pushing his hands away, I try to soften my face and look into his eyes, imploring him to understand.

But Max isn't listening, or he chooses to ignore me. His response is to move his hands down to fondle my breasts. Oh, God, please, no.

'We must do something to make you feel better then, mustn't we?' He leans in to kiss me.

Max has had a drink at lunchtime. I can smell the beer on his breath. He pushes his tongue inside my mouth. I want to bite it. I want to choke.

Kissing is an unbearable intimacy. I can't bear having his putrid mouth on mine. He moves his right hand and lifts up my short sundress, clawing at the waistband of my knickers. I tense and pull his hand away. Max's eyes cloud over briefly with confusion at the rejection as if it's dawning on him that I don't want this.

'Please, Max, not now. I'm not well. I'm having my period.' I clutch at brittle straws. I keep my voice calm. 'You're so impatient. I can't. Another time.' I impart my message in a chiding tone Cate would use.

Max ignores me. He doesn't speak. His breathing is getting heavier. He pushes the gusset section of my knickers aside so that it digs into me. He hastily unzips his shorts. I turn my head to see Ted, my son, who is oblivious, playing happily with a pile of colourful building blocks. Can I do this? Can I fuck this man and continue to pretend that I am Cate? To keep the pretence going to preserve what is mine. To keep my baby.

I'm not going to be given the choice. Max forces himself inside me so violently, I'm torn apart. His mouth starts licking and gnawing at my neck as he continues to thrust with force. His body presses down on me, forcing sounds to escape. Max takes it as a sign that I'm enjoying myself as he pounds into me harder and harder. The clamminess of his skin touches mine with every thrust. My eyes fill with tears as I succumb.

I focus on removing myself from my body. Take myself away to a higher plane. I close my eyes and tell myself I can survive this. Willing my mind to be calm even though my heart beats irregularly against my ribs. I refuse to take part in what is happening to my body. I despise myself for having to go through with this, for not being strong or smart enough to dispel Max's advances. This is my punishment for what I have done.

By the time Max finishes, all the air is knocked from my lungs and uncontrollable tears stream down my face. Max zips up his fly as he turns away from me. With the most intense physical and mental weariness I have ever felt, I try to rearrange my clothing and collect myself. I need to remove Ted and I from the presence of this man.

Cersei starts to play with the laces on his work boots; one lace has come undone and is trailing on the ground. She bats it with her paw before leaping on it. Max bends down and picks her up by the scruff of the neck. He squeezes her, forcing a painful mew from her tiny body before throwing her back on the ground. I feel my chest tighten, the hands at my side clench. I find my voice.

'Max. No. Stop it.'

I force my aching body to stand. He'd better not be about to kick a defenceless kitten. I believe how people treat animals is a view into the recesses of their inner soul. And, as I now know to my cost, Max's is very dark indeed.

On hearing me shout, Max looks at me. His face clouds and his eyes narrow to tiny slits.

'Well, someone's woken up, haven't they?'

He turns away from me. I move forward, fearing he's going for Cersei again, but he strides past her and heads for Ted who is crawling around the garden blanket. He picks him up. Panic rises in my throat. I take a sharp intake of breath, but it doesn't want to leave. I can't exhale. *Please don't hurt my precious baby.*

To my surprise, Max lifts Ted up gently and pretends to throw him up in the air while still holding on to him tightly. Ted giggles.

Max turns to look at me, ensuring he's got my full attention.

'There's my boy. Come to Daddy.'

CHAPTER 32

Adrianna

I have to know. Is Beth still alive? Is she masquerading as Cate? I've asked myself a thousand times — why would she? Leave her home, her life, give up David? But from everything David has told me, the answer is simple: to have the baby. If this is true, and it wasn't Cate I saw play-acting as Beth in a traumatised way, then she's taking one hell of a risk. She's got guts — I'll give her that.

Do I tell David? I've been asking myself the question for weeks and weeks now. How do you explain that you suspect his sister-in-law is his wife? *Didn't you notice the similarities, darling?*

This is all so tangled that I've been doing something weird. Once David has left for work, I sneak off to the cemetery whenever I can. It's become part of my routine and I've regularly visited over the last month or so. I've got a hunch. I've missed her so far, but the grave keeps drawing me back. Nothing has changed there yet but I think it's where I'm going to find answers.

'What are you up to today, my sweet?' David asks as he plants a kiss on my cheek while simultaneously reaching for the milk out of the fridge.

'They've asked me to help out at the box office again. I'll be back before you get home, though.'

'You don't have to work, my love. I've told you that. We can manage.'

'It's only for a few days. Keeps me occupied.'

'Oh, I can think of something to occupy us.' David pulls me into him as he deftly places the milk carton on the counter while untying my dressing gown. He manoeuvres me towards the kitchen table and pushes me back. I wrap my legs around him, taking in this man who doesn't rightly belong to me. Am I going to let him go? I'm not sure how to play things. I need to know what I'm dealing with first, so another day's vigil at the cemetery it is.

After David's left for work, I change into leggings and a tee, slipping on a slouchy hoodie over the top. I catch a glimpse of myself in the mirrored wardrobe door. I look like I'm about to go and rob a bank. Oh, if only it was something that simple. I fear everything is going to be shattered. Being in a steady rather than a scamming relationship with David, even though he doesn't know about my past, has allowed me to start healing these past months. It may turn out to be everything but a normal relationship. After getting my life back on track, I could end up with nothing. A skull full of splinters.

Before I go for the bus, I grab my ready-packed backpack containing some cloths and a brush for cleaning headstones, an assortment of artificial flowers I bought at the pound store, and a Marian Keyes novel to help while away the time. I'll be waiting for Cate — or should I say Beth? I'm convinced she's going to appear eventually. I hope I've not missed her.

* * *

The early autumn sun warms my face as I sit waiting on a wooden memorial bench at the far side of the cemetery. I have a good viewpoint from here. The cemetery is vast, but I'm well positioned to observe the main entrance while being hidden from direct view by a row of hawthorn bushes.

Shortly before eleven thirty, a red Mini enters the main gates. My heart gives a little flutter. *Finalmente.* Finally. It's her. I recognise the car from when she visited the house. She drives cautiously down the entrance road and pulls off to park down an artery road not too far from the Mildenhall graves. She finds a small space between parked cars and reverses in with ease. I recall David saying, 'Cate is a crap driver. You should see her try to do a three-point turn.'

I leave the seclusion of my bench and walk around the cemetery perimeter. I don't want to get there too soon. Cate is taking her time. She places items in the carrier basket beneath a buggy. Then comes the baby. She takes great care strapping him in and covering him with a blanket.

A shimmer of cool wind creeps through the trees. I stop to peruse a row of gravestones. I pull my hood up. A few early fallen leaves dance around my feet. I bend over and pick up a stray leaf, and crush it in my hand. I'm biding my time.

Cate is on the move, so I remain out of sight by walking around the far side of the small gothic chapel. As I reappear, Cate is positioned by the two graves. She leans over the buggy and removes items from the basket. I need to get closer. I take a circular path, not wanting to draw attention to myself. Other than Cate, there are only two other mourners in the vicinity, although a burial is taking place in the far north-west corner, hence the volume of cars parked up. I stop short of where Cate is, four rows behind and off to her left at a previously selected grave. I have a view.

I lay my rucksack on the ground and take out the brush and cloths. I dampen one of them with a bottle of water. The gravestone of the dearly departed Emerald Jackson is about to get a clean-up. I start with the wire brush to loosen some of the dirt and lichen. I crouch down, but always keep Cate in line of sight.

She stands motionless in contemplation. I catch snippets of conversation, but I can't make out what she is saying. Is she talking to the baby again or addressing someone else? She's got something in her hand. I'd put money on it being a trowel. She takes a plastic bag and walks with purpose, pouring its contents along the raised soil mound of the children's grave. She turns over the soil with the implement in her hand and mixes it in.

At a glance, you see a grieving mother planting something on her children's grave. But it's too early for that — the ground is far from settled. I don't believe this woman is their mother. She is their aunt reuniting them with their actual mother's remains. That's what she was looking for in the house that day — the ashes.

After leaving some flowers, Beth, for I'm now certain that's who she is, pushes the buggy back towards the car. I've crouched down, hood still up, and scrub away at the foot of Emerald's head-stone with vigour, breaking into a sweat as my head pounds with the confirmation. I don't look up. I don't glance around. After a while I hear her car drive away.

With the coast clear, I can't resist taking a look at the Mildenhall graves. Up close, the ground of the children's grave has been disturbed. The grave of Giles Mildenhall looks firmer — slightly crusted over.

My head spins with the implications. I don't know what I'm going to do. I can't help but admire what Beth has done. The lengths she's gone to in order to reunite Cate with her children was a selfless act. My problem is that she's David's wife. Has Beth plans to reclaim him and play happy families. He was originally attracted to one sister, after all. Why not the other?

I think back to David's response about not wanting to adopt the baby. It convinces me even more that this is Beth. She would have known the gift of her sister's baby wouldn't have sat easily with him. I'm so distracted with questions spinning in my head that I don't realise I've got company.

'Hello.' It's a female voice.

I spin around. It's her — Cate. I mean, Beth. She stands right in front of me. Staring at me with the sharpest of green eyes. I've been tricked. She's not left the graveyard. I glance over at where her car was parked. The space is empty, but I see a flash of red where she has parked further up the road. She thrusts out a hand. I tentatively take it.

'Cate Mildenhall. And you are?'

'Adrianna. Adrianna da Silva.' *Fique calma.* Stay calm. Should I pretend to be a burial fanatic — the equivalent of a train spotter for cemeteries? To my surprise, a smile begins to light up her face.

'Pleased to meet you. I think you must be a friend of David. I saw you at my husband's funeral. About time we got to know each other, I think. Don't you?'

I'm flummoxed, frantically racking my brain for a suitable reply, when she turns and walks away. After a few steps she stops, turns her head nonchalantly to face me over her shoulder.

'Come on, then. What are you waiting for?'

Merda. She's expecting me to follow her.

'Where are we going?'

'Coffee. Maybe lunch. My place. This way — I can't leave my son in the car. Do you need a lift?'

CHAPTER 33

Beth

Well, well, well. I wasn't expecting this today. She's here, in my kitchen. Her name is Adrianna. David's whore. She's so breathtakingly beautiful it's not true. Flawless cappuccino skin. Long, dark, lustrous hair. A gorgeous figure. That natural kind of beauty that gives you the confidence to feel comfortable without make-up. Not a hint of the type of foundation I don't dare leave the house without.

How did David land her? Talk about having your back turned. God, I've been blind. Blind to what my quest for pregnancy was doing to David, to us, to our relationship. Even before I *died*, I was traded in for someone younger, more beautiful. I'm not sure I can lay all the blame at David's feet anymore. And do you know something else? It's laughable. I like her. How bloody crazy is that?

The question, though, is what was she doing in the cemetery? We were caught up, Ted and I, in finally laying Cate to rest with Charlie and Georgie. A task I should have done weeks ago but after Max raped me, I haven't managed to summon the strength to go out until today. I'm glad it's done now. It was the right thing to do. Tucking her in with her children. I was going to scatter some of Cate in with Giles too, but then thought better of it. I could hear Cate in my head.

Oh, for God's sake, Beth. I'm one, not two! Don't divide me.

I was wishing Cate bon voyage, generally having a solemn moment, when I became aware of a noise behind me. An abrasive scratching sound gradually became more vigorous. I glanced backwards for a fraction of a second to see a figure working on a headstone. I thought nothing of it. Assumed it was being cleaned. It was only when we were returning to the car that something made me look across again. I was surprised at how small the person looked, even in baggy clothes. And then I saw it. A long, sleek, dark tendril of hair escaping from the hood of her sweatshirt. I might have only seen those locks twice before, but they were unforgettable.

When I got back to the car, I made up my mind to confront her. I drove away to make her think I was leaving, then parked further up the road, hoping to take her unawares. It worked. By the time I was on my way back, Adrianna was at my family's grave. Was she that voyeuristic?

What do they say? Keep your enemies close. To be honest, I have another reason for inviting her back apart from trying to suss her out. In a word, Max. I never know when he's going to appear. I now spend so long shadowing Magdalena around the house that she must think I'm weird.

I don't want to be alone. And I can't invite Cate's friends over yet, if ever. It's too risky and I'll trip up. There'll be plenty of time to make new friends in the future — maybe when Ted starts nursery and school. There should be a good pool of like-minded mums then. This Cate is going to have to build a new life, but, in the meantime, befriending the mistress may be the best I can do.

'This is a friend of my brother-in-law. Adrianna. She'll be staying for lunch,' I say to Magdalena who walks through the kitchen with a bathroom bin bag.

'Very pleased to meet you,' Magdalena says, grinning broadly. She has no idea that we don't know each other. She's probably grateful that I've chosen some company for once so I'm not bothering her.

'Likewise,' Adrianna replies. 'Please let me help you?' she asks as I open the fridge door and pull out some cold chicken, cheese and salad. I put the oven on to heat a semi-baked baguette.

'You can lay the table if you like?' I say, pointing to the cutlery drawer.

'Mrs Mildenhall. Mr Max left a note for you.' Magdalena pulls a sealed envelope from her tunic pocket.

As soon as I take it from her, it scalds my fingers. I place it in my handbag to read later. Or maybe burn. That old nausea rises in my throat again. I've got to get rid of Max. But how? I'm so scared of him. It comes to something when you resort to inviting the woman who stole your husband over for lunch as a protection barrier.

Once Magdalena has left the kitchen, I set on preparing a large bowl of mixed salad.

'This is very kind of you. Unexpected,' Adrianna says.

She takes in the size of the kitchen, running her hand along the gleaming worktops.

'You've got a wonderful house. Have you lived here long?'

Thankfully I know the answer as I can bookmark it — it was around the time David and I first started trying for a baby. And Cate was already pregnant with Charlie.

'Must be coming up to nine years. So, tell me. How long have you known David? I don't remember Beth mentioning you.' I might as well go for it and test her reaction.

'I never knew Beth.' Adrianna looks down at her feet and I think I detect a sharp intake of breath. After a couple of seconds, she lifts her head again and pointedly looks me straight in the eye.

'David and I met a few months before Beth passed away. Back in the early spring. We've become very close since she died.' Adrianna purses her lips, hesitating before she continues. 'I'm sorry. This is awkward — you being her sister. I can't say I'm proud of it, but I think you deserve the truth. You've got enough going on without me lying to you or pretending it's something it's not.'

I'm disarmed by her honesty. By 'we've become very close', I presume she means *I've since moved in and am sleeping in your sister's bed with her husband.*

Oh, the irony of it all. *If only you knew, Adrianna.*

I should want to scream at her. Call her a bitch, tug at her revoltingly gorgeous hair. But somewhere along the line, the fight has started to leave me. I can't have it all. And I need my strength to dispose of Max. I can't be at war with Adrianna too. It's not easy. I have to grudgingly accept she won that battle even before that fateful day. My back was turned and I didn't even realise the door was open.

My mind drifts to a couple of lines from a nonsense poem that our grandfather used to recite to us as children. *Back to back, they faced each other. Drew their swords and shot each other.*

That was us, David, wasn't it?

'I appreciate you being candid with me,' I say, putting the lunch plates on the table. 'I'm not going to judge. Beth had started to suspect something was going on before she died. I saw the way David looked at you at my family's funeral. I guessed it was you.'

Adrianna looks at me pointedly.

'I'm sorry, Cate. I truly am. I never expected to end up with David this way. You've lost a sister as well as your family. I can't believe you're still standing. You're very brave.'

Something is bothering me.

'Can I ask what you were doing at the cemetery? I somehow can't believe you're a grave historian.' I make the quip, trying to keep it light.

Adrianna laughs. Her face lights up. No wonder David was captivated. In love, I suspect.

'I recently discovered that my great-aunt is buried there. I went to check it out a while back, and realised her grave and headstone are rather neglected. I finally made it back there this morning to try to clean it up a bit. It turned out to be rather more of a task than I anticipated, but I've made a start.'

I'm not sure how plausible a story this is but I don't know Adrianna or her family history. I want to hate her. Despise her even. No one knows she's in my house, save for Magdalena who is currently looking after Ted. I could stab her with one of Cate's oversize kitchen knives, chop her up and put her through the ridiculous mincing machine. Send her to David as a box of burgers. Leaving him forever wondering what happened to the new love of his life. *Consumed by love, David. That's what happens.*

So, what do I do? I open a bottle of chilled Sauvignon Blanc. And then a second. Sauvignon was Cate's favourite. It tastes a bit sour to me, but Adrianna doesn't seem to notice. We spend the afternoon getting tipsy. We laugh hysterically as she regales me with stories from her varying theatre jobs and failed auditions, before moving on to how you can tell the difference between a man who is buying perfume for his wife or for his mistress. Adrianna is effusive, warm and funny. Delightful company. I hate and love her. It's the best time I've spent in ages.

As we approach six o'clock, Adrianna says she should get going. We exchange numbers and promise to meet up again soon. I've made a new friend. Pathetic, desperate being that I've become.

I show Adrianna out the front door and my light-hearted afternoon ends abruptly. Max's Garden Butler van is parked up in the driveway. No sign of him though. He must have gone around the back as we came out the front. Impossible, crap, predictable timing. I want to run back inside and lock all the doors.

My stomach is sinking. I wish I hadn't drunk so much. I need to be in control.

What I want to say is: *Can't you stay for dinner? Help protect me from the abusive, sexual deviant who is currently loitering in my back garden. The one who comes and goes as he pleases, even though this is supposed to be my house. Oops! Silly me — I'm forgetting. I'm the imposter so have no right to complain. I've taken a baby and brought this on myself. My bad, right?*

The ground starts to sway. Adrianna says goodbye and walks down the driveway, but as she passes the van she stops dead in her tracks. I notice her clenching her fists. She heads back towards me, looking startled. Has she read my thoughts?

'Do you . . .' Adrianna points at the van. But she doesn't finish, as though she's lost for words. She pauses and envelops me in a hug. Taking a step back she looks directly at me with concern on her face. 'Stay safe, Cate. Please, look after yourself and be vigilant,' she says as her voice cracks.

Adrianna pulls up her overhanging hoodie to hide her face and makes a swift exit, breaking into a run before disappearing down the road. It's as though she can't escape fast enough.

CHAPTER 34

Beth

There is no need for Max to work this late. I can't see him in the garden, but the lawnmower is out so he's probably in one of the sheds. I consider going out to tell him to leave. Mowing the lawn is too disturbing when I've settled Ted down for the night, but I don't want to face him.

A creeping fear closes in on me. I remember the note that Magdalena gave me earlier. The corner of the envelope protrudes above the zip of my bag. I'm tempted to tear it up without reading it, but like a car alarm it's growing louder and getting more persistent.

I tear it open. It's another postcard. A picture of a red deer stag. Like the ones in Richmond Park. Nothing on the back. *What the?* What is he trying to tell me?

I have, have, have to get rid of this man once and for all. I've let things slide for far too long because I don't know what to do. How to act. How to deal with this. The creep literally has my life in his hands. He is controlling me, calling all the shots.

I've thought of calling a locksmith and getting the side-gate key code changed. Telling him to leave for ever, get out of our lives. But I can't take the risk of how he could react. He's obsessed. How deeply involved was Cate with him? And for how long?

I have to allow for the fact it's possible Ted is Max's son. In which case, Cate and Max were going on for well over eighteen months. Maybe longer. But even if that was the case, how would Max know that Ted was definitively his? Giles and Cate were still having sex; I heard them at the cottage. And Giles never showed any sign of suspecting that Ted wasn't his son. I pray that Giles is the father. I intend to get Ted tested. DNA testing was not part of the plan, but I've got no choice.

I'm staggered about how little I knew my sister's life. It all seemed so perfect, but maybe it wasn't for her. We had plenty of secrets we shared, Cate and I, but I never realised she kept so many from me. *Thanks for that, Cate.*

I go to lock the doors from the kitchen to the garden, but I needn't have worried; they're already locked. Magdalena must have done it before she left, thank God. Good girl — she's a treasure. I sigh with relief. I'm going to have a leisurely soak in the bath. Maybe light a few candles and get myself an early night. My head is still swimming from too many glasses of Sauvignon. Exhaustion is tugging at every sinew.

A pool of soft, dappled evening light reflects on the glass doors. I catch sight of my own pale, haunted reflection in the windowpane. I drag my fingers over my cheek. My skin looks like uncooked pastry compared to Adrianna's.

I jump as I think I catch a movement, but I still can't see Max in the garden. My skin prickles as though I'm being watched. Where the hell is he? I see a movement again, but still no Max. My brain feels fuddled. I curse my afternoon drinking when it finally dawns on me. I'm not seeing a movement outside, I'm seeing a reflection. I'm not alone in this room.

I spin around with a cold chill creeping up my spine. Max leans against the far kitchen counter, arms folded across his chest with a smirk on his face. I can't read him. My head is throbbing, but *I muster my strength. I have to be you, Cate. I must look pleased to see him.* I force a smile.

'That's naughty.' I chide him, putting my hand to my chest in a feeble attempt to stop my heart from palpitating. 'You made me jump. How did you get in here?'

Max remains leaning against the counter, but opens his arms as if expecting me to run into them.

'Same as always, of course,' he replies with the look of a satisfied Satan.

Christ. Does he have a way into the house too? *You've got to be kidding me — he can't seriously have a key?* Or is this another test? I can't think quickly enough to know how to react.

'Come, come here, my girl.' Max takes one step towards me with his arms still outstretched. 'I think someone needs a hug. Let me smooth away all your troubles.'

He is waiting for me, making me go to him. I don't know the rules to this game. I have an unfair disadvantage. But I was the one who rolled the first dice, wasn't I? I'm painfully aware of that. I could deliver a masterclass in building personal armour to protect yourself from self-appointed superior siblings, but I'm not equipped to deal with this man standing before me, waiting for me to fling myself into his arms.

I walk towards him. Slowly. As I get near, he leans forward, grabbing me by the wrist and pulling me towards him. I have no choice but to allow him to embrace me. I force myself to put my arms around him. I rest my head on his shoulder so I don't have to look at him. I'm suffocating. His grey T-shirt smells of the garden, faint sweat and yesterday's aftershave. I try to relax. I can't let him feel how tense I am.

Max reaches for below my chin, clasps my face in one large hand and turns it upwards to meet him. He leans in to kiss me. Despite my efforts, my whole body tenses. I smell his foul breath as his tongue searches mine. Breath that could strip paint. Involuntarily, I gag. He pulls away from me, a dark frown creeping across his face. I've blown it already.

'Max, I'm sorry. I'm still not well. About us. Please, I've got to have time to—'

'Don't you worry, princess.' Max pushes me backwards up against the island counter, the cold, unforgiving granite digging into the small of my back. In one swift move he lifts me up onto the counter, pulls my legs apart and wraps them around his body. He grips me by both legs and squeezes them so hard that I wince. I know what's coming next. He starts grinding himself into me, but he hasn't yet undone his trousers or made an attempt to remove my jeans. Is this his idea of a turn-on?

Max's eyes hover intently on me. He watches my every move, trying to catch my every emotion. He grapples with my zip and waistband, and pulls my jeans down roughly. He tugs brusquely at my knickers. I'm too scared to do anything but acquiesce. He undoes his belt and fly, and his fully erect penis emerges, the head cresting out over the top of his underwear. His dark and flinty eyes fix so firmly on mine it hurts to return his gaze. Max removes his penis fully and starts to jerk himself. Am I to be spared? Is my role to watch here? *Don't be a fool, Beth. This isn't over.*

Max grips my jaw with his free hand and slips his fingers inside my mouth. I try to resist the urge to bite hard on them. I want to, I so want to. Shall I? But I can't now as he's pressing his fingers hard down on my tongue, locking my jaw. I begin to choke and saliva escapes my mouth and dribbles down his hand.

'Good girl,' Max says as he removes his hand and uses my own saliva to lubricate me. In one swift action he pushes me back, simultaneously pulling me towards him so that my lower half is tilted below the worktop. I'm conscious of the pain in my unsupported lower back as Max thrusts into me. I focus on the stabbing pain in my spine. I force myself to disengage from my body once again, waiting for it to all be over.

I think of David, our lovemaking of old and how I allowed it to become mundane, purposed only for procreation. *Oh, David. What have I done?* You think you're unhappy with your lot until something worse comes along and you realise you were happy after all. I didn't know what happiness was. But then I think of Ted. I have to continue with this Grade A shit-fest. It's all for him.

After what feels like an eternity, with the pain in my back escalating to such an extent I'm going to pass out, Max releases his grip and my feet land with a thud on the kitchen floor. I hurriedly bend down to pull my underwear and clothes back up, already feeling the sticky ooze seeping into my knickers. I long to wash myself clean of this man. I don't know how to do it, but I've got to find a full-stop.

As Max zips up his trousers, I look at him as if trying to see inside his core. *What the hell were you doing with this man, Cate? Was this the kind of sex you had with him? Rough and opportunist.* Were they a lock and key that found each other? As a pair, Max and Cate, I sense that something putrid was being released into the world.

I've been contemplating Max for too long. My vision starts to refocus and I realise he's staring straight back at me.

'Your enthusiasm has dwindled rather, hasn't it?' He clasps my face again in one hand, his steely eyes boring into me.

I can't help myself.

'What do you expect? You know what I've been through. I've lost almost my entire family. It's difficult to heal. Being here. I shouldn't be doing this.'

Max steps back and places his hands on his hips, surveying me.

'Is that a fact?'

Anger starts to bubble up inside me. Whatever the nature of his relationship with Cate, he has shown zero compassion. I cannot believe anyone could be that heartless. Whatever her relationship with Giles, *Cate* has lost two of her children. *I* deserve some sympathy.

'I've been thinking of going away. I can't breathe in this house; it's too difficult. Too many reminders. It's killing me.'

'Oh, I don't think you'll be going anywhere, do you?'

'What are you talking about? Why wouldn't I? Surely you can see I need to?'

'I'll tell you what I see, shall I? I see an opportunity. An opportunity for you. And an opportunity for me.'

'The soil hasn't settled on my husband and children's graves yet, for Christ's sake. It's all so wrong and disrespectful.' I pray that there is some decency somewhere inside him.

'Ah, there's the rub,' Max says with an exaggerated waggle of his forefinger.

'What? What are you talking about?' I stammer with the Cate confidence completely draining from my voice. I've gone too far. I've pissed him off. I've made a bad move.

Max's eyes flicker over me like flies crawling on my skin.

'The husband — and the children. See, the thing is they're not yours, are they?'

I feel a chill like a sharp knife blade scraping over my skin. *Think, Beth, think.* This is pivotal. I can't give up now. I will protect Ted until every last ounce of breath has left my body. When I go to speak, my mouth is dry.

'What the fuck are you on about? Seriously? What do you not get about this monumental tragedy and my loss? Have you even got a heart in there?' I poke at his chest.

There is coldness in his eyes before it gets masked by the return of the smile. His response takes me aback.

'You're a dull shag. Do you know that?'

'Strangely, I'm not feeling too responsive right now. Get it?' I muster as much vehemency and sarcasm in my voice as I can.

Max shakes his head.

'Nice try. Boring Beth.'

A bomb explodes inside my head. Cate used to call me that when she wanted to be cruel: Boring Beth. Shrill, whining sounds of warning start to whirr at speed. Can Max read my panicked thoughts flitting through my brain, not finding a direction? I'm dumbstruck.

'You see, Beth, this little game of hideaway of yours doesn't fool me. Not anymore. I bought it to start with, grant you that much.' A sardonic laugh escapes from his now snarling lips. 'But I've been watching you. It's not about privacy in your time of mourning. It's about secrecy. Isn't it now?' A spittle bubble bursts in the corner of his mouth. 'My Cate is dead. She wouldn't treat me like this. You're a poor imitation, by the way. But I expect you know that.'

'I think we're done here, Max, and I'd like you to please leave my house.' I'm screaming as I point to the hallway. I want him out the front door for good.

'I'll leave all right. If that's what your ladyship wishes,' Max says in a mocking tone. 'But let me make one thing very clear. I am offering you a serious opportunity here. But there will be consequences if you don't take it.'

'What? What are you on?'

'Oh, I'm going to have some fun with you. Time for fun of a different kind, I think.' Max reaches out and helps himself to a red apple from the fruit bowl. 'We're going to play a new game, you see. And here are the rules.' He takes a crunch of the apple and chews. 'I'll give you two weeks to transfer twenty thousand pounds into my bank account. That'll do for starters. You have the details, don't you, *Cate*?' He takes another bite. 'You see, I can call you that if we're going to carry on with this pretence. Your choice. But I wouldn't think about it for too long if I were you. Consequences. Consequences.'

There is a glint in those dark, malevolent eyes.

'Get out. Get out!' I shriek at him and shove him in the direction of the front door. To my relief, Max mocks a salute, turns and heads for the hallway, kicking Cedric who's crouching in the doorway. He yowls in pain. Bastard. I follow to make sure that Max is leaving. He opens the front door as I hover in the kitchen doorway, cuddling the cat in case he decides to go for one of us again. His final words float back to me.

'Has it not occurred to you that my son is the sole heir to the Mildenhall estate? I want my share. As I said — opportunity for you, opportunity for me. Two weeks, *Cate*.'

CHAPTER 35

David

We're snuggled up on the sofa watching *Gogglebox*. We've shared a bottle of red and are now all sleepy and chilled at the end of another working week.

'I've got something to tell you,' Adrianna says.

'What's that, sweetheart? Got some good news?' I reach for the spicy tortilla chips and slump back against Adrianna. Maybe she's been called for an audition or something.

'I don't know if you'll think it's good, necessarily.'

'What's up? Hollywood's come calling, has it?'

'No. There's nothing up. And thanks for the vote of confidence,' she says. I'm surprised at how snappy she is.

'Sorry. Didn't mean it like that. It came out all wrong. What's happening?' I say, utilising my best goofy face. Beth would have smiled, but Adrianna's expression doesn't change.

I move my outstretched legs from resting on the coffee table and plant them on the floor. I sit up straight and turn to face her so she knows she's got my full attention. I don't want to mess with Adrianna. She gives me a look, the kind I've not seen from her before. A sort of 'you're not going to like it, but' look.

'I've met Cate.'

Major heart spasm. Fear creeps in like a cold breath on the back of my neck. All I can think is WTF!

'Cate? Seriously? When did this happen? You didn't mention it.'

'I'm mentioning it now, aren't I? It wasn't planned or anything.'

'Did she call the house phone? Or come here?' I laugh, but the kind borne out of manic anxiety rather than humour. What was said? Is Adrianna about to tell me she knows what happened on the afternoon we scattered Beth's ashes?

'Relax. No. She's not been here. We met in the graveyard yesterday.'

Call me dim, but I am confused.

'In the graveyard? I'm not following.'

'There's nothing to follow, David. We bumped into each other, that's all. Struck up a conversation and she invited me to lunch. Thought it was sweet of her.'

I can't quite compute all this.

'Hang on. Backtrack a moment. You happened to be walking through the cemetery and you clocked each other and started to chat, culminating in a girlie lunch?'

Adrianna now seems distracted. 'Something along those lines, yes.'

What the hell is Cate up to? God. Why the hell did I do what I did that evening? This is going to come home to roost, I can sense it. Smack me quite squarely on the jaw.

'I thought you said you were helping out at the box office?' I try not to sound too sarcastic or accusing. Adrianna blinks rapidly.

'They called to say they didn't need me after all, so I went to the cemetery. I have a relative buried there, you know. Thought I'd pay my respects.' She says this nonchalantly, as if popping to an old grave is an everyday occurrence. Maybe it's my guilt making me smell a rat, but I know better than to push it.

'Good lunch, was it?' I say as a way of trying to keep the lid on things. 'How's Cate doing?'

'As well as can be expected. She was kind and welcoming.'

Cate must have had a personality transplant. She's up to something. Adrianna finishes the last drop from her glass and places it on the coffee table.

'She knows you and I are together — and before you say anything, she's not mad about it. She said no judgements.'

I smell a faint aroma of fear and sweat; it's me. Cate is whip-smart — this meeting was no accident. I can't fathom what her game is, but I'm assaulted by memories of what Cate and I did. Why couldn't she just leave it be? I thought we both agreed that it shouldn't have happened. We got caught up in the emotion of the moment, that's all.

'David, are you even listening to me?' Adrianna says, interrupting my thoughts.

'Yes. Of course I am, sweetheart. Sorry, sorry. It's been a long, tiring week.' I fake a stifled yawn. I want this conversation and nightmare to come to an end and for us to go to bed. To envelop Adrie in my arms and for her to love me.

'Do you know something?' Adrianna purses her lips. 'It was a bit weird if I'm honest.' She lets out a big sigh.

'Weird?' I realise Adrianna has been off since yesterday. Withdrawn and quieter than normal. Hard to gauge.

'I couldn't help but imagine I was having lunch with Beth.' She turns to face me. Gazes directly at me and locks her beautiful eyes on mine. 'Your *wife*.' Adrianna elongates the word 'wife' to give it emphasis, as if to throw a spotlight on it. 'How ridiculous a thought was that?'

Has meeting Cate made Adrianna jealous of Beth? Better than her knowing what I did with Cate, I suppose.

'Well, they do look the same,' I say. 'And it's all a bit strange for you, this whole after-Beth situation, I know.' I take her hand and lean in to kiss her. Adrianna ducks under my arm and leaps off the sofa.

'Where are you going?'

'I fancy a shower to clear my head. I'm not feeling too great. I'm heading up.' Adrianna picks up her empty wine glass off the table. She stops in the doorway and turns to look at me.

'And you seriously need to clean your teeth. Those tortilla chips make your breath stink.'

I'm embarrassed. After she's gone, I blow into my hand and give it a sniff.

I decide to give Adrianna a bit of space, so I watch TV for another hour then head upstairs. She's already in bed asleep, her back turned away from my side of the bed. I cocoon myself around her; she doesn't stir. She could be feigning sleep, but I dare not wake her — in case. We've not made love to kick-start the weekend. I can't remember that ever happening before.

CHAPTER 36

Adrianna

I'm glad the weekend is over. I thought at one point I wouldn't be able to make it. My head has been spinning since Thursday. Finally, though, I'm alone. David has left for work, and I've taken myself back to bed with my laptop and a strong cup of coffee. The mornings are cooler now, but David is refusing to put the heating on yet. Tightwad. I prop myself up on pillows and pull the duvet up around me. I cradle the large, white Ikea mug to warm my hands and take a sip. How did I get here? And what on earth am I going to do?

I need time to think, plan. Escape. I thought I was finally healed. Ready for another relationship. But now I'm not so sure. Not after lunch with Cate. I mean, Beth. I don't even know what to call her in my own head. This is one gargantuan mess.

Worst of all, it's not even David's fault. He hasn't a clue what's going on with me, never mind my romance-scam sideline, but I'm beginning to find him unbearably clingy. Like a toddler and his cuddly toy. I don't want to be anyone's comforter. This whole weekend he's been behaving like a limpet. But he's someone else's husband, even if he doesn't know it. I don't want to be part of this screwed-up situation. Not after having met *BethCate*. And not after seeing that van outside her house.

Since Thursday it's like a switch has been flicked. I don't want to be touched. Nothing even close to intimacy. David sensed my distance, so responded with being increasingly needy. He wrapped his arms and legs around me in bed. Snuggled up to me on the sofa, came up behind me in the kitchen, smothered my neck in kisses and blew in my ear. 'Fuck off,' I wanted to say to him yesterday. I managed to bite my tongue and continued to stir the scrambled eggs.

The darkness creeps further and further towards me. It's taking all my strength to stop it from reaching me. I will not drown a second time.

'Is everything all right, sweetheart?' David asked me this morning, pulling me into his arms as the alarm went off.

'Of course. Why wouldn't it be?'

'You've seemed a bit distant, that's all. I want to make sure you're okay. I love you. I can fix things,' he said, attempting to stroke me in between my legs.

You'll never fix this, I thought as I reached for my dressing gown.

'David. *Um*. One — just because you've not had sex this weekend doesn't mean there has to be something wrong. Get over it. And *dois*. Two — in case you haven't noticed, the alarm has gone off.' I tied up my gown. 'Haven't you got a meeting or something to go to?'

'Adrie, tell me we're okay?' David grabbed hold of my hand, trying to pull me back towards him. I instinctively jerked away. 'Ow.' He looked hurt and cradled his finger, and I realised I was overreacting.

'Someone's being silly. No need for the paranoia.' I tried to soften my tone as I smoothed down his mop of bed hair. I leaned over to kiss him gently on the lips, but placed my hand firmly on his shoulder so that he couldn't pull me in again.

I open my laptop and wait for it to light up. I've needed the space to be able to do this. I type in *The Garden Butler*.

I wanted to believe that after you've experienced the ultimate invasion, confronted your worst possible demons and defeated them, that everything will work out fine. But I was wrong. It's not the case at all. Over the last few days, I've been haunted by unwanted memories. And every detail that re-emerges is another grain of salt ground into my once-healing wounds. Something dark and rotten crawls below my surface.

I remember the first time I found the courage to ask Sol why he treated me like that. I needed to know, to understand. Do you know what he said? He said he wanted to know what it felt like to make love to someone who was fighting back. To experience what would happen if he took me by surprise. He showed no remorse for his actions.

'Now I've done that, perhaps the next stage is while you're unconscious,' he said. 'Add a bit more excitement. Huh?'

He treated it as a joke. Or was it a veiled threat? And what came after unconscious?

I started to plot my escape. But there was no leaving Sol the easy way — he made that very clear. I had to plan. I had to bide my time.

I was raped four more times before I had the courage to leave. Twice in our bed at night, once on the living-room floor and once over the wooden kitchen table where he pinned me down like a beetle on a board. I tried to wrench away from him, but he just tightened his grip around me and it served to only make him more forceful — so I stopped trying and gave in.

And he would always tell me, again and again that, if ever I tried to leave, he would come after me and kill me. In between the sexual attacks he remained controlling, but could be kind and gentle in other ways. He'd buy me flowers and little gifts, run me a bubble bath, cook me a delicious dinner. All to appease his guilt, I presumed — to convince himself he was a caring, loving partner.

I finally escaped across London to Arnos Grove, where I rented a short-term studio let, sight unseen. It was somewhere to hide and miles away from the Lewisham flat Sol and I shared. I was safe, but the trauma then truly set in. I didn't go out. I stopped eating properly. Sleep was always fitful. All life brutally ripped from my body.

From that first rape on, I stopped seeing the world in the same way because nothing is the same as before. I'm a changed, damaged person. I know that — I'm not denying it. I'm not proud of the person I have become. But having your sense of self and safety stolen from you alters you in ways you can't account for. Nearly seven years on, I still can't.

The old cliché of time being the healer is true, but only in part. I was ready to meet a David and to try a proper relationship again. I'm steaming towards my thirtieth birthday and thought I wanted to settle down, but now I'm not so sure. There's a sickness inside of me that won't go away and David is not the cure. I am damaged beyond repair. I see that now. Sol has made sure of that; he continues to destroy everything and take everything away from me.

How I've tried to consign Sol and what he did to me to a deep, hard-to-reach place. To keep it marked as *unremembered*, or, better still, *deleted*. Memories scrubbed out like faint stains. And I was succeeding. I finally had the upper hand until that day at Cate's house. I saw that van, and it's as if the floodgates have opened and the violent memories are going to assault me all over again. Kill me, even. As he promised.

I look down at my laptop, suck in air and click on the link. He's there. His picture. His services. Testimonials. Sol has moved to south-west London and set up his own business, as he always said he would. It *was* his van I saw parked on the driveway at Cate's house. On the side there was a yellow sun motif. Symbolising Sol: Maximillian Solomon — The Garden Butler.

I want to run. I shouldn't have chosen this part of London. *Estúpida*. Stupid. This city will never be big enough — I need a new country. I could pack, leave now and be on a plane by tonight. But I know I'm not going to. Not yet. I need to get some more money together first and start to set up a life somewhere else. How much should I take off David? Fleece him totally or part empty his accounts? I *do* care about him — but not enough to stay. I'll have to keep up my pretence for a while longer. How can he not see what's happening right under his nose? Not just me. Beth.

My other dilemma — I can't stop thinking about *BethCate*. Is she safe with Sol at her house? I'd be amazed if he hasn't taken an interest in her. Should I warn her? What would I say? *Beware of your garden man — he's a psycho.* I pick up my mobile and find her number in my contacts. *Cate Mildenhall. Except you're not, are you? You're a deceiver like me. A fellow interloper.* My thumb hovers over the *call* icon.

I throw the phone back on the bed, peel back the duvet and leap up. I've got other stuff to do. She's not my problem — she's part of the problem.

CHAPTER 37

Beth

I'm sprawled out on the sofa, propped up by cushions. I'm too afraid to go out again since my confrontation with Max. His deadline is looming. Ted plays with a wooden Noah's Ark and some toy cars on a play mat. Normally, I'd be down on the rug with him. We'd be exploring the toys together and I'd be encouraging him to fill the Ark with the varying-size animal shapes that fit the different holes in the roof. But today I only have the strength to watch as his little pudgy fingers grasp the animals. He gives the grey elephant a good suck before he bashes it against the Ark's roof.

'I know how you feel, buddy.'

Ted looks up at me and grins. A gorgeous smile that dimples his cheeks, making my heart melt. I have to find a way to go on for his sake. I can't let him be taken away from me. But what do we do about Max?

You'll think of something, Mummy. Don't worry — we're a team.

I've hardly slept. I'm going to fail. Fail through circumstances I could never have predicted. Fail through odds I cannot overcome. Fear takes complete hold of me now, like icy fingers stroking my skin. I'm exhausted, constantly nauseous and I'm so terrified I want to pee all the time.

I'm trapped. I'm such an idiot. Max knew Cate — he was intimate with Cate. And I've been behaving like the Ice Queen. Appearances might deceive, but this journey never had a road map showing me all the side roads, cul-de-sacs and dead ends. Would I have embarked on it if I'd known? I could have avoided Sleepless Street and Terror Terrace if I had. Too late now. I painfully, truly, now know the meaning of the phrase, 'Be careful what you wish for'. I'm miserable, lonely, isolated and traumatised by rape. Only Ted keeps me going.

I've spent too long pretending I can pull this off, but many more days like this one and I fear my courage and bravado are going to desert me completely. Now Max has called my bluff. *Help me, Cate, please! You seem to have abandoned me of late. Tell me what to do about Max?*

Magdalena appears and loiters by the sitting-room doors.

'May I come in, Mrs Mildenhall? I throw out some of the old newspapers?' She points to a pile of Sunday papers and supplements built up on the coffee table.

'Sure. No problem. Come on in.'

Magdalena gets down on her knees to sort through the pile. Does she too suspect I'm not Cate? She's here most days. She's observed me more than anyone, but she's never uttered a word. Magdalena has been only deferential, kind and respectful. Magdalena the house fairy was another of Cate's secrets. I'm reminded of the time back at the beginning when Jess, my appointed FLO, asked me the cat's name. Magdalena came to the rescue. Did she step in to save me that day or was it pure coincidence?

'Sorry, I should be helping you. I'm feeling a bit useless and unwell today.'

Magdalena gives me a knowing smile.

'My job,' she says, bobbing her head down as if it is capable of its own curtsy.

'Magdalena, can I ask you something?' She looks up at me expectantly. 'Why do you give Max money?' Her expression changes. She looks sad, forlorn . . . guilty? I can't fathom which.

'Mrs Mildenhall, I'm so sorry.' The expression is now fear. 'I-I—'

'It's okay, Magdalena. You're safe here. No judgements.' I clasp my hands together and bring them to my heart to demonstrate reassurance. I almost said, 'No secrets,' but thought better of it. Magdalena puts down the pile of papers and inhales deeply. She goes to speak, but nothing comes out, her mouth frozen open.

'Whatever it is, I promise you can trust me.'

'I don't have proper working visa, madam. It's fake.' She pauses and sips in a breath.

'I will leave. If madam thinks that is better? Whatever madam wish. So sorry. I never meant to be—'

'No way. Ted and I would never manage without you. You're not going anywhere. But where does Max come into all this?' I think I already know. 'Is he blackmailing you?'

Magdalena nods her head disconsolately.

Seriously. Am I trying to convince myself that I knew nothing about this? Of course I knew. Somewhere in my heart I acknowledged something untoward was happening between Max and Magdalena. I've seen her handing him money, for God's sake. And I've done nothing about it. I've been so busy playing Cate that I'm becoming Cate.

'But how does he know?'

'My fault. He ask me about how long I be in England. Where I work before. I got muddle. The words came out wrong. I got scared. My face tell too much.' She gesticulates her hand around her eyes and cheeks.

'You poor thing. Max has no right. I'm very angry with him. How much are you giving him?'

'It's now four hundred a month. It's very difficult for me now to manage.'

'Four hundred? You've got to be kidding. Oh, Magdalena, no. This is terrible!'

'What to do?' Magdalena says, shaking her head. 'I have no choice. Mr Max report me.'

'No, he won't. Leave it with me. I'll put a stop to this. I promise. I will. And I'll pay back whatever he's taken from you.' Magdalena bows her head and puts her hands together in thanks.

'I'll also look into how we can get you a proper visa. I'll be careful — don't worry,' I add, seeing alarm spreading on Magdalena's face.

Michael will be able to help with this, I'm sure. 'Anything you need, only ask,' he's always telling me. He used to work in a government department of some sort. He'll know what to do.

'It's not an area I know much about, but we're going to get this sorted,' I say, heaving myself up on my elbows and swinging my legs over the edge of the sofa, planting Cate's seriously expensive mule slippers on the hideously expensive rug. I skirt around to the side of the coffee table where Magdalena is crouched and rest my hand on her shoulder.

'No, back down — sit, madam.' Magdalena rises and puts a hand up towards me. 'You will be needing this rest. Yes? And I very, very grateful. Big thank you.' She puts her hands together again as if in prayer. She then does something strange. She pats my stomach and looks up at me with a little smile.

Magdalena registers the surprise on my face and looks crestfallen. Panic spreads across her face.

'So sorry. I thought—'

'Magdalena . . . you think . . . what?'

Blimey. She thinks I'm pregnant? I must be getting fat through being a couch potato. *Magdalena, if only you knew.* I have never, in my life, been pregnant. I only wish. I've lost two children in the most tragic of circumstances and my baby is right here playing happily on the rug at my feet — but I have never carried a child. Magdalena continues to look at me nervously.

'Madam has been very tired. And sick, yes? Mr Ocado man — he not bring any of the Tampax for a while. And I not see the little tubes and green papers in the bin.'

I instinctively raise my right hand to cover my mouth in disbelief. My brain calculates and goes into overdrive. *Oh, my God. Oh, my God. Oh, my God.* I don't know whether to laugh, cry, jump for joy or scream. Could I be? I try to remember when I last had a period. I normally write everything down about my cycle to the exact minute, never mind hour, but since that fateful day I've not given it a second thought. I can't remember. The last few months have been such a blur. I've a vague recollection of some light bleeding at some point, but that might have been a while ago. Anything else, I've put down to stress.

Time to go out for a little stroll, Ted. We need to pay a visit to the pharmacy.

* * *

I'm in the en-suite bathroom sitting on the loo seat, watching the two-minute counter I've set flick by on my phone. The indicator stick is perched on the edge of the sink. *Six seconds, five seconds . . . four, three, two, one.* Time to look. I take a deep breath. Pick it up. I have a plus sign in the window. It's positive. Okay, I believe it now. I'm finally beginning to believe that this is happening as I lay the stick down next to the other three I've already peed on. Four sticks, four plus signs, one pregnancy.

I have waited a decade for this moment. It's finally here. Blood rushes to my head with the maelstrom of emotions circulating. The euphoria of knowing a new life is growing inside me is weighted down by my sordid situation.

I can't be sure who the father is. Is it David? After ten years of trying to conceive with that man, he finally gets me pregnant when he thought I was Cate? Or, a thousand times worse, is it Max? It's too soon to be from the recent, brutal kitchen-counter sex, but it could be from the garden back in the summer.

CHAPTER 38

Beth

The morning is as sharp and crisp as a Granny Smith. Fallen leaves crunch under the buggy's wheels.

'Hear that?' I say to Ted. 'Shall we see if we can find any conkers in Richmond Park? And I'll show you acorns. Ooh. And I wonder if we'll get any snow this year? You wait until you see snow, little fella. It's amazing in the park then. We can build our first snowman together. And when you're a bit older we can go sledding. You'll love—'

Stop wittering. What are you going to do? You need to be prepared.

I peer down at Ted. I do know he's not really talking to me. Like Cate doesn't either. But what harm does a little imagining do when I spend so much time on my own. Sad, I know, but it helps me think things through. That or I'm seriously unhinged.

'You're not old enough yet to start the backchat.'

Max's deadline passed a week ago and I've done . . . nothing. Zero. Zilch. *That's my plan, Teddy, to do nothing. Call his bluff. I will not be blackmailed if he turns up again.* Cate wouldn't buckle and nor will I. I am Cate. What can he seriously do? I'll accuse him of being an opportunist, a chancer. I'm praying that he's not Ted's father and I'll find out the parentage soon.

'Thanks for the swab and hair by the way.'

Thank God Cate and I share exact DNA. Biologically I *am* Ted's mother. I figure there's only one way Max can prove I'm not Cate. My tattoo. Did he ever see Cate's? It's a serious gamble, but I'm guessing that Cate's relationship with him was more of a snatched moment in the shed thing rather than a full-naked-romp-in-bed opportunity. There's nothing I can do about it now. No decent tattoo parlour will work on me pregnant and it's not a risk I'm about to take. My plan to completely metamorphose into Cate will have to wait.

Once inside the park, we head straight for the Pembroke Lodge café before it gets too busy. I'm hungry and Ted always is. This time we have no problem in getting a table. After we've finished, I'm piling our plates back on the tray when I hear a voice behind me.

'Well, if it's not Cate with a C.'

I spin round to be greeted by a pair of smiling, piercing blue eyes framed by a mass of dark blond dishevelled hair. Harry is wearing ripped grey jeans with a navy pea coat and a red plaid scarf artistically draped around his collar. He's holding Abbie's hand. She is clutching her big white bunny.

'Harry. Hi. And Abbie.' I bend down to greet her.

'It's lovely to see you again. How are you? How have you been holding up,' he says with concerned kindness, reaching out to grace my arm with a soft touch.

'We're good . . . but it can be tough . . . well, you know . . . small steps . . . one day at a time.' I'm flustered. I'm out of practice talking to anyone, particularly attractive strangers.

'You're doing the right thing, Cate. It's not an easy journey, but it does get more manageable.' Harry pauses. 'Cate, can I ask you something?' A tingle touches me between the shoulder blades. 'Have you got time for a walk? It's lovely out there. Only if you'd like to, mind. Don't want to intrude.'

'Why not,' I say, while thinking, *you bet*. 'That would be lovely. We were planning a walk and would welcome the company.' I'm praying I don't blush as I notice the freckles underneath his eyes and on the bridge of his nose. I've got those too.

We follow a path to make it easier for me to push Ted. The parkland is a riot of colour, the trees standing proud like towers of red, yellow and gold. The intermingling colours flare against the low autumn sun, which warms our faces. Turns out, now that Abbie has started nursery, they've switched their Richmond Park day to a Wednesday. It's a fortuitous encounter. Since first meeting Harry in August, I never did make it back here on a Tuesday. Not after Max. Harry has been good enough not to mention my no-show.

We walk back to Pembroke Lodge where Harry has left his car. My phone vibrates with a message from Mum's care home. As I put it back in my pocket, Harry says, 'May I?' and indicates my phone. I hand it over. His fingers skim over it. His golden mop flops across his eyes as he's looking downwards. He flicks it back with a swift head movement as he hands me back my phone.

'Now you have me, Harry, under H,' he says with a cheeky grin.

* * *

'What a lovely time,' I say to Ted as we walk back through the Richmond Park gates.

Admit it. You like him, don't you? You were definitely getting a little bit flirty-flirty!

'I so was not. Was I? Seriously — is that what it looked like? You've got me worried now. What must Harry think of me? I'm a widow and bereaved mother of only four months — I shouldn't be flirting with cute sculptors. He's probably got a girlfriend anyway.'

But he did give me his number, I think with a warm glow as we head home.

It doesn't last long. As I approach the house, the fear and paranoia start to crawl across me again. Like an itch I can't reach. We've just had the most amazing time in the park with Harry and Abigail — a few snatched hours where I could pretend this sordid mess doesn't exist.

I lift Ted, still in his buggy, up the limestone steps to the front door. I'm relieved to see Max's Garden Butler van is not parked in the driveway.

'At least it will just be us and the kitties.' It's Magdalena's afternoon off. 'Gosh, you're getting heavier. Won't be long and I'm not going to be able to carry you like this anymore; you'll be walking up on your own.' I don't get a response. Ted must be getting bored of my little chat game.

With Ted safely in the hallway, I close the front door with a satisfying click. How I love to shut the world out. I want to continue to bask in the glow of having spent a few real-time hours with Harry and Abigail.

I bend down to pick up the post off the jute mat that's inlaid around the doorway. It's arrived. There's a white A4 envelope stamped with the logo of the DNA testing centre.

'Brace yourself, Ted.'

I stare at the envelope, addressed to Mrs Catherine Rose Mildenhall. I've gone for the full-works testing in case Cate has any more surprises lurking in her closet. Ted starts to writhe in his buggy and lets out a disgruntled whine.

'Sorry, sweetheart. Let's take you to the lounge. I think I want to be in a comfortable spot in case I fall over when we open this.'

Ted and I settle among the cushions on the sofa. I'm still staring at the envelope. Acid gnaws at my insides. It's like getting your exam results, only worse. Ted leans to grab the envelope as if telling me that he will open the damn thing if I won't.

'OK. Hint taken. Let's do this.'

There's a covering letter and numerous sheets of test results. I frantically scan each one, but can't focus for the panic. Tables of numbers were never my thing. They start to swim in front of my eyes, coagulating into a fuzzy blur.

Take a deep breath, Mum. Read the covering letter.

It's explaining how to read the genetic-system tables included, something to do with allele sizes. I move through the sheets more slowly. I see the term *Alleged Father*, meaning Giles, in a column above a series of unfathomable numbers. Adjacent is Ted's name with more numbers.

Then I see it. *Probability of Paternity: 99.9998%.*

Thank you. Thank you!

'Ted . . . look at this,' I say, pointing out the number. Max has been playing me.

I scan the other sheets. I am the biological mother of all three Mildenhall children. Who knew? I never doubted it, but Giles is also the father of Charlie and Georgie. *Sorry, Cate, thought best to check.* Hair and toothbrushes having allowed me to do so.

I leap up with Ted and swing him round. If I wasn't pregnant, then I'd be cracking open a bottle.

'What's that? You want some juice, Teddy Boy? Juice coming up,' I say, planting kisses on the top of his head as we walk through to the kitchen. 'This day is getting better and better, wouldn't you say, Ted?'

I feel like I'm floating on air. I still don't know the father of the baby I'm carrying, but this is a positive start. I can feel the tide turning.

'The size of this kitchen is ridiculous,' I say to Ted as I gently lower him into his playpen that is set up in one corner of the room. 'I've now got to walk a quarter of a mile to get your juice out the fridge. I'd better set out. See you sometime later this afternoon, buddy.'

The house seems very quiet without Magdalena here. I do miss her when she's not around. It's such a gargantuan, imposing house and Ted and I rattle around in it. Even when the new baby comes, we do not need six bedrooms. I crave something more low maintenance and a garden that doesn't require the services of a garden butler.

I contemplate moving on. A more modest home. Still south-west London, but somewhere people don't know our story. New neighbours, a different school for Ted than the one Charlie and Georgie attended. Anonymity. Harry eulogises about Putney, so maybe a house with a river view? I determine that I'm going to contact a few estate agents, start with having the house valued. It will get me thinking about the process anyway.

As I cross the kitchen, my foot catches on something shiny and sends it spinning across the floor. A little bell tinkles as it does so. I bend to scoop it up. It's Cersei's reflective collar. The little minx has managed to get it off. I place it on the central island to reunite her with it later, I don't want her going out after dark without wearing it. As I open the fridge door, I catch sight of one of our breakfast bowls on the floor too. There are the remnants of some-thing brown and sludgy inside. I pick it up and tentatively give it a sniff. My nostrils respond with a quiver. Fishy and unpleasant. It's cat food, I think.

What on earth is it doing here? Our cats have dried food. I look around and spot an orange package on the counter-top on the opposite side of the kitchen. Picking it up, I see they're cat treats. Our cats do get given those. A few of them have spilled out onto the worktop. This isn't like Magdalena. Why would she have given them soft food and left the treats out? The answer is . . . she wouldn't.

I cross over to the glass doors and look out onto the garden. Cedric isn't in his usual napping spot underneath the rosemary bush in the herb border at the edge of the decking. There's no sign of Cersei or Jaime either. It occurs to me that we haven't seen any of them since we returned home. That's unusual.

Checking that Ted is settled and secure, I run up the stairs, taking two at a time.

'Cedric! Where are you? Jaime! Cersei!'

I run into each room, shaking the treat bag as I go. I even go into the guest suites in case Magdalena has accidently shut them in. I check the linen cupboard, laundry baskets, washing machines, wardrobes. They're not here. All three must be out. That must be it. It's a coincidence, that's all.

I head back downstairs, but a knot of misgiving tightens in my stomach. Even if all three did happen to be out, it still doesn't explain the wet cat food and the Dreamies.

I walk around to see if there's anything else I've missed, opening cupboards and drawers. I look in the bin. I look in the pantry, the recycling, the ovens. I go over to the glass doors again and open one of them. The sun is now low in the sky and the contrasting coolness from outside slaps me in the face. I shiver.

'Where are you guys?'

I make clicking noises by pushing my tongue to the roof of my mouth and sucking in. No response. No little kitty comes running as they normally would and I'm sure they'd hear me if called. They should think it was feeding time by now. After a few more minutes, I close the door.

With my back to the garden, I survey the kitchen again. What, if anything, is out of place? Magdalena always keeps it immaculate. Everything was as it should be upstairs. The bread bin is in the usual position. So is the knife block, the chopping boards.

My eyes alight on the sous-vide machine. There's a little red light on. And the lid is not one hundred per cent in place — it's raised slightly and fractionally skew-whiff. I step towards it.

Tentatively I reach out to raise the lid. There's something inside. I can't work out what I'm seeing. I peer closer.

The sous-vide lid drops to the floor with an almighty crash. It startles Ted who begins to whimper. He's expecting me to rush over, and reassure and comfort him. But I can't. I try to fight back the bile that is rising in my throat. There's something in there. *Please, God, no! Don't let it be.* I grip onto the counter-top to steady myself for another look. My hand shakes violently as I reach inside the water. I lift out a shrink-wrapped package. I can't make out what I'm seeing at first, then I realise it's a cat collar — Jaime's. This is Max's work — what has he done?

I look around the kitchen again. What have I missed? I can't remember if I looked in the microwave, I definitely checked the ovens. It takes me a full thirty seconds before I can summon up the courage to open it. I close my eyes as I press the button. The door springs open. I force myself to look. It's empty.

I need to look outside. I run around as I experience the garden through smeary lenses and ears plugged with cotton wool. Standing in the middle of the lawn, a surge of emotion so forceful bends me double. *Breathe, Beth, breathe.* Then I hear it. A tiny mewl. Where's it coming from? From the corner of my eye, I detect a small movement by the summer house. Could it be a white paw — Jaime?

Running like I've never run before in my life, I reach him. Jaime tries to get to his feet when he sees me, but collapses. Gathering him in my arms, I look around for Cersei. The door to the summer house is slightly ajar. Cersei lies inside, motionless except she's breathing rapidly. *No, no, no!* Am I too late? Standing on the pink plastic play-table is a cannister of antifreeze. The vile monster has poisoned them.

Propped up next to the antifreeze is a Polaroid photo. I pick it up. It was taken outdoors somewhere — there are trees and grassland. I squint. I can see a family walking in the distance. Parents with two children. I scrutinise the outline of the figures.

It was taken today. It's of Ted and I with Harry and Abigail in Richmond Park.

I sink to the floor, still clutching Jaime and cling to him like a frightened child. *I am so, so sorry. This is all my fault.* Everything dips and swims around me. The tears fall and fall and fall.

I am defeated. I summon the strength to remove my phone from my back pocket. I open Cate's banking app and transfer the sum of twenty thousand pounds to Max Solomon, trading as The Garden Butler.

CHAPTER 39

Beth

The light sensor by the mirror in the en-suite bathroom detects my presence and bathes me in a yellow light. It's 6 a.m. and over a week since the kittens came home from the vets. They survived, but it was a very close call. We could so easily have lost them. Mercifully, they didn't leave the garden and I found them within a few hours of ingesting the poison, otherwise the vet said they would have suffered kidney failure and it would have been game over. To my immense relief, Cedric reappeared the next day unscathed. The wise old puss has learned to avoid Max.

I peer at my reflection and wipe the day-old mascara and tidemarks from under my eyes. I look gaunt, with the sockets of my eyes clearly defined. Every shadow and blemish on my face is exaggerated.

I am deflated and crumpled. In blind panic, my intellect became unfocused. The components of the mess I have created continue to orbit around me. I thought Ted was a gift, but sometimes it feels like he's been wrapped in layers and layers of punishment. What more is there to come?

I thought it impossible to cry any more tears, but since last week I have become undone. I've been unzipped and someone has taken all the stuffing out of me. Leaving me a shell of the person I once was. I had to tell Magdalena what happened as Jaime and Cersei were absent for a few days.

'No. I can't believe this. Very bad man,' she said, shaking her head in disbelief and wiping tears from her eyes.

Max hasn't returned to the house since — maybe the one good thing to come out of this horrendous episode.

I get a sudden urge to take a closer look at the three sheds that store all of the gardening and house-maintenance equipment. I check on Ted; he's still sleeping. Taking the baby monitor, I head for the garden. The sheds stand in a row, each painted a different colour like beach huts. The blue one reveals general maintenance tools like drills and decorating paraphernalia, the green everything for the garden, and the yellow, the biggest of the three, contains all the larger items like the lawnmower, step ladders, a workbench. Half of B&Q is housed in here. In the months since I moved in, I've only ever peered through the door. Stepping over the threshold feels like getting closer to Max, something I want to avoid. But I'm looking for answers. I'm not sure what I expect to find — keys to the house maybe, or a creepy wall covered with photographs of other women. Proof in case I do go to the police.

There is nothing of the kind. Each shed is kept immaculately. Not a gardening implement, paint pot or tool is out of place. In fact, it's so tidy and orderly, it's almost disturbing. Tools are lined up in rows in size order, equally spaced and attached by clasp attachments on boards to the walls. There are large concertina boxes with fold-out trays that house rows of hammers, screwdrivers and drill bits, again, all in ascending order. Boxes with small drawer compartments containing screws, nails and Rawlplugs. Guess what? All in size order. It's like a masterclass in filing and order management. Everything, right down to the doormat placed at the entrance of each shed, is clean and immaculate.

Max is definitely a neat freak. Lots of people like to keep things tidy, but this is bordering on the obsessive. Did Cate get Max to order her walk-in larder? God, that would be weird. I sit down on a small stool placed in the corner of the third shed and cradle my head in my hands. More and more I've been getting a dizzying feeling of my own insignificance in this world. Of the infinity of the universe beyond.

Are you out there, Cate?

I resent her for leaving me with this mess. *What the hell were you thinking of, getting involved with Max?*

It was the sex, I hear her say. *Simple as. Believe me, after nearly fifteen years of sleeping with Giles, any intimacy with that man felt like downing a cup of cold sick.*

I thought I could cope with every version of you, Cate. But this?

The last gasp from a flatlining sex life of a marriage. Something to stir the pot. You know me.

Life with Cate always was like skating on thin ice, never knowing when it might crack and I'd be plunged into the icy depths. Who thought it would still be happening aged thirty-nine.

You are a squashed bug on the windscreen of my life. Do you hear me, Cate? I smile inwardly as I remember her saying that as a child.

Cate always made an impact on those around her. *Max got it bad, didn't he, Cate? He'd started to behave obsessively with you, hadn't he? Wanting more.*

I think back to that weekend at the New Forest cottage. Cate was distracted, distant almost — even for her. And she was on her phone even more than usual. Was the strain of Max starting to take its toll, I wonder? And I'm convinced it was him on the motorway that day too. The police concluded no collision had taken place, but Max could have caused Giles to brake too hard and lose control. Had Cate spotted him? I try to make connections. Is that why Cate and Giles were arguing? Or was it because Cate had undone her seat belt?

I need to get back to Ted. I leave the sheds with a hardened resolve. I don't find anything of physical significance, but I do learn something. Max is a man who likes to be in control; everything evidently has its place in his ordered world. Was he obsessed with Cate? Yes. And my version of Cate, post the trauma, has affected his equilibrium — destabilised him, perhaps? He's been trying to take back control. I can't wait for him to make another move. I have to find the strength to call the shots and make change. I used to be a functioning adult with my own decision-making capabilities; it's time to become that person again.

Back at the house I have time for a quick shower before Ted wakes wanting his bottle. Always hungry, my boy. I'm about to step in when I catch sight of myself in the full-length bathroom mirror. For once it's not the reminder of my tattoo that's made me stop and look at my reflection. It's my body shape. My breasts look fuller, firmer. I like them. I've never really had much boob. I run my hands over my belly, feeling the skin and imagining what lies within my womb. A tiny little foetus; my own baby. It's still a miracle that I am carrying a child. *I will nurture and love you whoever you are. Whatever the circumstances of your conception.*

I stand sideways looking at my belly, cradling it in my hands. It's definitely swelling. For a second I imagine a slight flutter, almost like a butterfly tickling my insides. But it's too soon yet; I can't imagine it's much bigger than a broad bean. *Bean*. I like that.

'Maybe I'll refer to you as Bean. May I?' I say out loud, aware this is the first time I've spoken to my growing baby. 'You're not too young for me to start talking to you, are you Bean?' This is ok, I think. Nurturing starts now. 'We're going on an outing today, little Bean. We'll get your due date and one of those adorable little images because we're going for your very first scan. Maybe that will give us a clue?'

I make a vow to love this baby whatever the outcome. Either way it will need my protection.

CHAPTER 40

Beth

Five hours later and I've contacted two security companies for quotes on changing all the locks. Including the side-garden gate that has an entry code I don't know. I'm stupid for not having done it sooner, but God knows what it could have initiated. Both companies are sending surveyors tomorrow. Sorted. I've also contacted three estate agents and arranged for appointments with assessors next week to give me valuations. Tick. I'm making decisions. Progress.

And now for the moment of truth.

'Mrs Cate Mildenhall, please?'

'That's me,' I say, holding up my patient card and leaping out of my seat to follow the smiling sonographer.

'Are you on your own today, Mrs Mildenhall?' she says, peering back out through the door in case she's about to shut my husband out.

'Yes. Only me.' I don't think now is the time to explain.

'Welcome. I'm Samantha. Make yourself comfortable on the couch and we'll get started.' She takes her seat in front of the screen.

'I hope you've got a nice full bladder for me so we can get a good picture of baby,' she says as she's busying herself twiddling dials and knobs.

I hoist myself up on the bed and lie back to rest my head on the blue-paper-covered pillow. I pull my baggy shirt up and loosen my trousers. I can't believe I'm finally doing this. How many times did I envisage this scenario in my head while trying to get pregnant with David? There's an empty wipe-clean chair on the other side of me. I wish he was here with me now. He could be the father and he's absent because he doesn't even know I'm pregnant. Yet. And because I'm Cate. If I'm about twelve weeks, then it's Daddy David. If it's less, then it's Daddy Max. Even after everything he's done, I pray for the former.

'Is this your first scan?'

I stop myself from blurting out: *Yes. First ever!* I need to be careful what I say. Hospital records will show differently.

'I have a nearly eleven-month-old at home.'

'You'll know the procedure, then. I'm going to apply a small amount of the gel. Be prepared for the cold on your tummy. Ready?' She smiles at me.

'Ready.'

With the gel applied, she turns back again to look at her monitor and deftly uses her right hand to manipulate a rolling-ball device while scanning over my belly with her left.

The positioning of the couch allows me to see the screen. Is this real? I can't believe I've reached this moment. I dare not look yet. Instead, I tilt my head sideways and look at Samantha's crisp white medical overcoat. My gaze moves up to focus on her left earlobe. She's wearing a gold stud. Neat and clean like her dark pixie cut. A few feathery bits of hair are folding around her ears. I bet she's already booked herself a haircut.

The transducer rolls around the cold gel on my tummy. It tickles as though I'm being polished. I can hear a few clicking sounds as Samantha is working her control panel.

'I can see Baby,' she says.

I inhale deeply and steel myself to look at the lunar landscape on the screen. I want to remember this moment. *My* baby. Not one I have *acquired*. There's *my* baby. It's a grainy picture — all fuzzy, but I can make out the outline of a tiny, developing, actual human being. It's beautiful. I can hear the heartbeat. *Thump, thump, thump.* It's like horse's hooves galloping underwater. I experience a sensation that I can only describe as a true unfurling of happiness. That's my *Bean*.

'Hear that? Healthy heartbeat we've got there.'

'It's wonderful.' I feel so emotionally choked I think I'm about to burst.

'Shall I show you around? The guided tour of your uterus, so to speak,' she says.

'Please. Yes . . . Lovely.'

Samantha points out the baby's hands, feet, spine, beating heart. As if reading my thoughts, she says, 'Would you like to know the baby's sex? I think I can tell.'

I open my eyes wide in surprise and nod enthusiastically. I wasn't expecting this yet. Wow. Technology.

'See here?' she says, pointing to the image. 'He's showing us his wares. Congratulations, Mrs Mildenhall. Looks like you've got a boy in there.'

'I'll have two sons,' I say brimming with happiness.

'Just one thing,' Samantha says.

She's looking at her screen, but even from my side view I can tell she's got a quizzical look on her face. A sense of dread envelops me. My emotions are on a rollercoaster ride. After all this, she's going to give me some bad news. More punishment. She's found something. Something's wrong. I can tell. She's not smiling. I take a long, slow blink to prepare myself for what's to come.

'Your notes suggest July as your last period date. Do you know when exactly?'

'It is . . . um . . . all a bit of a blur, to be honest. Mid-July, I think. It was light, but I've been grieving, you see. I thought . . . Is there something wrong?'

'Oh, no,' she says, breaking into a smile again. 'Most definitely not. All very healthy, in fact. I was just trying to ascertain your baby's true due date. I'm going to check a couple more measurements and then I'll be able to tell you.'

The relief floodgates open.

'Mrs Mildenhall, I think your July period might have been a bit of spotting. I'd say your baby is more advanced than you were expecting — approaching twenty weeks, so I'm going to give you a due date of . . . the twenty-fourth of February.'

I'm speechless.

As I'm leaving, Samantha hands me my ultrasound image of Bean.

'Take care now.'

I lean against the white wall in the corridor to compose myself. To compute this monumental, unexpected, marvellous curveball. My baby's father isn't Max or David. It's Giles Mildenhall.

CHAPTER 41

Beth

I sit at the kitchen table with a mug of strong tea and a cushion supporting my back against the chair. I'm still contemplating my earth-shattering news as Laura and Michael pull up in the driveway with the return of my number-one son Ted. I told them I was visiting Mum today. Not a complete untruth as I did pop in to see her briefly after my scan. Thankfully there hasn't been a repeat of Mum insisting I'm Beth. I'm not sure she knows anymore which daughter is visiting.

Laura and Michael were only too happy to help with Ted today. I've grown so fond of them both and I can't wait to tell them the exciting news. They don't even know I'm pregnant yet.

I couldn't get my head around how I was going to handle it before, conceiving after their son's, my *husband's*, death. It would have had to have been a very long gestation period. But I don't have to lie now. They are genuinely going to be grandparents once more and Ted is going to have a biological brother. Talk about dodging a bullet. I am so happy. I couldn't have wished for a better outcome.

I never thought for a minute it would work when I artificially inseminated myself on the Sunday morning at the cottage. Turns out Giles Mildenhall had super sperm. As the seconds ticked by after the noises next door stopped and I heard the latch on the bathroom door click, I found myself imagining exactly what Giles was doing. The toilet flushed and I heard the swing of the bathroom bin lid. *Ah . . . condom*, I thought. He's not flushed it down the toilet? And then: *Ah. Sperm. Freshly ejaculated sperm.*

I needed a pee anyway, so thought I might as well go and take a look. I sat on the toilet staring at the bin, which was within reach. I opened it, being careful not to make a sound. There was a full condom in there. What a waste.

I did try to dispel the thought but it remained there, enticing me, like the last chocolate in the box. I couldn't resist the urge; it had my name on it. I reached in and picked it out between my thumb and forefinger, and laid it carefully on the edge of the sink on top of a piece of toilet paper. Question was — how to unite the sperm with one of my eggs?

I couldn't go downstairs to rummage in the kitchen drawers for a turkey baster. Giles was down there. I'd be surprised if a rental would have one anyway. I had to be creative. Then I recalled Cate giving Ted some Calpol with a syringe the previous day as he was teething. Cate's oversized designer washbag sat on the window ledge. Lo and behold, the Calpol pack complete with syringe was packed inside.

Georgie took my phone to her room so I inseminated myself back in my bedroom with my legs up against the wall, while getting stewed up about David and his affair. If things were okay with David, I don't think I would have done it. But I was desperate. The opportunity presented itself, so I took it. I didn't stop to think about how I'd explain a pregnancy to David — with zero sex for the previous month at least. But then I didn't stop to think about anything I did that day. I honestly haven't given what I did that morning any more thought. I've been focusing only on what I did in the afternoon.

The doorbell rings.

'There you are.' I swing the door open, my arms wide. Laura leans in to pass me Ted who throws himself at me enthusiastically, nearly off-balancing her tiny frame.

'Whoa. Steady on, tiger,' I say, secretly thrilled that Ted has unconditionally accepted me as his mother. 'Have you had a lovely time with Grandma and Grandad?'

I smother his face in kisses. Ted giggles and buries his head in my shoulder.

'Come on in. Fancy a cuppa? I've not long since made some tea.'

'That would be lovely, Cate, thank you,' Laura replies, stepping inside. 'How is Rachel? I do hope she's okay?'

Before I can reply, we're distracted by Michael who has followed us in, laden down with baby paraphernalia.

'Shall I put it down here?' he says, indicating the contemporary take on a church pew that is backed up against the hallway wall.

'Perfect. I'll sort it later. Come on in to the kitchen. I've got something I need to tell you both.'

I catch a look of concern pass between them.

'Is everything all right, dear?' Laura asks.

'Oh, yes. It's good news. Promise. But I think you both need to be sitting down first.'

'Oh, my goodness, what is this about?' Michael asks, pulling out a kitchen chair. 'You've heard from the insurance company?'

I can hardly contain myself. But I'm going to hold back for a few seconds more. I want to cherish this moment and I need to strap Ted in his high chair first.

'Let me get you that tea and then I'll tell all.'

As I place two more full mugs on the table, I notice Michael's jaw quiver. Laura notices it too.

'Whatever is this news? You've got us dizzy with anticipation,' Laura says with a nervous little laugh.

I sit down between them and take a hand from them both and clasp tightly. Michael gives my hand a little squeeze.

'Giles has left us with the most precious of gifts. I'm pregnant. You're going to be grandparents again.'

'Oh, my giddy aunt.' Laura leaps to her feet and pulls me towards her in a tight embrace. 'Oh, Cate. I know this baby can't replace Charlie and Georgie, but what wonderful news.'

'Well, bless the Lord,' Michael says, reaching for a cotton handkerchief from his trouser pocket and proceeding to dab the corner of his eye.

'Goodness, well, you must be . . . ?' Laura says.

'Twenty weeks, according to my scan.' I reach for the image where I'd hidden it beneath a table mat. 'Due February 24th. Meet your new grandson.'

'It's a boy. Do you hear that, Laura? A boy. We're going to have another grandson.'

'It's a miracle. This is unbelievable.' Laura grabs hold of the chair back to steady herself before sitting down and tenderly picking up the scan image.

'You're the first to know. I only found out recently. I hadn't realised. I thought I was unwell. All the sickness. I can't quite believe it myself.'

'Well, we're absolutely thrilled. Aren't we, Michael?' Laura says, addressing her husband but not taking her eyes off the scan photo. Michael is still dabbing at his eyes. I know they're tears of happiness and my heart swells for them both.

Laura reaches across the table and takes both my hands in hers. Her face is a burst of warmth, and her voice soft and precise as she turns to me.

'Cate, Giles would be so, so proud of you. We're proud of you. You've been so resilient. It's been incredibly tough on you, but you've held it together. You're a wonderful mother — you truly are. We think you're remarkable.'

I don't want anything to spoil this moment. Guilt is such a furtive emotion, lurking in the shadows and waiting for the chance to steal the limelight. I will not let it. I push it away. I seem to be acquiring Cate's ability to pack away unwanted emotions.

'I think I could say the same about you too. It's been hell on earth for us all. I'm so grateful for everything you've done for me. All your support.' I reach for Michael's hand too. 'I honestly wouldn't have coped without you.' I am grateful to be linked to this kind, selfless couple.

'And if any good has come out of this unbelievable tragedy, then it's us, isn't it? We feel so much closer to you. Silly really, but we've got to know you so much better. We're a tighter family,' Laura says.

'We love you, Cate, like the daughter we never had,' Michael says.

'Like I said, family.' Laura gives my hand another squeeze. I don't think I've seen such a big smile on anyone's face. Not in a long time.

Our little triangle is broken up by my phone lighting up as it buzzes a message. It's on the central-island worktop, so I stand and head over to retrieve it. As soon as I see the screen, the veins in my skull pound.

MS: *Time for the next payment.*

Panic flutters in my throat. I was a fool to think he wouldn't be back for more. I seem to be one for clinging on to vain hope. Another message comes through.

MS: *£50K. Don't take too long.*

I know I was stupid to transfer Max money in the first place. By doing so, I admitted to him that I was Beth. But he succeeded in pushing me to the edge. It was like when you stand on a bridge and it crosses your mind that you could jump. You know that you shouldn't, but you can't quell the notion. That afternoon, when he poisoned the kittens, led me to the edge of the precipice. I was standing on the clifftop and was ready to join the water. To be swallowed up in the foam and sucked under to the murky depths seemed like a welcome relief. For a split second, I was done. I was ready to throw in the towel. Not anymore.

CM: *No more. This is finished.*

Three little dots dance with the promise of a reply.

MS: *I said, for starters.*

Another message closely follows.

MS: *Don't fuck with me, bitch.*

Tightness travels from my stomach to the rest of my body like an elevator. I can't reply. I don't know how to.

'Is everything all right, Cate, dear? Bad news? You've gone awfully pale.' Laura is looking over at me, concerned. Her voice draws me back to the present.

'Yes. Fine, thanks. I'm a little tired, that's all. From all the excitement. It's a few reminders from Mum's home. Stuff I need to sort. I said I'd deal with it.'

'Always available,' Michael says, raising his right arm and waving his hand about.

God, I love him. *If only you could deal with this for me, Michael. I don't think you can fix this for me unless you run a sideline as an assassin.*

CHAPTER 42

David

Adrianna leaps out of bed before I can even roll over and touch her. She pulls the curtains open with a flourish, flooding the room with sunlight. Dammit, it's not summer anymore. Why is the sun out? I wince and protect my eyes with the duvet. My mouth tastes sour and there's a dull ache behind my eyes.

'What a glorious day. I'm going for a run. I'd suggest you come with me for the exercise, but there's not enough time before work.'

'I'm gonna call in sick. Didn't sleep too well. Think I'm going down with something.'

'Can I get you anything?'

'Some fresh water and a couple of paracetamols would be good. I'll get up soon.'

'Coming up,' Adrianna says. 'You stay put.' I sense a faux breeziness about her. Trouble is bubbling underneath.

She leaves the room without kissing me. Not even on the forehead. She reappears five minutes later with the water and pills, and wearing her running gear. She places them on the bedside table and takes a step back away from my arm's reach. Still no kiss. I want a kiss.

'Won't be too long, but not sure what time. There's an open-air fitness class in the park I might join. Hope you feel better.'

She closes the bedroom door without looking back. Where the hell is she running to? Away from me. I know, I can sense it. I should have bottled that when-we-first-met feeling. I'd like to trap her in a jar so she can never leave. But I'm not like that. I'm going to have to let this little bird fly — maybe she'll come back to me. Filthy, sordid misery has enveloped me and Adrianna's not even left me yet. My life is being pulverised. Just desserts, I guess. There won't be any sympathy for me. I don't deserve any.

Sleep has eluded me since — since forever, it feels like, but after an hour I force myself to get up and go downstairs. My brain is so fogged up. After I call in sick, I flop on the sofa, remote in one hand and a coffee in the other, flicking through crap daytime TV. Something I've not done in years, but I can hardly put one foot in front of the other this morning. It's as if my body has become a leaden weight I drag around with me since Adrianna's attitude has changed. I'm losing everything. I contemplated going on the run, to show interest, but today it was going to be a physical impossibility. Not that she wanted my company — that much is clear.

I need to pull myself together. Behaving like Adrianna has already left isn't exactly going to endear myself to her. But I'm struggling to get my mojo back. I badly need a shower, I smell stale sweat on me. But first I have a phone call to make. After three rings she picks up.

'Cate. Hi. It's David.'

'I know. I do have your number in my phone.'

'Yes, of course. Um, how are you?'

'Well, actually I'm . . .' Cate hesitates.

'Sorry. Have I called at a bad time? You're probably about to go out.'

'No. Not that. David . . . I'm pregnant.'

She comes out with it just like that. It's like an invisible boxing glove has punched me full on in the stomach.

I didn't see this one coming. Jesus wept. A lump develops in my throat; saliva evaporates from my mouth. Hellfire. This is all I need.

'David, are you still there?'

I didn't think things could get any worse. They have.

'Yes. Sorry. Just a bit shocked. How did this happen?'

'I had sex, David. Sexual intercourse.'

'I know we did. I meant — well, I presumed you'd be on the pill or something.'

'I'm not. These things happen.'

'Cate, I'm so sorry. This is a mess. We're going to have to talk about this. I guess.'

Son of a bitch. I'm shitting myself. I can't stop my right leg from shaking. There are so many emotions crashing through my brain. What will Cate want from me? A relationship? To play daddy? Financial support? Not that she needs it. Fuck and damnation. I'm dead. Her voice brings me back.

'What are we supposed to be talking about, David?'

'Well, that kind of depends, doesn't it?'

'On what exactly?'

'On whether you . . . you know.'

'No. I don't know. Enlighten me.'

'Jeez, Cate. Don't make me say. I wasn't expecting this.'

'Aren't you happy for me?'

'Yes. Of course I am if you are? But it wasn't exactly planned. It was a mad moment. I thought we'd both agreed on that. This is a hell of a bomb to drop on me right now.'

'To drop on you? I never said the baby was yours, did I?'

'What? The baby's not mine?'

Talk about being let off the hook. Suddenly I can breathe again.

'No. It's Giles's, of course. The father of all my children. I'm due late February. You do the maths.'

I let out a nervous chuckle and sink back into the sofa cushions as the tension evaporates from my body.

'Phew. I thought there for a moment—'

'I know what you thought, David. But how did you think you could possibly be the father when you never managed to get Beth pregnant over the best part of ten years?'

Ouch. Bitch. Cate's famous acerbic tongue can still lash out. Nothing's changed then. She played me there; it's what I deserve. I can hardly blame her for taking a poke at me. Cate knows I was unfaithful to Beth and she's met Adrianna. She also knows first-hand what I'm capable of. I want to ask whether she dropped a hint about our liaison to Adrianna. I need to know. Things can't seriously get any worse.

'Well, congratulations, Cate. Amazing news. I'm so thrilled for you. You deserve this.'

'Yes. Yes, I do. And thank you for saying that.'

'Cate, can I ask you something?'

'What?'

'I know you bumped into Adrianna at the cemetery and you guys had lunch. She told me.'

'Yes. Wasn't a problem, was it? She seems lovely.'

'No. Nothing like that. Well, she's been a bit off with me since and I wondered whether you'd said anything about the day we scattered the ashes? Inadvertently, of course.'

Cate laughs. 'It might surprise you to know that you were hardly mentioned. If Adrianna is off with you, then it's nothing to do with me. I promise you that.'

'Okay. Thanks. Sorry, I had to ask. And congratulations.'

'Bye, David.'

I repeatedly run my hands through my hair. My neck is getting too tired to even hold my head up. The tension seeps into my temples again. I'm still none the wiser and nearly had a heart attack in the process.

'I wouldn't keep doing that. *Seu cabelo vai começar a ficar ralo!* Your hair will start to thin.' Her voice is sharp.

I turn around, startled. Adrianna is leaning in the doorway. Arms folded. Her glossy hair is swept back off her face in a ponytail. A thin veil of sweat covers her forehead. But her breathing is steady. How long has she been standing there?

'You made me jump. I didn't hear you come in.'

'Apparently not.'

Self-disgust starts to fill me from the bottom upwards. I'm a mess. I pulled on old trackie pants to come downstairs and grabbed a stale T-shirt from the wash bin. I wish I hadn't done that. Adrianna stares at me, ice maiden written all over her face. She's waiting for me to say something. How much did she hear?

'Did you have a good run?'

'Fine.'

I pause, waiting for her to say something else. She doesn't. Adrianna doesn't move. Her gaze is rock steady. Other than a slow blink, she's frozen. I can't stand it. I capitulate.

'Adrie. Please. I don't know what you thought you heard, but I can explain.'

She unfolds her arms and gives me a half-nod gesture, barely discernible, just a slight incline of her chin upwards.

'Is that right?' she says.

She surprises me by breaking into a smile, but as it unfolds it's apparent it's a mocking smile. I've fucked up big time. I can taste the hate I have for myself at this very moment in my mouth. Before I can galvanise my brain to come up with a plausible version of events, Adrianna turns in the doorway.

'I don't need an explanation. I'm going for a shower,' she says as she walks away.

The third stair creaks with her tread and I catch a mutter in Portuguese. '*Cretino.*'

CHAPTER 43

Adrianna

I close my eyes, head tilted towards the showerhead, and allow the water to cascade over my face and trickle down my body. The temperature is as high as my skin can withstand; it's on the brink of scalding. I want to be cleansed. I like the steam condensing on the shower screen and the bathroom mirror. It envelops me in a warm, comforting fog.

I heard every word of David's conversation with Cate. Or should I say Beth? He was so self-absorbed, he didn't hear me come in or close the front door. I wasn't especially quiet about it. I kept waiting for him to turn around and see me standing there, eavesdropping, but he remained oblivious. David is a man with other things on his mind. He was gripping the phone; I could see the whites of his knuckles. I couldn't see his face at that point, but I could imagine his tense expression. His right foot was tapping out a violent rhythm on the floor.

When David finally turned around, he froze, looking like a Labrador that had pissed on the carpet. Despite what I heard, I wanted to laugh. Whatever David might think, I'm okay about it. The situation suits me. I don't belong here and I'm out. I've been paid for a few shifts I managed to get at the theatre box office and

David hasn't yet noticed the cash I've been withdrawing on his card. He's sloppy. It's better if he thinks his infidelity is the problem. I'm best gone to leave David and BethCate to work things out on their own, whatever the future holds for them.

I sense more and more my real life is happening somewhere else. I need to find it and become part of it. I'm ready. Time to close the repercussions of the Sol chapter of my life completely. Goodbye to David and goodbye to London. No more romance scamming and no more married men. Particularly ones who think they are widowers, but whose wives are still very much alive.

The bathroom doorknob twists repeatedly.

'Babes. Adrie. Please can I come in?'

I turn the shower off and reach for my towel.

'I need to talk to you. Please. I love you.' The door handle rattles again. 'Why have you locked the door?' David continues trying to open it as if by magic it's suddenly going to spring open.

'I'm showering and I don't exactly want the company right now.'

'Don't shut me out, Adrie. Please let me—'

'David. Go away.'

'I know I've messed up. I'm not going to lie to you.'

'But you've not exactly been telling me the truth, have you?'

'Open the door. Please. I can explain. I—'

'David.'

'Yes, sweetheart.'

'*Vai embora.*'

'What's that mean?'

'Piss off.'

He whimpers like a little dog as his body slumps to the ground. It's barely audible but I make out, 'No. Adrie. Please. I lost Beth too. Oh, Beth.'

I envisage him propped up against the bathroom door like a rag doll, the spineless man that he is. I finish drying myself, brush my teeth and put my robe on. As I open the bathroom door, David springs to his feet.

'Babes. I can't tell you how sorry I am. Can we talk?'

He rubs his mouth with his hand, looking at me expectantly. His jaw clenches, serving to highlight the dusting of stubble on his chin. He's waiting for me to say something. He looks tired; his whole face is like a sinister bruise of worry. He's been a prick and knows it, but it's not his fault for the way I am. I've used him. He's confused, can't work me out and I can't blame him. I don't know myself half the time. He looks at me intently as though he's trying to gather up information on my feelings, on what I'm going to do next.

'Come here,' I say.

He steps towards me tentatively and I allow him to take me in his arms. I don't want him to kiss me, so I nestle my head into his shoulder. I can hear the thud of his heart. David cradles me in his arms and strokes my hair as though it will smooth away what he sees as the issue between us. With the warmth of his body and the muscles in his arms wrapped around me, I try to relax into his embrace, to give him something back. But all I can sense is further resolve; it's clutching at me, tightening its grasp. *You don't belong here, Adrianna. It's time to leave.*

I pull myself away. I want to be firm and decisive.

'David, I'm going to get dressed, then I need to go out for a while. Let's grab some dinner later — if you feel up to it, that is? And then tomorrow—'

'You're saying goodbye, aren't you?'

'Yes. I'm going away. Travel, I think. Dig out the old backpack.'

'Let me come with you? It could be fun.' Desperation covers his face.

'No. I know it's not what you believe you need, but you should spend some time alone. Allow yourself to grieve. You've been burying your grief. Work out what's happened. Give yourself that chance.' Dare I say any more? 'Trust me — you owe it to yourself. And you never know what you might find.'

'What I need is you. I'm in love with you, Adrie. I thought you loved me too?'

'I'm sorry. I can't do this anymore. It never was right, it is over. You'll come to understand you're better off without me. I'll be leaving tomorrow.'

I give his hand a squeeze and brush past him to get dressed. I'm going out. Before I depart, I want to see BethCate one more time. Something is forcing me to do so. I'm not exactly sure what I'm going to say, but I want to let her know I'm out of the picture. Apologise. The rest is up to her. And if I can find the courage, I should warn her about the garden-maintenance man she employs. I owe her that much. Max Solomon is a very dangerous man.

CHAPTER 44

Adrianna

It's nearly three o'clock by the time I reach BethCate's road. Trying to extricate myself from David proved rather difficult. He thinks if we talk about things incessantly, he's going to be able to change my mind. I know differently.

'Please, give me another chance, Adrie?' David kept repeating this as though if he asked the question often enough, he'd erase his mistakes and I'd agree.

He's booked us a table for dinner at our favourite Thai restaurant, miraculously deciding he feels better enough to be able to dine out. More romantic declarations and persuasion to come, no doubt, but I can cope with one more evening. But tomorrow, I'm going for sure.

The sky is low and woolly-looking. The pavement turns wet; raindrops whisper pitter-patter on roof tiles. So very English after a beautiful morning. I'm going to head for more sunshine. I quicken my stride until I'm standing at the foot of Cate's driveway. I try to gather myself, to think through exactly what I'm going to say. Inform and warn is my message.

Two cars are parked in the driveway — BethCate's Mini and a blue Vauxhall Astra. She must have a visitor. My timing isn't good.

I'm debating whether to retreat and come back later when the front door opens. A man's voice instils panic that it might be Sol. I dart behind a large bush the other side of one of the ostentatious pillars framing the gravelled drive.

BethCate is talking to a man who is now standing on the steps that lead up to the portico. He's wearing a navy-blue suit with black shoes. He's carrying a clipboard under one arm and gesticulates animatedly with the other. BethCate comes and joins him on the steps; they both step back and are looking up at the house. He looks like an estate agent with his smart suit and coiffured silver-fox hair. I hope they won't be long.

BethCate guides the man around to the far side where there's an entrance key-code gate. It beeps as she punches in the numbers. I'm about to go and wait by the front door when a black van turns to swing into the driveway. The Vauxhall Astra is blocking the entrance. I make out some yellow lettering. *Merda!* It's The Garden Butler van. This really is Sol. I close my eyes, willing away the fear rising in the pit of my stomach.

He drives a short way down the road to a parking space. I can see the van reversing. What to do? Run or stay. I have to see this through. I want to leave London for good tomorrow and I owe BethCate this much. I look up at the house. The front door is open a fraction. She's not yet reappeared from the side entrance, although I can hear voices. I don't want Sol to see me. I'd rather be savaged by a rabid dog than come face to face with him again. I have to make my move now. I walk briskly towards the front door and slip inside. I'll tell BethCate that the door was open, that I called out but there was no reply. I came in to check that everything was all right.

The voices are getting louder.

'That's kind. You've got my mobile, haven't you?' BethCate says.

'Yes, Mrs Mildenhall. The valuation should be through tomorrow. I want to consult with my colleagues. Thank you for the opportunity. I'll be in touch. Now let me get you those brochure samples out of the car.'

I think I've made the wrong call here. I should have cut and run. Sol is about to appear. I don't know if he goes around the back or comes in through the front. He mustn't see me. If I'm standing here . . . I can't. I dart into a room off the hallway and push the door to, but ajar enough that I can hear what is happening. I'll either slip out again and ring the doorbell, or reveal myself safely as soon as I know BethCate is alone.

Looking around the room, I see I'm in a very neat home study. A desk inlaid with smooth green leather sits below a large, bright, shuttered window. Everything on the desk looks like it's been laid with precision, each item evenly spaced as though measured out to within the millimetre. An elegant, gleaming brass desk set of a paper hole-punch, letter opener and paperweight sits in one corner. A red retro telephone with a notepad and Montblanc pen occupies a position on the opposite side of the desk. A sleek silver laptop lays closed precisely in the middle.

I peer through the shutter. BethCate is raising her hand as the Astra backs out the driveway. She turns and heads towards the front door. I'm about to go and stand in the hallway when I catch sight of a movement by the driveway entrance. A figure stands behind the pillar, pavement side. He's leaning with arms folded. I only need a glimpse to know it's Sol. He does work here, so why is he loitering? Doesn't make sense. It looks like he's spying on BethCate. Or did he see me out in the street? Does he know I'm here? His body is turned towards the house now and he's staring directly at me. *Merda!* Surely, he can't see me through the shutters.

The front door clicks shut with a weighted thud and I can hear the echo of BethCate's footsteps. I've not made it out into the hallway before she's re-entered the house. Now it's going to look like I was snooping. A quick glance out the window and I can see Sol striding up the driveway. My chest tightens; my skin is clammy. My palms are sweating. The sight of him heading in my direction after all these years instils such fear in me that my knees buckle and I sink to the ground. I'm becoming breathless with fear. A tight, invisible band has wrapped itself around my chest and is squeezing tight. I crawl into the footwell space below the desk and curl myself up into a ball. I try to steady my breathing as I rock back and forth.

CHAPTER 45

Beth

Estate agent number two has left. It's good to be making some progress. Magdalena walks out of the kitchen as I close the front door. She's clutching Ted who's wrapped in a black towel and smeared with yogurt. Literally all over. His baby hair clings to his head in a white mass, it's in his ears and smeared across his gorgeous little face. He licks his fingers. He looks like he's just been born except he's far too big. He's grown so much he looks like a baby panda in Magdalena's arms.

'Oh, Ted. What do you look like? Someone's been having fun,' I say, unable to stifle a laugh.

I'm not sure what Cate would make of Ted bathing in yogurt (probably not allowed), but it's proved a useful distraction while I've shown the estate agents around. Large plastic sheet, a litre tub of Greek yogurt and throw in a naked baby. Result: squeals of delight. Where's the harm in that?

'Shall I?' Magdalena says with her foot already on the bottom stair.

'Great. If you don't mind getting Ted in the bath? I'll be up shortly. I need two minutes to take a quick look at these brochures.'

I sit down at the kitchen table when the doorbell rings again. Getting up, I spot the estate agent's collapsible umbrella on the sofa. He must have forgotten it. Grabbing it, I head for the front door.

I swing the door wide open. 'I only spotted it—'

There's a dropping sensation in my gut, like I've driven over a humpback bridge at speed. I go to shut the door again quick. I'm not quick enough. Max pushes his heavy work boot up against the door and puts an arm out to easily stop me slamming the door in his face. I wasn't prepared for this. He's got both feet over the threshold now and pushes me backwards into the hallway. He slams the door shut behind him.

'You've changed the side-gate lock. Why did you do that, *Cate*?'

'Something I should have done a long time ago.'

'I told you not to fuck with me.'

I sidestep him and reach for the door latch. Max grabs hold of my arm and swings me around.

'Get the fuck out of my house.'

'You don't get rid of me that easily. I want my share, *Cate*. Don't make things difficult.' He pulls me towards him and cups my chin in one of his hands. He squeezes it, making me wince. I know he's warning me. I know he's capable of so much more.

I consider calling out for Magdalena. Max won't realise she's in the house. He thinks I'm alone — that's why he's here now. It's Wednesday, usually Magdalena's afternoon off but she switched this week to look after Ted while I have the house valuations done. But she's got Ted in the bath. She can't possibly leave him. Best I stall for time and get him to leave when Magdalena comes back down. He can't do anything with her here. She won't be too long. I'll call the police if necessary. I need to stall him for a bit.

'You've got this all wrong. I've tried to explain what I've been going through. Come into the kitchen. I'll make tea,' I say, attempting calm and confidence in my voice.

Max lets go of me and allows me to walk into the kitchen. He follows.

'Where's the baby?' he asks bluntly.

'The baby', I note. He doesn't say 'Ted' or 'my son'. He was always bluffing. I consider saying he's having his afternoon nap, but I think it safer if Max thinks he's not here for now. It will give me the upper hand.

'At his grandparents. They'll be here soon,' I say with conviction. My armpits are sweating.

'Good. We're alone,' he says, standing close to me again. He traces his fingers down the side of my face as though he's trying to reassure me. I can't read him at the moment; his face is as expressionless as a blank piece of paper.

My body tenses at his touch. I do not want his hands on any part of me. The hairs on my arms stand up in response with revulsion. I gulp and turn my face sharply away from him.

'I know what you've done, Beth.' It's as if saying my name is pulling at the corners of his mouth. I'm going to face up to Max once and for all. This has to end.

'Stop calling me that. Just because you're too insensitive to understand—'

'I don't drink tea. Cate would know that.'

'I meant I'll fix us a drink. That's all. I drink tea.'

'You must be very dense if you think you can fool me. Stop the fucking pretence. I have a claim here.'

'Ted is not your baby. He's my husband's. I can prove it. Our relationship is over, Max. Everything has changed. I'm telling you to leave me alone. You're totally misunderstanding everything.'

Max stands in front of me, motionless. His eyes glint like sea glass. For a nanosecond I think I can see his tense jaw loosen, his hunched shoulders relax. He's listening to me. Maybe I'm finally getting through. I've got to keep going. Not much longer now. *Magdalena, please come soon.*

As if a switch is flicked, he clenches his fists at his sides. It sends a slight shudder through his body and a wave of terror through me. Fear flushes through me, rising up my cheeks and flaring on my neck and chest. As I take a step backwards and turn to move away, I see his arm in slow motion in my peripheral vision. He punches me hard in the face. My brain jolts inside my head like I've been on a swirling rollercoaster ride.

There's whistling in my ears from the sensation. My mouth starts to fill with blood. I taste iron. I instinctively touch the side of my face. I look at him with disbelief. *Who are you, Max? What has turned you into this violent monster?*

I retch as the blood hits the back of my throat. I swallow it quietly, I mustn't incite him further. He takes a step forward. I put my hand out towards him as though to put a barrier between us.

'Max. Please, no more.'

My own voice sounds muffled, the ringing in my ears distorting all sound. The air has become treacly, slowing my brain and reactions. I want to run, but tortuous terror has sucked all strength from my limbs. What is he going to do next? I pray for Magdalena. I continue to back away. I choose flight, but he's blocking my run for the door. God help me.

'Show me you're Cate. Show me.' He's screaming, his anger boiling up now like bubbles in a kettle.

Maybe Magdalena will hear Max yell. This is a big house — but maybe? If I scream, he'll get to me before Magdalena can react. Ted . . . bath. As Max starts to unbuckle his belt, realisation hits as to his next move — the meaning of *show me you're Cate*. I can't. I can't do it. Not again. I have to protect my unborn baby. The fear of what I'm faced with sits in the hollow at the base of my ribs like a physical rock. I wish I could cut it out and throw it back at him.

Max lurches towards me and with one swift movement he's spun me around and pushes me towards the central island. I try to resist, but he's tugging at my hair with one hand and has my arms pulled together behind my back with the other. He grips my wrists tightly as I'm propelled forward. The island overhang pushes into my pelvis with a thud as my face slams against the counter-top.

There's a bruised ache now that runs from my cheek down my body. I writhe and wriggle, trying to escape from his grip as he snatches for a zip on my trousers but they have an elasticated waist. *No. No.* I want to scream now, but Max is pushing my face into the worktop and I gag again with blood trickling down my throat. All I can manage is choking noises. *You fucking cockroach.* With every fibre of my being, I know I have to survive this. For my son who's blissfully splashing away in his bath upstairs and for my growing baby still to be born. I will not lose what is mine. Whatever it takes.

As I try to gulp in air, a rasping ragged noise escapes from my body. I try to speak, but his hand grabs the back of my neck and the other catches the waistband on my trousers as I'm flipped over to face him. His left hand moves up around my neck as he's pulling at my trousers, trying to drag them down. I can't breathe again as I find myself forced backwards, looking up at the ceiling. A jarring throb of pain stabs into my back as my body resists the position I'm pinned into.

I hear Cate's voice. *Your arms are free.* I flail wildly. It's enough for him to change his position. His head comes into view and I tighten my fist into a ball and swing with all my might to punch him square in the face. I twist my wrist on impact to smack him sharply on the nose. A single line of bright blood dribbles from his nostril, reaching his top lip. Max releases his grip and wipes his nose with the back of his hand. I leap to my feet.

'Fucking bitch.' He looks at the red, sticky splodge smeared on his hand.

His eyes look mad and his face is streaked with blood where he's rubbed it. I've made things worse and this is the most scared I've ever been. He moves towards me again. As the panic rises in me like lava in a volcano, so does my self-preservation instinct. I scream out and punch and claw at his face. I feel a piece of his skin under my nail. I'm grateful that Cate always kept her nails long. I want to punch his lights out.

Max's arms reach out and grab me by the throat. Slowly, deliberately, he starts to squeeze his fingers around my neck. I've heard that strangulation is the most intimate form of murder; is this how it's all going to end? I'm forced to stop throwing punches at him as I frantically try to prise his fingers away from my throat. Just as my strength ebbs away, he releases his hands and spins me around again to face the kitchen island. We're back where we started.

Max has my head pulled back by gripping my hair tightly in one hand while his left arm is clamping my chest. He's so much stronger than me; I don't know how I'm going to get out of this. I need Magdalena. *Where are you?* I try to scream but my lung capacity is so reduced; my breath is ragged and painful like I've been running. I'm not sure if any sound is coming out. Can anyone hear me?

Max hasn't yet pushed me over the counter like I was expecting him to. Maybe he's contemplating how to murder me rather than rape me. How do I break this? I can't move; my arms are pinned to my sides. I can't compete on strength. Cate's voice echoes in my head once more.

Use your legs.

I arch my back and as Max supports my weight, I lift my legs up to waist height and get purchase on the counter with both feet.

Start the backstroke race.

With a huge heave I push myself off as if in the swimming pool. We propel backwards. It catches Max off balance and we launch off, hurtling towards the floor. We land with a heavy thud, me on top of him. I hear a crack as his head strikes the floor. He releases his grip. Please let this be over.

'Jesus. Bitch.'

I scramble to my feet, but Max is only a fraction of a second behind me. We're way into the kitchen and it's too far to the hall-way. Curse this massive room. He'll catch me before I make it to the door. Darting sideways to the food preparation area, I snatch at the largest butcher's knife in the block and turn to face my assailant. I hold the knife up and tighten my grip. I can't believe I'm doing this, but I'll die fighting to protect my children. Max catches sight of the glinting blade and stops in his tracks. He looks over my shoulder to see if he can get past me to grab another knife.

I take a step forward, knife tip pointing towards Max. If he lunges at me, he risks getting stabbed. He's obviously thinking the same thing as he puts his hands up and takes a step backwards.

'My, my. A bit of Cate pluckiness after all.'

I push the blade towards him. He continues to take tentative steps back. I need him to keep focusing on me.

'Leave me alone.' *Don't look behind you.* 'That's all I want. All I'm asking.'

I'm babbling. Must keep talking. Distraction.

'Do you understand me, Max?' We need to make it to the far end of the kitchen. 'Leave me alone. Do you get it?'

Max's eyes dart around. He's got blood on his navy sweatshirt now; it's been dripping from his nose. Dark shadows are splattered across his chest. He's wondering if he can overpower me. I can tell. I don't allow my gaze to wander from those molten chocolate eyes. *Focus on me.* Only a few steps more. Slowly does it.

Once we are a step away from our destination, I make a sudden lunge at him with my knife arm. On command he takes a jerky, deep stride backwards. Perfect. Max looks confused as he can't understand why his booted foot hasn't gripped the stone floor. He slips, so takes another step with his other foot to balance himself. Even more perfect. He has no connection with the ground now as his feet are slip-sliding all over the place. My baby accomplice has done a brilliant job of evenly distributing the yogurt on the plastic sheet. He's turned Max into Bambi on ice.

Max's feet slide from underneath him and he crashes to the floor with a heavy thud.

Run, Beth, run.

This is my chance. I have enough time now, with Max in a sticky mess on the floor, to make my escape. By the time he can get to his feet again I'll be halfway across the kitchen. That's enough of a head start. Do I run out the front door or lock myself in the study and call the police? I mustn't run upstairs. Protect Ted at all costs. I turn. I can see my exit route. The walnut hallway floor is gleaming. One stride. I'm on my way.

My left leg won't move. Something is gripping my ankle and I'm being dragged back. Max has launched himself across the floor and has my leg in a vice hold. He's tugging at me. I'm losing my footing. I fall heavily, but twist myself so as not to land directly on my tummy. The knife escapes from my hand and skids out of reach across the floor like a curling stone. The pain in my hip sears through me like a red-hot poker. I'm winded. Every bit of air from my lungs has been squeezed out.

Max drags me across the floor like fresh kill. His hands are on me again as I'm forcefully rolled onto my back. He sits astride me, the weight of him heavy on my thighs so I can't move my legs.

'You won't be getting out of this one, little lady.'

His hands are around my neck again now. He starts to apply pressure. Slowly at first, then he turns up the dial. His eyes are manic, telling me he's going to squeeze the life out of me. He's saying something. Repeating it over and over again.

'No one leaves me. You don't get to leave me. No one does.'

His hands squeeze tighter on my throat; it feels like I'm watching this happen to someone else. I try to focus my mind back. I will not watch my own execution. Max is using the ultimate form of power, demonstrating control over my next breath as he relaxes his fingers, allowing me to gasp in air before squeezing tight again. He's torturing me. I will my body to react for a final attempt at survival here. I writhe, contort and twist in the hope I can buck him off of me. I try to scratch his face.

'You don't get to leave me.'

It's useless. He's too heavy. He grips tighter. I'm pinned and I can't breathe. I'm starting to feel dizzy. Spots dance at the edge of my vision until they blur around the edges. There is pressure in my head like overinflating a balloon. *Magdalena, you are my last hope. Take care of my baby . . . I tried . . . I'm sorry.*

I feel the blood leaving my brain. It's peaceful, like I'm falling asleep.

CHAPTER 46

Beth

Something has changed. I heard a muffled noise in a tunnel. Like a popping sound. Max's hands have released their grip around my throat. A rush of blood is returning to my brain. I'm able to gasp in air. And another one. I'm breathing again. I can hear gurgling sounds. Am I choking? It doesn't feel like me — I'm breathing, filling my lungs with life-giving air.

My vision refocuses. I can see Max. He's still astride me, but his hands are around his own neck now. His eyes are bulging out of their sockets. His mouth is open and I can see a metallic glint of something sharp pointing towards me out of the blackness of his mouth. He's starting to topple towards me. I try to move my limbs. I can see another arm; it's not mine. Max is pushed and falls sideways onto the floor with a thud. I'm not alone anymore. Magdalena has come.

'You piece of shit!'

The butcher's knife that skirted across the floor pierces Max's chest, tearing through flesh and bone. A mist of red explodes from his wound and he stares blindly at the blade protruding from his chest for a moment before looking up at his assailant. She's standing over him. Looking like she's ready to twist the knife if necessary. A look of shock registers on his face as well as mine. And is that recognition on Max's face? It's Adrianna. Adrianna is here?

CHAPTER 47

Beth

My brain can't work fast enough to fathom why Adrianna is here.

'You okay?' Adrianna crouches down on the floor beside me. She pulls me up into a seated position and puts her arm around me to support my back.

'Take slow, regular breaths.' I do as I'm commanded. 'That's it. Nice and slow, to regulate your breathing back to normal. You're doing great.' Adrianna rubs my back gently as if to soothe my trauma away. 'Don't try to talk yet. Your throat is going to be seriously sore.'

I grip Adrianna's arm, imploring her to look. I point at Max, lying in a pool of blood on the floor. I'm scared he's going to come for me again. Like in films when you think they're dead but they're not. Adrianna reads my thoughts.

'Don't worry, he's not going to be attacking anyone ever again. I've made sure of that. Do feel ready to stand up? Just nod.'

I move my head up and down in acknowledgement. My neck is sore and bruised.

'Let me help you.' Adrianna tucks her hand under the top of my arm and places her other hand around my wrist. 'Easy does it. Lean on me as much as you need to.'

Adrianna helps me to my feet as Magdalena rushes into the room. She stops dead in her tracks at the sight of bloodied and stabbed Max, and me covered with blood and yogurt. With a look of horror, Magdalena makes a sign of the cross.

'Oh, Mother of Mary. I hear noise. What happened?'

'He attacked Cate,' Adrianna replies, wiping a tear from her eye. 'I stabbed him. With the letter opener and then the knife. I had to.'

I want to thank her. She has truly saved me. I want to know why she's here — how did she get into the house? So many questions, but I know they'll have to wait for a while longer. I try to find my voice and manage a croak. 'Ted?'

'He's okay. Do not worry. In his cot. As soon as I hear trouble. We only just left bathroom. Radio was on,' Magdalena says, shaking a little.

Max makes a gurgling sound. We all stop to stare at him. He's not dead. He looks at us with imploring eyes. I think he's asking for help. Or maybe he's asking for atonement for his sins. Who knows? Red blood bubbles are popping on his lips like milk froth. Adrianna holds my hand as we both approach him.

'I know him,' she says, looking at me like she needs me to understand. 'Sol. He's a rapist. My rapist.'

'Mine too,' I whisper.

I feel so tired. All my energy is spent. It's as if all the pent-up emotion from the last five months is being released from a holding tank. The tap has been turned on full blast. Out it floods. I sink to the floor once again; the tears come as the realisation dawns I have come within a whisker of death and it is David's mistress who has saved my life. I feel compelled to say it. I can't keep it in any longer.

'I'm not Mrs Mildenhall.' I look at Magdalena. 'I'm Beth, Cate's sister. David's wife,' I say, turning to Adrianna.

There is silence for a moment, like the very thought of it is suspended in the air. Magdalena is the first to speak.

'No matter.' She shrugs her shoulders nonchalantly. 'I much prefer this Mrs Mildenhall. Think we keep her.' There's a touch of a smile on her face.

'You knew?' I say in disbelief, my voice still sounding raspy.

'This Mrs Mildenhall left a haircut in bathroom bin. Makes me coffee. Empties the dishwasher. Gives me mornings off. Very good mother. Is very kind lady. She stay?' Magdalena puts her hands together as if praying that I will keep up the pretence of being Mrs Mildenhall.

Max groans and his body twitches. Magdalena looks at him, then walks over to the row of copper saucepans hanging from a ceiling frame above the central island. She selects a pan. Jiggles it up and down, tapping the bottom with her hand as if testing its weight. She strides over to Max, takes a swing with the pan and hits him sharply on the crown of the head with it. Crack.

'For poisoning the kittens. Now we all involved. I tell no one.'

'Well, I certainly won't be,' Adrianna says. She rests a reassuring hand on my shoulder.

'You saved my life. I'll never be able to thank you enough.' I reach up for her. Adrianna sits down beside me. She puts her arm around me. It feels so loving and comforting. I lean into her. Together we watch the final dregs of life ebb out of Max. The blood has dwindled to barely a trickle like a lawn sprinkler having lost its pressure. His eyes have rolled back in their sockets, and his skin looks clammy and tinged with blue. His chest is soaked in blood. Visible terror on his face. Max Solomon is finally dead.

I'm ashamed to say I can't help feel elated Max has gone. Looking at my co-conspirators, I don't think I'm the only one.

'Mrs Mildenhall,' Magdalena says pointedly. 'What we do now? Bury him in garden?' She's ready for action, having already put on her rubber gloves, and has fetched bleach and a mop and bucket for the clean-up operation.

'No. Too risky,' I say, shaking my head. 'I think I've got a better idea.' I look at Adrianna. 'We need a proper grave. And I happen to know where to find one. We can bury him after dark.'

'Great idea, but the cemetery is locked at dusk, isn't it?' Adrianna says. 'We'll never get away with it in daylight.'

'Lucky then, as the owner of two graves, I'm entitled to a key.'

CHAPTER 48

Adrianna

We put SolMax's body in one of his own garden-refuse bags. After dark, we drag it to the front door and it takes all three of us to haul him up onto the backseat of BethCate's car. I cover it with a blanket. We make a plan and every part of the process is discussed and dissected. We painstakingly make a list and collect together shovels, a rake, a broom, plastic sheeting, more bags and a wooden board.

Luckily SolMax didn't park his Garden Butler van in the driveway so if anyone asks, he hasn't been working here today. I saw him park a way down the road. He works for plenty of other homes around here. He must have been visiting one of them.

I don a beanie, tucking all my hair underneath. I put on one of Giles's coats with a few jumpers underneath to bulk myself out.

'How do I look?'

'Like a murderer,' BethCate says.

'Perfect.'

Once we were assured that SolMax was dead, I took his car keys from his pocket. Around 8 p.m., I leave to drive SolMax's van to Acton. I park it in the street where he lives. I drop the keys into London's sewer system along with the cut-up SIM card from his phone. I rummage around in the van before I leave and find his passport in the glove compartment.

'I'm going to burn this,' I say, showing it to BethCate when I get back. 'It's best if it's never found. Leaves open the possibility that he's gone abroad.'

* * *

By midnight we're in the graveyard, both dressed like burglars in dark hoodies. It's fortunate that the grave isn't too far from one of the artery roads that run through the cemetery. It proves easier pulling SolMax out of the car than putting him in it. Just as well, as Magdalena has stayed behind to babysit — and bleach and anti-bac the kitchen yet again. To see the kitchen now, you wouldn't know what has taken place. Magdalena has inspected every inch for traces of blood and stray hairs. It's been mopped, hoovered, scoured and polished.

Between us, we manage to drag SolMax's body to the graveside. BethCate lets out a grunt.

'You okay? We can stop for a rest anytime you need.'

'Summoning the strength. I can do this.'

We work together to remove the topsoil from Giles's grave. We've brought a large plastic sheet that BethCate found in one of the garden sheds to lay the excavated soil on, so as not to leave any traces of loose soil on the grass area by the grave. It has to look as undisturbed as possible.

We set about shovelling spadefuls of soil. The ground has settled since the funeral, but isn't yet level and fully compacted. Recent rain may have helped, but we find we can dig in. Before long there's quite a pile by the side of the grave.

'How far down is he? Your *husband*.'

'The hole must have originally been about seven feet, I think. It's deep to allow space for Cate. Me, I guess.'

'Plenty of space for *cara de merda* — shitface, then.'

The grass in the cemetery is damp beneath our feet. I'm glad BethCate found me a pair of walking boots. We avoid using torches so as not to alert anyone to our presence. We only switch our phone torches on sparingly to look down to the depth of the hole we've dug. As we dig deeper, the musty smell of earthen soil invades my nostrils.

BethCate must feel the same. 'It reminds me of the smell on Dad's allotment when he used to dig up potatoes,' she says.

After we've been digging for nearly an hour, BethCate rests her hands on top of her shovel for a moment to take a short rest.

'Can I ask you something?' she says.

'Sure.' I throw down my spade. 'Ask away. I think you're entitled to.'

'Why did you come to the funeral? Giles and the children. It was you, wasn't it? I nearly fell in when I saw you.'

'You're right. It was me. How did you know who I was?'

'I saw you with David in Twickenham after my funeral.'

I put my hands on my hips and shake my head to reprimand myself. How much to tell her? After what's happened, I don't think there can be any more secrets.

'I needed to know what was going on with David and Cate, to be honest. Things had moved so fast. It's *complicado* — complicated. I'm sorry. It must have been shit. I haven't been thinking straight for quite a few years.' I put my arms around BethCate and give her a hug. 'David's all yours, by the way. If you want him. I'm leaving.'

I tell everything. My relationship with SolMax, how he treated me, my escape and then move into romance scamming. How I met David, ensnared him and what's happened between us since.

'*Estou ferrado*. I'm screwed up. Right?'

'No more than me. I'm sorry if *Cate* messed things up for you.'

'He is your husband after all. Trust me, you have nothing to apologise for. Good luck, Cate Mildenhall. I mean it, really.'

BethCate turns to look at the garden-refuse bag containing SolMax's body. 'What on earth created him?'

'His childhood hadn't been happy; I know that much. His mother abandoned him aged seven; she was pregnant with another man's child. She left SolMax behind with his uncommunicative father, but thought to take the family dog with her. He said the puppy was his best friend.'

'That resonates. Max kept saying — you don't get to leave me.'

'By the time SolMax turned nine, his father remarried. His stepmother was a cold, unloving woman by all accounts. SolMax was packed off to boarding school two hundred miles away, so weekends at home weren't possible. He told me he used to spend the summer holidays in the garden; nobody cared what he did. There was a derelict greenhouse, so he rebuilt it and started growing tomatoes and cultivating seeds. I guess that's why he treated plants better than people.'

'I think it explains a lot. But doesn't excuse it. Did you ever report the abuse you got from Max . . . Sol?' BethCate asks.

I shake my head.

'Why would the police believe me? We were partners, living together, and SolMax would only deny it. He could be very charming and *carismática* — charismatic. I couldn't face the investigation, the process. I focused on planning my escape instead.'

We pick up our shovels and resume digging. Once we've reached about three feet, plus a bit for good measure, we agree that's far enough. We roll SolMax in. He lands face down.

'Should we turn him over?' BethCate asks.

'No. Ass up, facing hell.'

'And poor Giles. Seriously sorry about this, mate, but needs must.' She smiles at me. 'You're right. This isn't laying to rest, but disposing of excrement.'

'I hear a noise at the edge of the cemetery.

'*Merda!*'

'What?'

I crouch down, grabbing at BethCate's arm to pull her to the ground with me.

'What the hell? What are you doing?'

'Get in the grave,' I say, keeping my voice low.

'Excuse me? No way.'

CHAPTER 49

Beth

I don't think I can take any more. Don't tell me after all this, Adrianna is a real psycho and she's going to bury me alive with dead Max.

Adrianna places her index finger across her lips. She purses them. 'Shh, people,' she mouths.

I look across to where she's pointing. There's a group of five or six exuberant youths darting in between the gravestones not far from the entrance. They must have scaled a wall to get in. A girl screams; one of the group is making ghoulish noises. 'Whoooo!'

'We have to hide. We can't risk being seen. Not even by drunk kids,' Adrianna says. 'Me first?'

She looks at me for acknowledgement. I glance across. They look like they're heading in our direction. I look around frantically. There's nowhere else to hide other than to squat behind gravestones. Too risky. It's too far to leg it to the chapel and we'd be seen. We don't have any choice. Adrianna drops down into the corner of the grave above Max's head.

'Pass me the tools.'

Thirty seconds later and I'm in the grave with her. We crouch down, huddled together in the dark, making ourselves as small as possible. Thankfully, there's enough room that we don't have to lie on top of Max's corpse. That would be too gross, not to say traumatic. The sodden earth smells musty. I realise we're directly on top of Giles. Oh, my God, the thought of what's below our feet. My heart is pounding enough at the fear of being caught, but this is making it leap out of my chest. I drink in the cold night air. *Calm, calm*, I tell myself. I place my hand on my tummy. I focus on my baby. *You're going to be a dad again*, I tell Giles telepathically.

The voices get louder. They invade the eerily quiet cemetery. A sweep of fear travels through my body. I can only pray. *Please, God, don't let us be caught.* My heart is palpitating like it does when you've woken up in the middle of a nightmare. Pure fear rams us up hard against the grave wall as we try to be invisible.

I recognise a sound, but can't quite place it. A light, tinny scrunch. There follows the sound of something being kicked along concrete. It rattles and skids. An empty beer can. They're on the artery road. At least that means they're not larking around the graves in this section. Laughter. Someone's making an owl noise.

A sweet, herbal, musky smell permeates the crisp air. Cannabis. The voices are getting quieter. We remain silent for a few more minutes until we can't hear any sound other than the distant traffic.

'I'm gonna take a peek,' Adrianna says. She gingerly peers out over the top. Looks in all directions. 'All clear. They've disappeared.'

I exhale with relief.

'Blimey. That was close,' I say once we're both on ground level again.

'Just kids having a joint and messing about. But even so.'

We pick up our shovels again and hastily start refilling the grave. A much quicker job than digging it out. The light of the moon is almost full, as though someone has taken a small bite out of it. It bathes the cemetery with a subdued luminosity. The night is clear, a vast, silky navy-blue, but the air is heavy with the lingering scent of earlier rain and damp autumn leaves. We work tirelessly until Max has well and truly disappeared from view and the grave is full to the brim. I've worked up quite a sweat now despite the chill; my T-shirt sticks to my back.

I've changed my mind. I make a mental note to write in my will I wish to be cremated. I'll request to be scattered in with the children. I never want to see this man again, even after death.

I use the wooden board to stand on and flatten the soil and we take it in turns to repeat the process to compact the top section as much as possible. We jump up and down, we dance on Max's grave. A great weight that I've been carrying around with me for months starts to lift. My body and limbs feel lighter. I'm free.

We redistribute the displaced soil we've purposefully placed in separate refuse bags. Adrianna has spotted a freshly dug grave waiting for its occupant a few rows away so we tip some in; the remainder we scatter as thin layers on the newest unsettled graves. Finally, we sweep around the edges of Giles's grave to tidy things up. We're done.

'Don't know about you, but that was one of the most satisfying four hours of my life I've ever spent,' Adrianna says as we head back to the car.

CHAPTER 50

The Following Year, 26 February

Beth

I used to think about the lucky women who had given birth and the euphoria they must feel. Today I am one of those women. It's exquisite. I am so filled with the most gigantic ball of happiness I'm going to explode like a mammoth firework display. *Wham! Whoosh! Whirr! Happy!*

My baby boy is cradled in my arms — two hours old, swaddled in a blanket and I have given my very first feed. Am I dreaming? I pinch the skin on my wrist and watch it fall back into shape. I ever so gently prod the little bundle; he shifts slightly, his eyelids flicker momentarily before closing again. He's real, alive. I can feel the fragility of his bones. I can see the blood trickling through his veins beneath the translucent skin on his delicate forehead. I will protect and cherish him to my dying day.

'You made it, precious. Despite the bumpy ride. Well done you.' I kiss his forehead.

I don't want to take my eyes off him. He's beautiful. I have two sons.

I steal a glance over to the hospital window. Snow is falling. There's a soft sprinkle of snowflakes building up on the windowsill already. We're on the fifth floor, my baby and I. I imagine the snow muffling the ground in the garden atrium below with a sparkling stillness. A protective blanket.

'You'll be able to build a snowman with your brother when you're old enough,' I say out loud.

He's so perfect, so innocent, so complete. He's survived the aftermath of a tragedy that happened in a split second. A chain of events that I still find difficult to comprehend.

The inquest recorded a verdict of accident. The coroner's report concluded Giles's car was travelling at excessive speed and he lost control of the vehicle, partially in response to having to brake sharply due to the proximity of another vehicle, which remained unidentified. All occupants of the Range Rover lost their lives due to the impact the vehicle suffered. One occupant, Elizabeth Brown, wasn't wearing a seat belt at the time which contributed to the severity of her injuries. The coroner also concluded, like the police had suggested, *Beth* had undone the seat belt to locate her phone, which was found in her jacket pocket. Her husband, David Brown, was ringing incessantly both immediately before and after the accident. I know the 'Mouldy Old Dough' ringtone for David would have driven Cate mad. He was telling the truth. *Great timing and too little, too late, though, David.*

Trying to recall everything around the time of the accident, all the minute details, is like trying to hold on to a dream. As time goes by, everything blurs around the edges. My memory is blank in areas. Maybe it's my built-in black-box recorder erasing it for my own good?

I have chosen an easy lie over a complex truth. You see, for me, being childless was like having a vital organ missing. I was becoming the merest outline of the person I knew I was meant to be. A ghost. Without a baby, I was never going to be whole. I was desperate, so I took him.

The guilt for what I did is still there, whispering in my ear like a hideous gargoyle, but I will not be held hostage for the rest of my life by the weight of it. I accept I will always have a tenuous relationship with truth. The further you get away from it, the harder it becomes to tell it. Lies beget lies.

And my tongue swells further with them. I received one call from the police about Max. It must have been about six weeks after we buried him. A Detective Sergeant Parish, I think he said his name was.

'Mrs Mildenhall. Sorry to disturb you. We're making enquiries about a Max Solomon. Is he known to you?'

'Yes. I use his services quite regularly. Gardening and house maintenance. He's The Garden Butler.'

'And when did you last see Mr Solomon?'

'Ooh. Let me see. It must have been around October, I think. Can't give you the precise date off the top of my head. I'd need to talk to my housekeeper.'

'I see. We're aware that you transferred a sum of twenty thousand pounds to him around that time. Can I ask what it was for?'

For no more than a nanosecond the truth gave a little dance on the tip of my tongue, ready to propel me into the abyss. *It was blackmail money. But luckily it was a one-off payment. I helped bury him in an existing grave in the big cemetery at Kew. Hope that's okay? He deserved it.*

'Sure. For some garden work and to order building materials. Timber and York stone. I've contracted him to re-lay the terrace and build a tree house.' I cleared my throat. 'Should I be worried, Sergeant? Is he in trouble?'

'No, madam. He's not in trouble. We're trying to locate him. A relative has reported him missing.'

'Oh, dear. I see,' I said, inflecting concern in my voice.

'Are you aware of any friends of his, or contacts?'

'I'm afraid not. He's an intermittent tradesman. He works for quite a few households around Richmond, I believe.'

I wondered whether I should say more. I decided to plant a seed. Seemed appropriate.

'He travels to Turkey quite a bit. He was there for a few weeks last summer. He was planning another trip, but I couldn't tell you when exactly. He's always very thorough and reliable, so I'm sure he'll reappear soon.'

'You've been most helpful. Thank you. I'll leave you my details in case you hear anything, if I may?'

'Of course.'

And that was the last time I heard the name Max Solomon mentioned. I won't be saying it. Those words will never touch my lips again.

Magdalena still insists on calling me Mrs Mildenhall. Michael has been helping her with an Indefinite Leave to Remain application. He's confident she'll be granted permanent residence based on the length of time she's resided in the UK.

Adrianna stayed with me for a couple of days after our night in the cemetery, sleeping, preparing for her next move and packing. I gave her a suitcase, let her help herself to any clothes she needed. Gave her some money to get herself settled.

'Where are you going to go?'

'Probably best if I just tell you travelling. Safer for you if you don't know — that way you won't have any links to me. Anyway, somewhere I can't be found.'

Early the next morning, Adrianna sent me a selfie in front of the departures board at Heathrow Terminal 5, with the caption *Adeus!* Goodbye. She could be anywhere from Mexico to Mumbai, Nassau to Nice. I haven't heard from her since.

I can't say the same for David. He kept calling me in the first few weeks after Adrianna departed. He was either in tears or drunk.

Or both. He was in a desperate state, devasted and crushed. Ironic that all the crying I did over our inability to conceive was also that: despair. Shame David didn't cry as much after Beth died, but I've now come to understand he was suffering from delayed grief. He turned to Adrianna, deliberately pushing his emotions away as a self-protect mechanism. He's in therapy and now mourns Beth as well as the loss of Adrianna. He's also grasped he was involved with a scammer, but says he deserved it. I've reassured him she did care for him too. It's a lot for him to come to terms with. I accept we both contributed to the downfall of our marriage and I genuinely hope David finds happiness one day. But it can never be with me.

I can't resist, though. I take a selfie with my new son. I type out the caption, still cradling my gorgeous bundle.

Dying to escape . . . in hospital with my baby boy! All well. And press send to David.

We will stay in touch, but, for both our sakes, I will keep him at arm's length. Anyway, who needs a David when I've got a friend like Harry. The thought of Harry Snow brings a warm glow to my insides as I continue to watch the snowflakes fall. Since meeting Harry, I've opened a new door into myself. I've discovered hidden parts of me I forgot about, like giggling, flicking my hair self-consciously, and butterflies in my stomach as I get ready to meet him.

'I've never had a first date with a pregnant woman before,' Harry said when he invited me to lunch in the glasshouse restaurant at Petersham Nurseries. It was only the two of us and afterwards we took a stroll around the wonderful shop and displays. There were lots of twinkly lights, wreaths and scented candles everywhere, giving a festive romantic ambience to the place. Harry insisted on buying me an enormous cheese plant.

'An early Christmas present. And to signify growth.'

'What sort of growth?' I replied with amusement, rubbing my hands across my swollen belly.

'Birth, friendship, new beginnings,' Harry said, laughing. A laugh as delicious as a truffle chocolate. I could see the significance of what he was trying to say still shining in his eyes.

Harry kissed me for the first time that day. A slow, gentle kiss. Harry's lips felt so different as they graced mine. The comfort of his arms around me, the tickle touch of his long hair as it brushed against my cheek. After so many years with David, it was strange. It was disconcerting at first, but then I relaxed into it — a bit like trying on someone else's clothes, initially feeling self-conscious, but very quickly they start to feel like your own.

We're taking things super slow. A snail has nothing on us. We're healing, Harry and I; we're our own little therapy group. Outsiders will assume for the same reason — Cate the widow and Harry the widower. We attract sympathy. Except my healing is very much of a different nature.

My babies and I will be moving from Richmond in the spring and, of course, Magdalena will be coming with us. Exchanging contracts on the house is imminent. I've found a wonderful smaller property within sight of the river, not far from Hammersmith Bridge. There are some great local schools for when the time comes and it's not far to visit Mum in Chiswick. Convenient for Harry and Abigail in Putney too. Oh, and only a short drive to the graveyard. To continue to lay flowers and to keep an eye on things.

There is a gentle knock on my hospital-room door.

'There she is. Or should I say, there they are?'

It's Laura, closely followed by Michael carrying an enormous koala bear.

'We couldn't resist him,' Michael says with the broadest grin on his face as he jiggles the koala about, before placing the toy on the bedside table. They both kiss me.

The look of joy on their faces warms my heart like a bowl of nourishing soup.

'Congratulations. Ooh, may I?' Laura says, standing by my bed, eagerly peering down at the bundle in my arms. I lift him up towards her.

'Artie, meet your grandparents. Laura and Michael — meet your new grandson, Arthur.'

'Did you say Arthur?' Michael says.

'I did.' I am proud of myself. I have learned that Michael's middle name is Arthur. I know that Cate would have chosen something on-trend like Lando, Enzo or Cosmo. I'm not going to do that to them.

'His name is Arthur Giles. But I'm sure he'll end up being called Artie. I hope you approve?'

'Arthur was my father's name too,' Michael says, leaning over Laura to look at the baby.

'Oh, Cate, what a wonderful choice. Thank you.' Laura looks up at her husband with a warm smile.

What a turbulent nine months it's been, but in times of crisis we are forced to get a new perspective on ourselves. To think about who we are and how others must see you. Life is resuming shape around me. I am fully Cate. But a different version of Cate. Maybe she was right all along with her mantra: 'After me, you come first'.

Except now it's: *After you, comes me.*

And as for my signifier tattoo? Once we are settled back home and it is safe to do so, I'll get my number 2 removed. Then there won't even be *After you, comes me*; there is no hierarchy anymore. It's just me now, Cate, travelling solo. For ever.

Cate once told me that true happiness is when expectations of your life are met. Well, I'm happy. Truly, deeply happy. On the way I've learned sometimes you feel you can't climb the mountain before you. You can. Sometimes you feel something isn't achievable. It is. And sometimes you feel that you don't deserve it. You do. I'm going to have to remain vigilant, but you can't always travel through life with certainty. And do you know what? Sometimes the unknown is better. There has been so much pain, but, now, looking at my new family — Laura and Michael, baby Artie and thinking of Ted safe back at home, I know there is also love. And where there is love, there is always hope.

THE END

ACKNOWLEDGEMENTS

I'm so delighted to be working with the incredible team at Joffe Books. Thank you all very much for everything you have done to bring my book into the hands of readers. Thank you to my acquiring editor Kate Lyall Grant and senior editor Kate Ballard. I'm full of gratitude. Authors write stories but it takes a talented team to shape them for publication and I'd particularly like to thank Krystyna Green for her editing skills and Suzy Clarke for being a brilliant copy-editor. Thanks to Tia Davis and the wider Joffe Books marketing, sales and production teams.

I want to do a shout out to my writing group — Anne, Dan, Derek, Dervla, Lou and Nia — aka the *Nashers*. What would I do without you? Your friendship and encouragement mean so much to me. I wish you all the utmost success on your own writing journeys. And posthumously, I'd like to thank the wonderful Wendy Williams — my very first beta reader who read my manuscript 'well into the night as I couldn't put it down.' I will never forget your enthusiasm for my book. Our Jericho Writers writing group came together under the guidance of our tutor and mentor Natasha Bell. Natasha — you are fabulous and your advice and nuggets of wisdom still sit with me.

A huge thank you to Marcela Tupinamba for her advice on the Brazilian Portuguese language. I am so grateful for your time and any errors are entirely mine.

Thank you to my wonderful family — husband Paul and children Amy and Matthew, to whom this book is dedicated. You have all supported and encouraged me on my writing path and I'd never have got to the end without you. I love you.

Finally, a heartfelt thank you for you, dear reader, for choosing this book. I hope to see you again soon and, in the meantime, may your lives be filled with fabulous fiction!

THE JOFFE BOOKS STORY

We began in 2014 when Jasper agreed to publish his mum's much-rejected romance novel and it became a bestseller.

Since then we've grown into the largest independent publisher in the UK. We're extremely proud to publish some of the very best writers in the world, including Joy Ellis, Faith Martin, Caro Ramsay, Helen Forrester, Simon Brett and Robert Goddard. Everyone at Joffe Books loves reading and we never forget that it all begins with the magic of an author telling a story.

We are proud to publish talented first-time authors, as well as established writers whose books we love introducing to a new generation of readers.

We won Trade Publisher of the Year at the Independent Publishing Awards in 2023 and Best Publisher Award in 2024 at the People's Book Prize. We have been shortlisted for Independent Publisher of the Year at the British Book Awards for the last five years, and were shortlisted for the Diversity and Inclusivity Award at the 2022 Independent Publishing Awards. In 2023 we were shortlisted for Publisher of the Year at the RNA Industry Awards, and in 2024 we were shortlisted at the CWA Daggers for the Best Crime and Mystery Publisher.

We built this company with your help, and we love to hear from you, so please email us about absolutely anything bookish at feedback@joffebooks.com.

If you want to receive free books every Friday and hear about all our new releases, join our mailing list here: www.joffebooks.com/freebooks.

And when you tell your friends about us, just remember: it's pronounced Joffe as in coffee or toffee!